THE MYSTERIOUS AFFAIR

The Mysterious Affair

by

Frederick E. Smith

Dales Large Print Books
Long Preston, North Yorkshire,
BD23 4ND, England.

British Library Cataloguing in Publication Data.

Smith, Frederick E.
    The mysterious affair.

    A catalogue record of this book is
    available from the British Library

    ISBN 978-1-84262-856-0 pbk

First published in Great Britain in 2010 by Emissary Publishing

Copyright © Frederick E. Smith

Cover illustration © Roy Bishop by arrangement with
Arcangel Images

The moral rights of the author have been asserted in accordance
with the Copyright, Designs and Patents Act, 1988

Published in Large Print 2011 by arrangement with
Frederick E. Smith

Dales Large Print is an imprint of Library Magna Books Ltd.

Printed and bound in Great Britain by
T.J. (International) Ltd., Cornwall, PL28 8RW

To my late beloved wife, Shelagh, without whose love and probity I might never have gained these viewpoints and beliefs.

ONE

If he had not lost his God before, Sean Hammond certainly lost his last remnant of faith in 1942. Not that he noticed or cared at the time. His other beliefs seemed more urgent and significant. Whether his colleagues noticed the change is debatable but in any case they were too young and too busy saving their own lives to indulge in such abstract concepts. It took his meeting with Linda Martin and the extraordinary year that followed for the mysterious affair to be resolved.

His first meeting with her was in the spring of 1943, on one of those rare evenings which the English like to believe are their very own, when the moon is near enough to be touched and the earth so still it can be heard breathing. When the birds nestle down in their nests and the trees cease their whispering to allow them to sleep. The kind of night when the very concept of war is a kind of lunacy.

He had come across the lake by accident. He had been following the footpath across the adjacent field but when he drew level with the stile with its private property sign, curiosity had made him see what lay beyond. Sean Hammond was a man invested with a natural curiosity but, even without it, an inborn resentment against private landowning might have prompted his act equally well.

The wood he entered was thicker than he had believed and forced him to follow a path that initially ran almost parallel to the field alongside him. Then the field disappeared among the trees and he believed he would soon come in sight of the house that dominated the estate. Instead the trees suddenly fell away and he found himself in an enclosed glade containing a small lake. Seeing a wooden picnic table with two facing benches and an old gazebo beside the lake and knowing he had already walked further than his hospital would approve, he glanced at his watch, saw he still had time, and made for the table. As he sank down on one of the benches he saw something stir from under the table's shadow. As it scurried away in the twilight he saw it was a hedgehog. He watched it until it disappeared under a clump of bushes, then lit himself a cigarette. As he sat back he noticed an old oak at the far side of the lake, its roots holding the soil like some loving and committed hand.

His first impression was the silence. Unaccustomed to it, he found it almost heavy on his senses. He could hear his breathing and the rustle of some small animal in the surrounding undergrowth. Then the silence returned, filling the space around him with its presence.

He gave an impatient laugh. It was quiet because it was sunset in private grounds and for a short while he was free of shot up airmen cracking dirty jokes. So what was so special about it? Why was he sitting there listening like some daft old lady waiting for a message in an empty church?

Yet he knew the reason even as his mind asked the question. The lake where he and Len had fished many years ago had been similar in size and its shape and silence were blips on the screen of time. His eyes lifted from the small clump of water lilies in the centre of the lake to the crimson sky that was streaked with vermilion clouds. The full moon above them was held in space only by the silence. Another childhood memory came back. A book read to him by his mother. A secret lake where fairies flew in at night on gossamer wings to relate their adventures. A place of magic at a time in childhood when magic was everywhere. Then he frowned at the recall and stretched out his injured leg, knowing only too well how pain brought back reality.

Even so, the distant bark of a dog came as a relief. He sat upright and listened. The sound was coming from the far side of the lake. He heard a scuffling among the trees and bushes, another louder bark, and then a woman's voice calling the dog. Half a minute later she and the dog emerged from the trees, dark figures silhouetted against the sunset.

Released from his leash the dog dived joyously into the lake. Then it noticed the intruder and with a loud warning bark began swimming towards him. The woman called it back but the dog continued swimming. Reaching the bank it dragged itself out, shook itself, and then with another bark ran towards Sean, only to skid to a halt as he extended his hand. Skirting the lake the woman had broken into a run. As she approached he saw she was young and graceful in her movements. A moment later he heard her breathless voice. 'I'm so sorry. Jason isn't very obedient when he sees strangers. Has he wet your uniform?'

He rose to his feet. 'No, I was well out of range. In any case I like dogs. Did you say his name is Jason?'

'That's right.' She called the dog to her who, after sniffing Sean's hand, moved towards her. 'I really ought to smack him. He should know better than to behave like that. Only he isn't used to seeing strangers when I take him for his walk.'

Now that she was standing close to him he

could see her more clearly. Dressed in a tailored suit, bare-headed, tall, slender, fair haired and beautiful, he guessed her to be a woman in her late twenties. 'It's my fault,' he said. 'I shouldn't trespass on private property, should I?'

She leaned down to pat the dog. She was smiling when she straightened. 'You're hardly a poacher, are you? Where are you from? Donnington?'

He nodded. 'That's my base. But I'm having a spell in Littleworth at the moment.'

'The cottage hospital? Are you a patient there?'

He grimaced. 'Hardly a patient. More of a scrounger having a week's rest.'

Her eyes were running over him now. Good looking, dark-haired, strongly-built, wearing RAF wings, she saw he was a flight lieutenant. 'I'm Linda Martin,' she told him. 'Mrs Martin.'

'Sean Hammond,' he said. 'Are you sure you don't mind? Shouldn't you and Jason be seeing me off?'

Unsure whether he was being sarcastic or making a joke, she ignored his comment. 'Have you been here before?'

'You mean have I trespassed before?'

'No. I mean have you been to my haven before. The place where my brother and I used to play as children.' As she was speaking she moved to the bench opposite him and seated herself. 'We had a little boat here. My parents didn't mind because the lake's only a few feet deep. We used to play all kinds of games.' She indicated the gazebo behind him. 'When it rained we'd play in there. We called it our log cabin.'

After a moment's hesitation, he returned to his seat. 'So it has happy memories for you?'

'Yes. Wonderful memories. But childhood memories often are, don't you think?'

'For some,' he said. 'Not everyone.'

'Yes, of course. I suppose I was one of the lucky ones.'

He watched her bend down and stroke the wet dog. 'Does your family own the estate?'

She nodded. 'My father does. He's the reason I'm home at the moment. He's been ill and I've been given time off until he's better.'

'Time off,' he said. 'Then you're not in the Forces?'

'No. I wish I were. I'm in the Food Ration offices. I hate the job but they won't release me.'

'What about your brother? Where is he now?'

She ceased stroking the dog and began fumbling in the small handbag she was carrying. As he offered her one of his own cigarettes he caught her expression. 'I'm sorry. I shouldn't have asked that, should I?'

14

She took a cigarette from him, allowed him to light it, then gave him a smile. 'You weren't to know. He was killed in early 1940. A few days before Dunkirk.'

'I see. Was he much older than you?'

'Only two years. He was in the regular Air Force. Joined it before the war.' She gave an embarrassed laugh. 'He was very similar to you in build. So I got a bit of a shock when I saw you sitting here. With most of our staff called up, hardly anyone visits the lake these days.'

'So you thought it was your brother sitting here?'

She nodded. 'It was your uniform and appearance. You know the way memories do these things.'

'You were very attached to him, were you?'

'To Mark? Oh, yes. We did everything together.'

'Have you any other brothers or sisters?'

'Just a younger sister, Susan. She's up in Edinburgh so I don't see much of her these days. What about you?'

'No, I'm the only one. No doubt I was such a brat my folks decided one was enough.'

She laughed. 'I can't believe that.'

'You would if you knew me. I'm one of those back-to-front characters who sees everything differently to other people. Apparently even when I was a kid I wanted to know why Father Christmas didn't come through

15

the front door instead of down the chimney.'

She laughed again. 'It seemed a logical enough question. It sounds as if you were a bright young lad.'

'I don't know about that but it taught me one thing. It doesn't pay to ask too many questions in this world.'

Although he was still smiling, his use of words puzzled her. 'Doesn't it? I'd have thought it something all intelligent people do.'

He reached down to pat Jason who was now nuzzling around his feet. 'I like the thought but wish it were true. Don't most of us accept the things we're told and muddle on the same way from generation to generation?'

She wished she could see his expression but as he was bending down patting Jason it was hidden from her. 'I suppose we do. But is muddling the right word? Haven't we sorted things out over the years and come to a general consensus of opinion?'

She was trying to analyze the quick glance he gave her before attending to Jason again. Was it one of dissent, she wondered? Realising she was enjoying the unusual conversation she asked another question to prolong it. 'Or is your question one of those back-to-front Father Christmas ones you used to ask as a child?'

He was smiling again when he straightened up. 'I suppose it is. The kind of daft question few people are prepared to answer.'

'How do you know that? Do you go round asking people?'

He grimaced. 'Hardly. An airmen's mess isn't the place for that kind of conversation. For that matter why am I talking to you this way? You should be shooing me out of here, not listening to my nonsense.'

Her reply surprised her. 'Perhaps I'm enjoying your nonsense. There isn't much of it in the general conversation these days.'

He gave an amused grimace. 'You shouldn't be so tolerant to trespassers. Or you could be swamped by them.'

As his cigarette glowed in the twilight she took another glance at him. His features were well defined and strong but she imagined sensitivity about his well-shaped mouth. There was also something she had not noticed before. He was wearing a DFC ribbon. 'That's hardly likely to happen,' she said. 'I think all the poachers have gone into the Services. Do you usually go for walks on your own? Or isn't the hospital full at the moment?'

He shrugged. 'No, it's got its usual quota. But they're all youngsters. Twenty year olds and younger. It's a relief to get away from their chatter for a while.'

For the first time she realised he was older

than the normal RAF pilot. Twenty-seven or twenty-eight was her guess. 'When does your convalescence end?'

'They expect I'll be fit for duty next week.' Before she could answer he ground out his cigarette and rose to his feet. 'I've talked too much. God knows why. It must be this haven of yours or perhaps it's because you're a good listener. I'd better go. Our matron doesn't approve of airmen who break her rules.'

She rose with him. 'I wouldn't think you're the type to be afraid of irate matrons.'

He grinned. 'You haven't seen our matron. She'd scare the hell out of the gorgon herself.'

She liked his sense of humour. It had a quirkish quality that appealed to her. As he gave Jason a final pat and then reached for his cap her sudden question amazed her. 'Are you coming here again or are you afraid of talkative dog walkers?'

He looked as surprised as she by her question. 'I hadn't planned to. Do you come here every night?'

Astonished by her words, which seemed nothing less than an invitation, she searched for excuses. 'I have to. Jason loves his swim even although he messes up the house when he gets back.' Seeing he was hesitating she went on: 'No one will bother you if you like it here. Our groundsman has been called up and I'm well and truly married.'

He smiled at that. 'Army, Navy or Air Force?'

'Air Force. We haven't our own home yet so we meet here when he gets leave.'

'Good luck to him,' he said, holding out his hand. 'And thanks for the talk and for being so patient with me.'

She liked his handshake. It was firm but not overwhelming. 'I wasn't being patient. I enjoyed your company.' Releasing his hand she took hold of the dog's collar. 'Say goodnight, Jason. Tell the Flight Lieutenant we might see him tomorrow night if he comes this way.'

She turned at the far side of the lake before taking the path to the house. He was still standing where she had left him and gazing after her. Then, noticing her glance, he turned and vanished among the trees. Frowning at herself, totally unaware of the massive difference the chance meeting was to make on both herself and the world around her, she put Jason on his leash and made her way home.

TWO

Sean tried the front door on his arrival, only to find it locked. Knowing it meant all other entries into the small hospital would be equally secured, he sighed, lifted back the old-fashioned door knocker and swung it down. Although the resonant clang that followed seemed enough to awaken the dead, he had to repeat the act three more time before he heard impatient footsteps clattering down the hall. A moment later bolts were withdrawn and the door swung open.

'So it's you, Flight Lieutenant. Have you forgotten patients are supposed to be in their rooms by ten p.m.?'

'No, matron. I hadn't forgotten. But I'd walked farther than I thought.'

A sniff followed. 'You've been told not to walk far, Flight Lieutenant. That leg isn't fully better yet.'

Sean felt her look withering him as he walked past. Matron Hastings wore her blue starched uniform like a suit of armour and it took little imagination to believe she was capable of swinging a sword at her delinquent patients. 'Sorry, matron. But it is a beautiful night.'

There was the sound of bolts being engaged again. 'Beautiful nights don't repair damaged legs, Flight Lieutenant. Please try to remember that in the future.'

Sean pushed open door 16. Taffy Williams was lying on his bed reading Tit-Bits as he entered. Taffy was a typical pilot of his time, young, reckless, and full of sex and mordant humour. Grinning at Sean, he laid down the magazine. 'Did I hear the old dragon giving you a bollocking?'

Sean shrugged out of his tunic and hung it over a chair. 'Yes. I can't blame her. She's still in her uniform.'

'That's her fault. I sometimes think she sleeps in it. Where've you been, sir? To the cinema?'

'No. I've been trespassing.'

'Trespassing? How the hell can you do that around here?'

Sean took off his shoes and pulled off his tie before answering. 'Towards Bessington. There's a private estate over there, with woods and a lake. I met a woman there and we had a long talk.'

At that Taffy laid aside his Tit-Bits. 'What sort of woman?'

'A woman. A young one. The daughter of the estate owner from what I could gather.'

'Good looking?'

Sean began climbing into his pajamas.

21

'Yes, I suppose she was.'

'What do you mean, suppose? Was she or wasn't she?'

'Yes, she was. Very good looking.'

Taffy sat up higher in bed. 'You've been having a ding dong, haven't you? With some society woman. What was it like?'

'I said we had a talk. Nothing more. How long are you going to keep that light on? I want to get some sleep.'

Taffy was not diverted as easily as that. 'It sounds as if she could be rich. Are you seeing her again?'

Sean dropped into bed. 'I don't want to talk about it. Hurry up and get that light out.'

'C'mon, sir. It's as boring as hell in this place. And I can't sleep this early. What happened with this woman? Are you seeing her again?'

This time there was no answer and the young pilot saw Sean's eyes were closed. He was an odd bastard, Taffy thought. A hell of a pilot but not one of the lads. Not someone you shared a pint and your love life with. Not with those crazy ideas he had about life and the way we lived. Maybe his age had something to do with it. He couldn't be that far from thirty.

Deciding he was flogging a dead horse in trying to work up a conversation, Taffy was about to pick up his Tit-Bits again when he remembered there was also a rumour Hammond had an uncertain temper. Deciding it might be wise after all to obey matron's orders, Taffy sighed, laid his Tit-Bits aside, and clicked off the light. He had no idea as he lay back that Hammond was still fully awake and seeing on the screen of his closed eyes the lake in the woods and the woman standing alongside it.

Linda mentioned Hammond to her father after dinner that night when he was settled in his favourite armchair. Courteous, grey-headed, with shrewd blue eyes beneath bushy eyebrows, Charles Shaw was in many ways as traditional as the smoking jacket he was wearing and yet a parent Linda had always found accessible and generous. She waited until he had taken a sip from his nightly glass of port and was preparing to light his pipe before mentioning the incident. 'There was a man in the estate tonight. I ran into him when I was out with Jason. He was sitting beside the lake on one of those benches.'

Charles Shaw continued to pack his pipe. 'You mean a trespasser?'

'Yes. But not a poacher or anything like that. He was an RAF Flight Lieutenant with a DFC.'

Charles pressed down tobacco into his pipe bowl. 'What was he doing there?'

'Nothing that I could see. I think he was

just enjoying the peace of it all.'

'Did you talk to him?'

'Yes. Jason spotted him and rushed over. But there was no trouble. He seemed to like dogs because he was patting Jason by the time I reached him.'

'How did he come to be here? Did he say?'

'He's a patient in Littleworth. He didn't tell me the reason but I noticed he had a slight limp. Perhaps he's had a leg wound.'

Charles made a face. 'We're a fair way from Littleworth, No wonder he needed a rest. Had he walked here on his own?'

'He must have done.' She hesitated, then made her admission. 'I don't really know why but I've the feeling he's a very lonely man.'

Charles took a glance at her over his pipe. 'What made you think that?'

'I'm not really sure. He didn't behave that way. Perhaps it was something he said about himself when he was young although he told it in a humorous way.'

Charles lifted a bushy, amused eyebrow. 'You must have had quite a conversation with him. What happened in his childhood?'

'It wasn't what happened. It was just the kind of child he was. Always questioning everything he heard.'

Charles struck a match, drew on his pipe, and was rewarded with a puff of smoke. 'It sounds pretty normal to me. You weren't much different yourself when you were a child.'

'Yes, but it didn't make me lonely. It has this man. Somehow I could feel it.'

Charles's eyes twinkled. 'Is he good looking?'

'Yes, I suppose he is.' Then her tone changed. 'What's that supposed to mean? That I've fallen for him? Don't be so daft, Dad. That's ridiculous.'

Among his many attributes Charles Shaw had an impish sense of humour. 'Why don't you invite him to dinner before he goes back on duty. Then I can question your mystery man and find out why he's lonely. If my guess is right he knows there's no better ploy than loneliness to win a good looking girl's interest. I know. Back in the last war I used to try it on every French girl I met.'

She laughed. 'From what Mum used to say I'm not surprised. But he wasn't like that. It wasn't what he said. It was the feeling I got.'

Charles Shaw was missing nothing of his beautiful daughter's curiosity. Examining the bowl of his pipe, he pressed down a rising flake before glancing back at her. 'I'd still like to meet your mystery man. When are you seeing him again?'

She knew there was no point in prevaricating. 'I said he could come again if he liked it here. I don't feel he's too happy at the hospital. But of course he might not bother.'

Charles grimaced. 'He won't be much of a man if he doesn't come back to see a lovely girl like you. If you think he's lonely he might enjoy dinner and company. Don't worry. I'll be sociable to him.'

'I know you will. I'll ask him although somehow I don't think he'll accept.'

'Why not?'

'I don't know. I just feel it, that's all.'

Charles eyed her, then pressed down another flake in his pipe bowl. 'I take it he knows you're married, does he?'

She gave a start. 'Of course he does. We introduced ourselves. What daft idea have you got now? That I'm having an affair with a man I only met tonight?'

Charles could never be at odds with his beautiful daughter for long. 'No, of course I don't. You feel there's a mystery about the man and you want to solve it. And you've always liked mysteries. I remember the trouble your mother and I had in finding you the latest mystery novel. Only don't forget how involved with them you always became.'

Laughing now, she crossed the floor and kissed him. 'I'm not going to get involved, Dad. Don't forget I'm happily married. So don't have any silly thoughts on that score.' She glanced at an ornate clock on the mantelpiece. 'I'm going to bed now. Don't be too late yourself. Remember what the doctor told you.'

He returned her kiss, then watched her slim, graceful figure leave the room. His eyes were still thoughtful as he took another sip from his glass of port.

THREE

Although Linda took Jason for his walk a few minutes earlier than usual the following evening Sean was already seated on a bench when she reached the lake. As Jason gave an excited bark, she released the dog from his leash. 'All right. Go and say hello.'

Before the words had left her mouth the dog was bounding towards Sean. She saw him turn and a moment later the dog was leaping up and trying to lick his face. Calming the dog down, he gave it something to eat. She laughed as she drew nearer. 'You've certainly made a hit with him. What's that you're giving him? He seems to like it.'

He returned her smile. 'One of the lads got some chocolate from the NAAFI before he came into hospital. I managed to scrounge a bar from him. Would you like some?'

She shook her head as she sat down. 'No. I'm not one for sweets. Keep it for yourself and Jason.' Leaning forward she laid a basket on the grass between them. 'I've brought something we can both have instead.'

He watched her lift out a bottle of wine and two glasses. 'It's red,' she told him. 'Is that all right?'

He was showing surprise. 'Yes, red's fine. Thank you.' He reached out his hand. 'Shall I open it?'

'It's all right. I've already loosened the cork.' As she poured out two glasses, Sean gave the dog the last piece of chocolate, then showed him an empty packet. 'Sorry, old lad. That's the lot.'

Although Jason seemed to understand, he still remained seated at Sean's feet. 'He's certainly taken to you,' she said, handing him a filled glass. 'What's your secret? Natural charm?'

He took the glass, then patted the dog's head. 'There's no secret. Just the opposite. It's what there is not that does it?'

'Is not? I don't follow.'

'Most people have some fear of large dogs. Sometimes it's no more than caution but dogs smell even that. So they're wary and it takes time to break down the barriers. But if there's no fear there are no barriers to break down.'

'And you haven't any fear. Is that it?'

'Not of dogs,' he said. 'None at all.'

Not of dogs, she thought. What had that slight inflexion signified? Or was it her

28

imagination? She wanted to ask the question but knew it was far too early yet. Instead she laughed. 'Anyway, it seems to work. Have you ever kept dogs?'

'Whenever I could. Life never seems complete without them.' He made a somewhat disparaging gesture at his uniform. 'But it's quite impossible these days.'

Without knowing why she felt on safer ground now. She took a sip from her glass. 'How's the wine?'

'Very good. But you shouldn't spoil a trespasser this way?'

The remark reminded her again of his teasing, quirkish sense of humour. 'How did you get on last night? Was the matron waiting up for you?'

He pulled a face. 'As a matter of fact she was. And still in her uniform. I daren't think of the report she's going to put in about me.'

'And yet you've come again,' she said, regretting her comment as soon as she made it. 'You must like our haven as much as I do.'

He seemed about to reply. Then, to her relief, he changed the subject. 'Is your mother still alive? Or shouldn't I ask.'

'No. She died six years ago. What about your parents?'

'My mother's still around. She's in Leeds. My stepfather's in Nottingham.'

Stepfather, she thought. As she wondered if there might be fertile ground there, he nodded at the lake on which, in spite of the lateness of the hour, the water lilies were still open. 'You're right about your haven. I can understand why you and your brother enjoyed playing here. It has something very special about it.'

Although his reversion back to the glade carried its embarrassments she was pleased by his comment. 'That's what I've always felt. A place where one can escape. A sort of oasis from the world.'

He turned back to her with an expression she could not define. 'I wouldn't have thought you needed an oasis. Do you?'

She did not know how to answer. 'I've never thought so. But don't we all need one at some time in our lives? A retreat where we can assess our thoughts and beliefs.'

His eyes were moving over her face as if he were seeing her for the first time. 'Do you do that very often?'

'Do what?'

'Assess your beliefs to see if they're still valid?'

His change of tone was puzzling her. 'Not as often as perhaps I should. But as you said last night – how many of us do, particularly these days when we have a war to fight.'

His nod gave his answer. His gaze stayed on her a moment longer, then he glanced back at the lake. 'Did I upset you last night when you thought I was your brother sitting here?'

'No. I got a bit of a shock but only for an instant. Why do you ask?'

'Does it mean you are religious?'

She gave a start. Until then conversation with him had flowed easily. 'What a strange question. Why do you ask?'

'It was your belief that you saw your brother again. It sounds as if you believe in the supernatural.'

The intrusiveness of his question made her frown. 'Don't we all have such feelings now and then?'

'No. I can't say I do.'

She wondered if his wartime role had corroded his sensitivity. Curiosity drew the question from her that she was to regret a moment later. 'Does this mean you're not religious?'

He gave a sudden start and his expression changed. 'Me? Religious? Good God, no. Whatever gave you the idea I believe all that damned nonsense?'

His accusation, expression, and change of tone shocked her and for a few seconds she was lost for words. Then she pulled herself together. 'I'm sorry. I suppose I shouldn't have asked the question. It was rude of me.'

His hostile expression faded at her apology. His short laugh indicated his earlier mood was back. 'Sorry. I shouldn't have jumped on you like that. Only I happen to be oversensitive about religion. I see its influence as harmful rather than benign. Nor, for that matter, has it done me any favours in the past.' As she was wondering what his last sentence signified he went on 'What about you?'

Although surprised, even shocked, by his reaction she knew she had left herself little choice but to give an answer herself. 'I'm a Catholic. I can't say I'm a good one but I try to live by its teachings. What happened to turn you against religion? Or would you rather not say?'

His momentary pause gave her the impression he had taken warning and was closing some portal in his mind. At the same time his reply carried its own logic. 'I've never needed anything more than religion's history to put me off. The times men have slaughtered women and children and burned one another alive simply because of their different ways of worshipping their same God. If there's one single thing that illustrates man is a sick animal it has to be how he has handled religion.'

She could not believe what she was hearing. 'That's a ridiculous thing to say. It's our religious beliefs that set us above the animals.'

He lifted an eyebrow, 'Sets us up? What

history have you read? What about the Cru-
sades? What about the massacre of Ancre?
What about Torquemada? What about the
Hundred Years War? Just a few of the hor-
rors Christians have carried out in the name
of Christ. Not that they're alone. The rest of
the sects have just as many battle honours to
their name. How can you possibly believe
religion elevates us? It's the fall back wea-
pon for every despot that ever lived. If he
can't get his people to do his dirty work on
his own he fires them up with religion. That
does the trick every time.'

She shook her head in astonishment.
'What sort of religion are you talking about?
My church teaches mercy and goodwill to
all men.'

'Then you're lucky. You might have a good
priest. But even so how far does his Christian goodwill stretch? To Muslims and Sikhs
and Buddhists and Jews? What was the em-
blem of the Conquistadors when they tore
natives apart with horses for not accepting
their religion? Or the Ku Klux Klan's when
they were burning some poor devil alive?
Stop me if I'm wrong but wasn't it the Cross
of Christ?'

His new outburst was stunning her. The
man she had seen so far as an amicable
stranger was suddenly digging a shovel into
her life-long beliefs and throwing them into
the air as if they were garbage. 'Those things

33

were done by fanatics years ago. We're not the same people today.'

'Aren't we? What about the slaughter of the Armenians? What about the blood sacrifices that are still practised? Religions started off well enough but they went right off the rails the moment politicians and financiers started making their own interpretations of them. The religions we have today are materialistic, prejudiced and divisive as you'll find out when this war is over. There'll be more wars and I'll lay you a pound to a penny that a high percentage will use religious fanaticism to serve their ends.'

She could not believe what she was hearing. At the same time it was a reminder this was no uneducated man launching his attack. Her inability to deny his historical facts kept her temper under control. 'You're talking about fanatics, as you said yourself. Not about normal people.'

He shrugged. 'Who are fanatics but people who have a stronger faith than the rest of us? The stronger the faith the greater the intolerance. Is that a defence of religion?'

Damn the man, she thought. She had always thought herself tolerant but he was getting under her skin faster than anyone she had known. 'You're attacking people for being religious when a need of it is part of our make up. We were born with that need so what's the point of attacking it?'

34

He gave a short, hard laugh. 'We were born with lust and greed and savagery. Does that mean we shouldn't control them too?'

'That's a stupid answer. Religion is a beautiful thing when its message of love and tolerance are obeyed.'

'But when are they? Isn't every sect taught to believe it has the only true faith and doesn't that by definition make it look down on all the rest? And what does that kind of arrogance lead to?'

Unable to deny his last accusation she fell back on a defence that seemed weak even to herself. 'You're arguing against human nature. Our history and culture have decided which faith we have. So how can we avoid the rivalry that comes between us?'

His sudden laugh came as a surprise. 'I've got a solution for you. Let's invent a common religion. As most of them believe in God, let's keep him on his throne but work out a way of worship we can all practice. Let's do an Esperanto, take the early and best parts of each religion, and then invent common rituals, a common prayer book, and common hymns.' As he spoke his voice became teasing. 'You know something? If that big man in the sky is as kind and merciful as our priests and vicars tell us, he might just prefer our fraternizing and buying one another bars of chocolate than pouring boiling oil over one another in the old fashioned way.'

To her surprise she found herself smiling. 'It's a novel idea but you know it can never happen?'

He leaned forward. 'Why not? Take the world's two largest religions, Islam and Christianity. Their links are so intricately bound that when you read the Koran you can sometimes think you're reading the Bible. Didn't even Saint John of Damascus believe at first that Islam was just a variation on a Christian theme? Didn't Christians, Jews and Muslims once live together as neighbours and friends within the Ottoman empire? I'd bet you that if an old Byzantium monk came alive today he'd have more in common with Muslims than our modern Christian evangelists.'

She shook her head. 'You're losing me. I don't know anything about Islam.'

'Then isn't that your answer? Modern nations discourage such knowledge. Working all the time to promote their own identity and importance they distort the differences of other religions until they appear alien. As a result we see nations with different religious ceremonies as rivals and sometimes as enemies. But if we ever found the sense to set aside our idiot patriotism and accept how much we all have in common we could cure our bigotry like any other disease.'

As she had listened to him one word had

rung in her ears above all else. 'What was that about patriotism? You're not attacking it too, are you?'

His eyes met her own in a challenge she would never forget 'Of course I am. It's as dangerous a poison as modern religion. In fact in many ways it's worse.'

FOUR

She could not believe what she was hearing. The man was a fighter ace with a battle award. 'You've lost me completely. How can you call patriotism a poison when you're a part of the Armed Forces fighting for your country?'

He shrugged. 'Patriotism has nothing to do with it as far as I'm concerned. I'm at war with a bunch of thugs and bullies called the Nazis. It's as simple as that.'

'But doesn't your country mean anything to you?'

'Of course it does. I like its villages and its pubs and its fields and its cathedrals. But I like French chateaux, Italian tenors, and German composers too.'

She was struggling to understand. 'You're saying you also appreciate other nations' assets and treasures? I accept that but doesn't this country have a special place for you?'

'Not in the sense you mean. I can't tub thump and put my hand on my heart because I'm English. When I go abroad I try not to be English but just be another human being.'

Her brow furrowed. 'I see your point. But is it possible to be so detached? Don't you feel something special when you hear your country's martial music being played or when your national football team wins a trophy. Don't you get a feeling of pride?'

To her surprise he nodded. 'Yes. And I dislike it.'

'But why? It's a natural feeling.'

'Perhaps it is but it's tribal. It's something we have to overcome if we're ever to have peace in the world. We have to re-write our history books and stop our governments and our culture brainwashing us. We have to see the world as a single house, not a squabbling block of a hundred apart-ments.'

She took a deep breath. 'You're an idealist, aren't you? You're a fighter pilot with a battle honour fighting for a country for which he has no special feeling. I take it you are English, aren't you?'

His laugh told her his sense of humour was back. 'So my mother and father told me.'

'Then how do you operate? What drives you on?'

'I've told you. I loathe bullies and particularly those who want to inflict their damned twisted culture upon us. Isn't that enough to drive any man on?'

'It wouldn't be for me. I need my love of country.'

He nodded. 'So do the other races. How does Hitler get his armies to fight so well? To fight and die for the Fatherland. Mix that with religion and you've got a drug more potent than heroin.'

'But why must you bring religion into it?'

'Why? Because padres deliberately mix it into the drug. Die for your country and you go straight to heaven. My country right or wrong. Was there ever a more unprincipled assertion?' When she did not reply he went on: 'Do you know that in the last war some padres used to bless the very guns that killed men in the other trenches. They're not quite so bad in this war but they'll still bless you and tell you to fight with all your might and bring the Hun to his knees. Quite a thought when you know other padres are telling the Germans the same things about us.'

'You can't blame religion for that,' she protested. 'Nor can you blame the padres. Some men need the comfort of a blessing before they go into action.'

His laugh was hard again. 'Then isn't it

time they all grew up? What happens when a Jerry and I kill one another? Do we shake hands and share a cigarette before we float up to heaven together? Or do we have another scrap before we go down to hell? Dr. Johnson had it right. There isn't a word in the dictionary that's killed more people than patriotism.'

She shook her head. 'I still don't know how you keep going with these views. Do you ever discuss them with your friends?'

He took a sip of wine before answering her. 'You're a protected specie, Mrs Martin. You obviously haven't lived on a station with a bunch of servicemen.'

'But there must be some places where you can meet people and have arguments and discussions.'

'There is. The White Hart in Lonbridge. Another abode of sanity and brilliant debate.'

She made a mental note of the name. 'Do you go there?'

'Only when I want to get drunk. And oddly enough that isn't often these days. I sometimes wonder why.'

'Perhaps you should go there more often. It might relax you.'

He shrugged. 'Perhaps I don't need relaxing. After all what are we? Only demented ants fighting over a scrap of tree leaf. I don't suppose ants need religion or patriotism to kill one another, so why should we?'

It was an answer that chilled her with its implications. 'Don't you value your life?' she asked.

The look he gave her was charged with a complexity of emotions she could not analyse. Yet when he answered her his mood was light again. 'You think I'm a dreamer, don't you? Or some kind of fruitcake?'

'Fruitcake? What on earth is that?'

'The service expression for a clown or idiot.'

She wondered how to answer and then took courage. 'No, but you are a revolutionary, aren't you? You attack things many of us believe in and rake up other things that some people feel in their hearts but never put into thoughts or words. So you can't expect to be too popular.'

'Does that mean I've offended you with my views on religion and patriotism?'

'No. My faith's strong enough to withstand criticism. And I do know that religious prejudice has caused crimes in the past. So you haven't offended me.' She picked up the bottle of wine. 'Let's finish this before you go. I don't want to take it back.'

As she filled his glass she remembered Charles' invitation. 'I mentioned you to my father last night. He said he'd like you to have dinner with us before you return to your squadron.'

He gave a nod of appreciation. 'He has a distinguished First World War record, hasn't he?'

The question told her he had been making enquiries, 'Yes, I suppose he has. He ended up on Earl Haig's staff.'

He made a humorous face. 'Your father on the General Staff, your brother and husband in the RAF... That's something to give Jerry a nightmare or two.' He pointed down at Jason. 'What his role? Military police?'

She was reminded again how his humour attracted her. 'No. Jason's a civilian through and through. He ignores all the DROs.'

'Good for him,' he smiled. 'A man after my own heart.' Then he changed the subject. 'No, it's good of your father but with my views he'd probably have me arrested as a fifth columnist. So perhaps I'd better thank him but say no.'

She was secretly relieved but felt obliged to make a protest. 'You don't have to bring those things up. I certainly wouldn't.'

He shook his head. 'They'd probably come out if your father is as good at exposing a man's beliefs as you are.' Then he paused. 'By the by, are you sure they haven't upset you? I didn't mean them to.'

'No,' she said. 'I don't share them but even if you were right, how could you bring about such changes when not one person is a million would agree with you?'

His smile was whimsical. 'Is that necessarily bad?'

'It's bad for your peace of mind, your social life, and your digestion.'

He laughed. 'So if I could just convince one person, it might help my digestion. Any offers?'

The challenge made her smile back. 'Yes, why not. You want some kind of Utopia and I suppose we all want that. So, yes, I'll go that far with you.'

His lips quirked. 'How far is that?'

'Until you start attacking my religion and my patriotism. That's when I stop.'

He gave her a mocking half bow. 'At least that's a beginning. There's hope for me yet.'

The unconventionality of his arguments and his willingness to discuss them with a total stranger gave her a sudden disturbing thought. Having found out that religion played a part in her life, were his attacks and arguments nothing more than a ploy to intrigue and gain her interest? It came as a relief to hear his apology when he picked up his glass of wine again. 'Sorry. I know I've talked too much. I'll finish this glass and go.'

'Do you know yet when you're going back on duty?'

'No, but we're having medicals tomorrow evening. As I'm sure they'll pass me fit again that'll only leave Friday before I'm back at Donnington.'

She could not believe it was she who was asking the question. 'Does that mean you'd like to come back again on Friday evening? If you would the haven will still be here.'

In the brief silence that fell an aircraft engine could be heard and his face lifted as he tried to trace its path across the moonlit sky. Then his eyes lowered to her. 'I could come on Friday. But only if you're sure I'm not wasting your evenings.'

'If you were I'd say so. Come on Friday evening and tell me more what's wrong with the world. Who knows? It might be good for me.'

Smiling, he rose with her. 'I doubt that. But as you've invited me, it's on your own head.'

This time she waited until he had left, sitting back on the bench and tidying up the glasses and the empty bottle. When she had finished she leaned against the table and tried to sort out her thoughts. Why was she doing this? Did she like the man or was she only fascinated by his iconoclasm? She had not needed to take his hint of a further meeting. She could have ended it there instead of behaving like a coquettish girl and virtually aiding him to invite himself. What was the point of further meetings? She was in no need of a lover. She was in love with Douglas and even if their meetings were infrequent she was still better off than

most women in wartime with their husbands and lovers often abroad.

Then why was she continuing to see a man
whose beliefs were so alien and opposite to
her own? What was the impulse behind it?
Had it any point in his life or her own?
Unable to see one she decided her father was
right. A lover of mysteries, she had come
across a man who seemed in total conflict
with himself, a man who seemed to bear a
grudge against God himself, a man who de-
spised the patriotism that made his colleagues put their lives on the line for their
country, and yet a man who was fighting
alongside them with such skill and courage
that he had won a battle award. Although he
had never lifted the sixth veil that hid his
bitterness, much less than the seventh, she
sensed in him a loneliness so deep it called
for help from anyone who considered
themselves a caring human being.

This was her reason, she told herself, and
surely not one that carried any guilt. After
all, she argued, her contact with him had not
been of her own making. Fate had brought
them together and she held the belief there
was usually a purpose behind such events. If
she were right and this odd passionate man
needed help, it was surely her duty to give it
and in doing so she might solve the mystery
that intrigued her, for she felt certain there
was a mystery behind his bitterness. Having

convinced herself with her argument, she put the leash on the impatient Jason and led him home.

She heard her father calling for her later that evening when she was drying Jason. Giving him a last rub she released his lead and went to the sitting room where Charles was in his favourite armchair with the radio alongside him. As she entered he switched the radio off and turned to her. 'Well, how did it go? Did your pilot turn up again?'

She dropped on the settee opposite him. 'Yes, he was there.'

'I never thought he wouldn't be. Did you get his loneliness sorted out?'

'I can't say that,' she said. 'I'm not even sure he is lonely. But if he is I think I know at least one reason for it. I also think he's had some bad experiences in his life.'

'What kind of experiences?'

'I don't know but I'm sure he's had them. Otherwise I can't see why he's so hostile to religion.'

'Hostile? Is he an atheist?'

'Very much so. Almost obsessively, in fact.'

Charles gave his impish grin. 'At least he doesn't sound boring. What other neuroses does he have?'

Finding it a relief to talk, she told him about her recent conversation. Relaxed as Charles could be, he only showed surprise when she mentioned Sean's views on patriotism. 'Did he really say that? You're sure he wasn't pulling your leg?'

'No. He meant them. He volunteered for aircrew only because he dislikes bullies. He thinks patriotism is tribal and divisive.'

'And he claims he's an atheist too?'

'Yes. Very much so.'

Charles reflected a moment, then nodded. 'Then he's almost certainly a Bolshevik. One of those characters who wants to drag down the Crown and install a Communist state. As long as I can remember they've always been around.'

'But where does religion come into it? He gives the impression he detests it.'

'Some Communists do, darling. They believe it's been used in the past to keep the working classes down. Particularly in Russia.'

She shook her head doubtfully. 'Somehow he doesn't seem the type. In any case why would he be fighting and risking his life for this country if he wants to bring it down?'

'Darling, Communists hate Fascism as the devil hates holy water. Like the Russians, they fight to get rid of Hitler. It's only afterwards they'll show their true colours.'

'I suppose you could be right.' Then she shook her head. 'No. I can't believe it of this man. He just isn't the type.'

Charles lifted a bushy eyebrow. 'Then what type is he?'

'I can't explain. His ideas aren't destructive when he talks about them. In their way they're calling for a more peaceful world.'

'Like abandoning religion and love of country? Come on, darling. It's the way all anarchists talk. Go along with them and we're in Utopia until they roll out their true colours. Stop seeing him, darling. It wouldn't do Douglas any good if it became known you'd become friendly with a man like that.'

She suddenly found herself wishing she had kept her second meeting a secret. 'He's no anarchist, Dad. He just sees life differently to the rest of us. And after all, whatever his views, he is risking his life for this country.'

Charles always found it difficult to argue for long with his favourite daughter but on this issue he held his ground. 'He's no mystery man or wounded animal, darling, so he doesn't need your help. He's a Bolshie and I'd prefer him not to trespass on the estate again.'

FIVE

Group Captain Douglas Martin, Linda's husband, arrived at Smalloaks the following morning. Linda spotted his staff car from her bedroom as she was teasing and combing her hair. Running downstairs she was at the front door before he reached it himself. 'Hello, darling. This is a lovely surprise. But why didn't you ring?'

Removing his cap Douglas gave her a kiss and a hug. 'I only found out I could get away last night when it was too late to phone. And I deliberately left early this morning in case something cropped up to spoil it.'

'How long can you stay?'

'That's the catch. I'll have to be back this evening. But a few hours is better than none, isn't it?'

She gave him another kiss. 'Of course it is. Give me your bag to take upstairs while you have coffee. You'll find Mrs Griffiths in the kitchen.'

A welcoming voice made them both turn. Charles Mason was approaching them with outstretched hand. 'Hello, my boy. This is a nice surprise. What's happened? Is the war over?'

Douglas clasped his hand. 'I'm afraid not, sir. But we're not doing badly. With luck we should be back in Europe soon.'

'Let's hope you're right, my boy. I'm getting tired of doing all these estate jobs myself.'

'I hope you're not doing too many, sir. You're supposed to be taking it easy, aren't you?'

Charles grinned and motioned at the smiling Linda. 'That's what she keeps telling me. She doesn't realize I only went sick to get her time off from that office. Now I'm trying to stay sick to keep her here.'

Linda's eyes were on the two men as they laughed and chatted. Her father, grey-haired and stooping slightly in spite of his efforts to retain his military posture; Douglas the archetypal RAE staff officer with immaculate uniform, brevet and ribbons, and the moustache that had become the hallmark of fighter pilots. For a moment a picture of the clean-shaven Sean Hammond flashed in her mind, to be dismissed instantly as she continued examining her husband. He looked well, she thought, even although there were a few grey threads mingled in his brown hair that had been absent two years ago. The effect was more distinguishing than aging and not for the first time she had a sense of pride at being married to one of the youngest staff officers in the service.

Her father's question brought her back to the present. 'What do the two of you want to do today? If you want lunch here Mrs Griffiths will need telling.'

Douglas met Linda's eyes before she could answer. 'I don't think we want to go out, do we? I've done all the driving I want this morning and in any case I'll have to leave no later than five o'clock.'

Linda had not missed the unspoken message Douglas had given her. 'No, we'll stay in, Dad. I'll talk to Mrs Griffiths about lunch.'

Charles, no amateur to the needs of the young, offered no argument and soon tactfully disappeared to leave the couple to themselves. Fully aware what Douglas wanted and although not averse herself, Linda persuaded him first to take a walk around the estate. 'It's a fine morning and you look as if you need some fresh air.' When Douglas gave her a rueful look she laughed. 'We've plenty of time and you know what Mrs Griffiths is like. If she finds we're both locked up there in the bedroom she'll have everyone around here sniggering. Wait until lunch is over. She goes home then.'

Taking Jason with them they walked round the estate and to the local shops and returned an hour later. When Charles heard them return he broke his self-imposed banishment and joined them in the sitting room for coffee. After chatting to Douglas about the war situation and the prospects of victory, he gave a chuckle and nodded at Linda. 'Has Linda said anything to you about the airman she met the other night?'

Douglas shook his head. 'Airman? No. Where?'

Charles chuckled again. 'On the estate. Apparently he doesn't take any notice of private property signs. That's one reason I think he's a Bolshie. That and the things he said to her.'

Douglas glanced at Linda. 'What sort of things?'

Charles sat back with his morning cigar. 'Tell him, darling.'

Caught by surprise Linda had to collect her thoughts. 'I came across him when I was taking Jason for a walk. He was sitting alone at that table by the lake. Jason barked and rushed up to him but quietened down right away when the man patted him.'

'What rank was he?' Douglas broke in. 'An erk? An ordinary airman?'

'No. He was a pilot. A Flight Lieutenant with the DFC.'

Douglas showed surprise 'A pilot? Just the same he shouldn't have been trespassing. Didn't you tell him so?'

'No. How could I? He wasn't doing any harm. I had the feeling he was lonely and enjoying the peace and quiet.'

'So what happened?'

She found it difficult to explain. 'He was polite and talking normally until we got on to religion.'

Douglas lowered his cup of coffee. 'Religion? What on earth were you doing talking about religion?'

'I honestly don't know,' she confessed. 'He suddenly brought it up and at the same time his mood changed. It gave me the impression he'd had some bad experience with it in the past.'

'He didn't insult you, did he?'

'Oh, no. Nothing like that. But he did say he thought religion and patriotism were twin poisons. Or something of that nature.'

Douglas gave a start. 'Patriotism! A poison!' He glanced at Charles and then back at Linda. 'Did you get his name?'

Realizing what was happening she was suddenly thankful she hadn't given Sean's name to her father. 'No,' she lied. 'I never asked him. But don't worry about it. I just think he's a man with different views to the rest of us.'

Douglas's clipped voice was dry. 'Very different. And you say he's a Flight Lieutenant?'

'Yes, with the DFC. So he can't be a fifth columnist or anything like that, can he?'

For a moment Douglas Martin was very much the staff officer. 'You're quite sure you didn't get his name? Did he give you his unit?'

Her alarm grew. 'No. He never mentioned it.' To cover herself she lied again. 'I got the impression he was from some squadron up north and was down here on leave. But I could be wrong.'

As the words left her mouth she saw her father's eyes settle on her and remembered she had told him Sean was a local hospital patient. Afraid he might correct her she went on quickly: 'He did say something about having been in hospital but I gathered that was some time ago.'

A slight twitch of Charles's eyebrows told Linda he had picked up her signals. Charles treated his two daughters as adults and if one of them chose to tell a fib he accepted she had a reason. To Linda's relief he added support to her story. 'To me he sounds like one of those bolshie northern characters. All radical and revolutionary but ready enough for a scrap when one comes along.'

She gave her father a grateful nod. 'You could be right. I think he had a slight northern accent.'

Douglas was not so easily satisfied. 'Do you think he's likely to come again?'

She hated the lies she was having to tell but could see no way of avoiding them. 'I wouldn't think so. Why should he?'

'Let me know if he does. And get his name

if you can. Our disciplinary unit are only too keen to get their hands on servicemen who spread that kind of talk about.'

Charles' laugh told Linda that he regretted his earlier mention of the intruder. 'Don't take it too seriously, Douglas. If the man's shooting down Nazis, what does it matter if he's an atheist or an anarchist? If he's locked up it only means some decent lad has to take his place and where's the profit in that? If he's good enough to win medals, let him go on until the Nazis get him. Then we've gained on the deal both ways.'

Douglas gazed at him, then shrugged. 'I suppose you're right. But it's not what the rule book says.'

Charles made a face. 'Since when did rule books win wars or shoot down Nazi bombers? If our intruder's doing that and doesn't believe in a hereafter then he's got more sand than I have. All that kept me from running away in my time was the thought of a cushy reward in heaven.' He turned to Linda. 'How about more coffee, darling? All this speculation is making me thirsty.'

She thanked him with her eyes as she picked up the tray. At the same time she realized for the first time the odd and precarious situation her curiosity was creating.

Douglas made love to her that afternoon in

55

their bedroom. He gave a sigh of relief when he threw off his tunic and began undressing. 'I was getting worried when I kept looking at the time.'

She smiled back. 'You didn't need to. I was keeping an eye on it too.'

'Thank God for that. I was beginning to think you'd gone off me.'

Laughing, she pulled off her slip and then her bra. 'How can you think that after the letters I write you?'

As she lowered her panties he eyed the lithe, naked and beautiful body before him. 'I need the real thing, darling. Letters are fine but they don't fill the needs I have.'

She was fully aware of that. She had always found him an eager and virile lover. 'Never mind. The war can't last for ever.'

He grasped hold of her and she felt his hardness pressing against her groin. 'I don't mind the war. It's done well for me. It's this part of life that I miss.' Bending down he kissed her breasts before easing her towards the bed. 'All these long nights in an empty cot. It's nothing but a damned waste.'

She feigned surprise. 'Waste? From a Group Captain helping his country to win a war?'

He grinned at her and pushed her on to the bed. 'Aren't war and sex supposed to go together?'

'Are they? Then it's a pity they don't

arrange things better between them.'

'I'll go with that,' he said. 'I'll make the point when I get back to Group.'

With that she felt him parting her legs. She wrapped her arms around his naked shoulders and drew him over her. 'Never mind. It'll all come right soon. We'll have our own house and...' She broke off with a gasp as he entered her. As he drove deeper she drew his face down to her own. 'I miss this too, Douglas. Just as much as you.'

He gave no answer. His loins were rising and falling and his breathing growing short and rapid. As her body responded she felt it was growing lighter and floating into space. She wanted to cry out things that had no meaning but his lips were now pressed tightly to her own, imprisoning whatever words were there. She wanted the moment to last forever but his eagerness was too great. His stabs at the core of her being became so rapid that for a moment he had to lift his head to take breath. In that split second, his handsome face seemed to blur and become clean shaven. The true image returned at once but not before a shock ran through her. Sensing it Douglas gazed down at her. 'What is it? What's the matter?'

She reached down his body and urged him deeper into her. 'Nothing,' she panted. 'Just go on loving me. Don't stop. Please don't stop.'

His thrusts began again and again she floated upwards towards the sun and the stars. When his climax came she wanted more of him but his deep sob of contentment was enough in itself. When his breathing quieted his head lifted to her. 'What happened? Did I hurt you?'

'No. It wasn't that.'

'I was too quick, wasn't I? Only I couldn't help it. It's been too long.'

She smiled at him. 'Four weeks.'

'Too bloody long,' he muttered. 'And I don't know when I'll he able to get up again.'

At moments like this she could never link him with the efficient disciplinarian she knew he was. 'Never mind. As you've said yourself, it can't last that much longer. Then you'll see too much of me.'

He dropped back on the sheets. 'Stop talking rubbish.'

She turned and stroked his face. 'You've been working too hard lately. Have a little sleep now. You've plenty of time.'

He was asleep in a couple of minutes. But she could not join him. She could not forget that momentary glimpse of a clean shaven rebellious face and the memory filled her with both disquiet and bewilderment. It also made her question again the wisdom of the plan she had made for the following evening.

SIX

Linda found the White Hart at the far end of Longbridge. As she parked Charles's car in the car park she saw a fighter flying low over the town, a sign that Donnington was only a couple of miles to the east. Finding to her relief the pub was open, she entered the public bar, ordered half a pint of beer, and found a table near the window. The only other occupants were two middle aged men whose appearance and behaviour suggested they were commercial travellers. Both had shown some surprise at her entry as had the somewhat flashy barmaid, but to her relief none made any comment although one of the two men kept making surreptitious glances in her direction.

It was the evening after Douglas's visit. Telling Charles she would like to visit some friends in Longbridge she had asked if she could borrow his old Bentley. She had feared that his limited wartime ration of petrol might deny her the loan but Charles used the car seldom these days and he had concurred with the only caveat that she drove no further than the small market town. She had waited until she believed the town's pubs would be open and then driven straight there.

She was disappointed to find the pub empty of airmen. As the minutes ticked by, she wondered if she had picked an evening when the airfield personnel were restricted by some operational duty. Nor did the occasional sound from the airfield of an engine under test do anything to reassure her. A further embarrassment was the curious glances the barmaid kept throwing at her as the girl flitted in and out of the bar. Although she was only sipping at her beer, the glass was now half empty and she could hardly remain in the pub without ordering another.

Seeing the curiosity of the two travellers was growing along with the barmaid she felt embarrassment and then impatience at herself. It had been a ridiculous project from the beginning, she thought. She had met a man who had spilled out far fetched ideas to her in a moment of loneliness and she had allowed her imagination and curiosity to do the rest. Her father was right. She loved mysteries and she was making one out of a man who, for all she knew, might be quite different when surrounded by colleagues and friends. He might be the anarchist as her father believed, or he might even suffer some mental derangement because of the war. On top of that the odds were that after tomorrow night she would never see him again.

For that matter did she want to? Their meetings had told her he was a very different man to Douglas and any involvement with him might create problems that might embarrass or even harm her marriage.

She was about to leave when she heard voices and laughter outside. Glancing from the window she saw a party of airmen making their way down the road to the pub. For a moment she hesitated. There was still time to escape and if she kept away from the lake the following night the entire bizarre episode would be ended. Then, as if disobeying her, her body sank back on the chair and she watched the half dozen airmen enter the bar.

Seeing from their brevets they were all pilots she feared for a moment that Sean might be among them. When she saw they were all younger men, she decided that having come this far it would be cowardly to quit now. Sliding her skirt a little higher above her knees she sat back, lit herself another cigarette, and waited.

She had little time to wait. The six men had already noticed her and kept casting glances in her direction. As they drank, their amused comments grew louder until a young fresh-faced pilot officer, accompanied by cheers from the others, made his way to her table. 'Hello,' he said. 'Can I buy you a drink?'

Deciding to play hard to get, she pointed at her glass. 'I still have one, thank you.'

He gave her a grin. 'That's nearly empty. Let me get you another.'

'All right,' she said. 'But only a half pint.'

Accompanied by more cheers from his colleagues he triumphantly brought another filled glass to her table and then sat down. 'What's your name, love?'

'Lucy,' she lied. 'Lucy Brown.'

'Why haven't I seen you here before, Lucy?'

'Because I haven't been here before. I've only just moved down to these parts.'

'Where from?'

'London,' she said.

Suddenly he looked uncertain and she guessed her upper class accent was confusing him. 'I thought you didn't talk like people around here.'

She shrugged. 'So what. You don't either. What's your name?'

'Jack. Jack Etherington.'

'What station are you from? Donnington?'

He nodded. He indicated the five men at the bar who were getting steadily drunk. 'We all are. This is our pub.'

She wondered if it were too early to make her ploy. 'I met one of your men the other day. A pilot called Hammond.'

His expression changed. 'Hammond? Where was that?'

'In a shop here. I was with a relation and

buying something when he came in. The shop keeper told us afterwards who he was. Do you know him?'

His young face was looking puzzled. 'Yes. I know him all right. Who doesn't? A tall Flight Lieutenant with a DFC.'

'That's him,' she said. She tried to make her words and voice match the lie she had invented. 'My relation fancies him. She'd like to get to know him.'

His earlier flirtatious mood returned with her explanation. 'She's got some chance.'

She gave a slight start. 'Why is that? Doesn't he like girls?'

'I don't know if he likes them or not. But I wouldn't think they like him.'

Her curiosity grew. 'Why is that?'

He shrugged. 'Because he's an unsocial bastard. Some say it's because of a girl, others because of a friend he lost. Whatever it was it's made him a miserable old sod.'

Her curiosity was growing. 'You say he lost a friend? In combat?'

'I suppose so although I don't know the details. It happened at Lemington before he was posted to us.' Etherington's indifferent shrug was the gesture expected of a wartime fighter pilot. 'But so what? It happens all the time. So why should it affect him that way?'

'What way?'

Etherington shrugged again. 'Taking bloody stupid chances. Flying too close to

Jerries before opening fire. Daft things like that.'

'You're not saying he's trying to kill himself?'

'I wouldn't go that far. But who knows?' Growing tired of talking about Hammond, the young pilot became impatient. 'It's all hearsay. It happened before we got him and he never talks about any of it. He's been in hospital recently but I'll lay odds it hasn't changed him. To be honest he's a morose bastard and most of the lads steer clear of him when off duty.'

She tried to laugh. 'I wonder what my friend sees in him.'

'I wonder too. Tell her if she wants to know more about him she should contact Peter Phillips, the Intelligence Officer at Lemington. I'm told he and Hammond used to play chess together until Hammond was posted to us. He should be able to give her more gen.'

She realised this was all the information she was likely to get without awaking suspicions. 'Thank you. I'll tell her.'

'She'll probably find it a waste of time. Hammond's such a back-to-front bastard I can't see any woman taking to him for long. In any case from the way he's flying he's not likely to last much longer.' As Etherington broke off to take another swallow of beer she saw his eyes moving over her body.

Under the table his knee brushed against her own. 'But why are we talking about Hammond? Let's have another drink and then go for a walk. There are some great walks round here and I've got friends in the village who'll give us a bite of supper.'

She wondered now how she was going to shake off this gauche young pilot. Conscious his colleagues at the bar were watching them she gave him a warm smile. 'I'd like to but I must get back to my father. He's not been well since we moved down and I can't leave him for long. Perhaps another time. OK?'

Disappointment was written all over his young face. 'Couldn't you stay a little longer? Half an hour or so?'

She drained her glass and then rose. 'No. I hadn't intended to stay this long. I'm sorry.'

'But how far have you to go?'

'Twenty odd miles,' she said.

He was showing confusion now. 'But how are you going to get there? Let me get a taxi. I don't mind standing the fare.'

Although under no illusions about his motive she felt touched by his offer. 'No. You keep your money. I've got transport outside. Thanks for the drink and the chat.'

She could feel the eyes of the other airmen following her as she walked to the door. The youngster followed her outside. 'When can I see you again?'

She walked to the Bentley and then turned to him. 'I don't know, Jack. It depends when I can leave my father. But I hope I'll see you again. Thanks again for being so nice to me.'

His eyes were on the Bentley. 'Is this your car?'

'No. It's my father's. But he lets me use it now and then.'

The sight of the expensive car on top of her accent proved his final embarrassment. 'I shouldn't have treated you like a pick up, should I? Only I didn't know...'

Feeling some shame at her deceit she put a finger over his mouth and then kissed his cheek. 'You've nothing to be sorry about, Jack. I enjoyed our little chat. Now go back to your friends and take care of yourself in the future.'

She took a quick glance back as she started the engine. He was still standing on the car park watching her. Once again she felt shame for her deception as she drove away.

SEVEN

Sean was late arriving on Friday night. At first she wondered if his posting back to active service had come earlier than expected but then told herself he would have found some way of letting her know if that were the case. As it was, she waited until the sun had set before turning to the impatient dog. 'Something's happened to your friend, Jason. Sorry, pet, but we can't wait much longer.'

It was then she heard the distant rustling of bushes. Relieved, she sank down on the picnic table and waited. Half a minute later Jason gave a welcoming bark and raced towards Sean as he came into sight. 'Hello,' she said. 'I was beginning to think you weren't coming.'

To her surprise he made no comment although he paid attention to Jason who was leaping up around him. As he neared the table his expression and posture betrayed a mood that both puzzled and disturbed her. Her first thought was that he had found out about her chat with the young flirtatious pilot earlier in the week. 'What is it, Sean? Is something wrong?'

He dropped on the bench opposite her

and lit a cigarette. In the flare of the match he struck she could see his eyes examining her. Puzzled, she tried again. 'Why are you looking at me like this? Why are you acting so strangely?'

For a moment it seemed he would not answer. Then he appeared to come to a decision. 'Your name *is* Linda Martin, isn't it?'

She stared at him. 'Yes. Of course it is. Why?'

'Who is your husband? He's not Group Captain Douglas Martin, is he?'

'Yes. Didn't I tell you?'

'No, you didn't. You just said he was in the RAF. And Group Captain Martin must be ten or more years older than you.'

Her bewilderment grew. 'What's so strange about that? Why are you making such a mystery about it? Do you know Douglas?'

He half opened his mouth to speak and without knowing why she braced herself. Then, as if he had won some inner battle, his tone changed. 'I know him officially but that's all. He was the C.O. at an earlier station of mine.'

'He was once at Lemington. Was that the station?'

'Yes. I'd six months there. In late '42.'

'It was when Douglas was at Lemington that we were married,' she told him. 'A few weeks later he was promoted and transferred. But what's the problem? Did he do something you didn't like?'

Again she felt conflict within him. As he leaned down to pat Jason a massive drone overhead told her an RAF heavy bomber swarm was on its way to Germany. The sound was fading in the distance before he straightened up again. 'No, he'd a good combat record before he moved up the ladder. But you must know all about that.'

It was only later that she realised he had not fully answered her question. For the moment it relaxed her until she remembered her talk with the young pilot. 'Then why did you sound so aggressive when you asked about him? Was there another reason?'

In the silence that followed she had the impression both were gathering their thoughts, she in defence of her visit to the Longbridge pub and he for some reason unknown to her. His explanation when it came left her uncertain whether it was an excuse or a reason. 'I feel you should have told me you were married to a staff officer. Particularly one I'd served under.'

She found it a weak excuse. Feeling the need to investigate the puzzle further she gave a smile. 'It never occurred to me because I never saw you as a man who gives a damn what he says. And in any case what does it matter if Douglas is a Group

Captain? Surely it hasn't any bearing on the things we've talked about.'

She could sense his resentment as he drew in smoke. Although she knew the reason could be a simple one of military caution, the knowledge she had gleaned about the man already told her it went much deeper than that. 'You have something against Douglas, haven't you? Won't you tell me what it is?'

His reply was abrupt and to the point. 'No. Forget about it.'

'How can I forget it? Douglas is my husband. If he has hurt you in some way I want to hear about it.'

In the few seconds he took to reply she felt once more he was marshalling his thoughts. 'No, he did nothing to me directly. In fact I never saw him do anything more than his duty, if that's what you call it.'

She frowned as she repeated his words. *If that's what you call it.* What does that mean?'

His eyes challenged her across the table. 'He did his duty as a Station Commander. Nothing more nor less.'

She felt her temper fraying. 'You're not being honest with me. You have some grudge against him. Why don't you be a man and admit it?'

His face set as hard as cement at her challenge. 'The only thing I've got against your husband, Mrs Martin, is that he is a regular officer of the old school. Nothing more than that.'

'And what's wrong with being a regular officer?'

'In my book quite a lot. But as you won't agree with any of it, let's drop the subject.'

'No. I want to hear it. My family has a military background. Not only my father but my brother and my husband. So I want to know what's wrong with regular officers.'

He frowned, then turned away. 'No. It's just another of my damned prejudices and I've given you enough of them already.'

Growing angry now, she pointed at his RAF brevet and his DFC ribbon. 'What are those things? Ornaments? Don't you fight for your country too? So what's the difference between you and regulars?'

'Leave it, Mrs Martin. I don't want to talk about it.'

'But I do. You must have volunteered for aircrew? So what's the difference between you and a regular? What makes you feel so damned superior?'

Challenged, he turned back to her. 'If you're saying I'm a hypocrite I agree with you. They don't come any bigger. But that doesn't stop me from seeing what a lunacy the military system is. We're all people living on the same small planet who not only claim to be intelligent but also to be the protégé of a peace loving God. Yet we've been beating our chests, rattling our swords, and slaughtering one another with our national armies since history began. Isn't it time we worked out better ways of settling our quarrels?'

Mixed with her anger was the acceptance that his accusations always carried an infuriating logic with them. The knowledge tempered her hostility. 'All right. When we get the Utopia you crave for, maybe we won't need our national armies. But until it comes in a thousand years time we'll need them as much as we need police forces to take care of our criminals. So stop condemning decent men who believe they are making sacrifices for their country.'

He made no reply. Instead he rose, moved to the lake, and stood gazing across it. Watching him she found her anger dying as once again she wondered if his argument was presented to hide a deeper bitterness. At the same time she could not hold back her comment. 'You hate war, don't you?'

She saw a sudden shudder ran through him. Although he did not turn, his answer seemed to burn the air between them. 'I loathe it. Every wicked murderous moment of it.'

The shock of his hatred forced the question from her. 'And yet you shoot men down. How in God's name do you come to terms with yourself?'

He swung round. His impassioned words

sounded like explosive bullets. 'I do it because I hate the bastards who worship their damned creed and nationality so much they want to make the rest of us slaves to it.'

'Then you agree it's a good war? One that has to be fought?'

'No wars are good wars, Mrs Martin. They're all filthy and obscene. But because the structure of our societies leads to bastards like the Nazis, it's one that can't be avoided.'

'Then why do you punish yourself so much?'

The intensity returned to his voice. 'Because it doesn't make me less of a murderer. Every time I kill I take another step into the pit of hell.'

She was both shocked and fascinated by his outburst. 'And you tell me you're not religious? For heaven's sake you're immersed in it.'

He gazed at her as if she had suddenly become his enemy. 'Don't talk like a fool. How can any man in his right mind live in this damned world and believe the hypocritical rubbish the priests give us. Don't insult me, please.'

Her mouth went dry. 'I'm sorry. But you feel so strongly about killing that nothing else makes sense.'

Her words seemed to calm him. 'I feel strongly about killing, Mrs Martin, because

I feel strongly about murder. Those men I fight and shoot down are no more guilty than I am. They're victims of the tribal system we talked about on Wednesday night. The damned system that's been encouraged and developed by those twin rascals, politicians and priests.'

She took a deep breath. 'I've never met anyone who feels so deeply about war. It must be a nightmare for you having to fly every day when you feel this way.'

For a moment his eyes examined her as if checking her sincerity. Then he shook his head. 'No. As I said on Wednesday I've long seen myself as an ant in a battle of demented ants, and so no more valuable. When you can accept your insignificance like that, it's no problem living and dying with it.'

She could find no words to follow bitterness of this kind. She watched him bend to pat Jason who had followed him and the act seemed to restore his humour. 'We're getting too serious. Let's talk about happier things.'

She was still too shocked to agree. 'I was right about you, wasn't I? You're an impossible idealist and it's all making you a lonely and embittered man. Isn't it true?'

For a moment she thought he was going to walk away and leave her. Instead, to her relief, he returned to the table, giving Jason another pat before sitting down. 'If you want to believe that, be my guest. I'm just sorry I've upset you with my stupid ideas.'

Her temper flared again. 'Don't go soft on me, for heaven's sake. I don't want your apologies. I'm not even sure I don't agree with some of the things you've said. But what can we do about them?' When he shrugged she went on: 'Why the hell don't you accept the world like the rest of us do?'

His sensitive mouth suddenly twitched humorously. 'You pack some fire power when you press the button, don't you? You're quite right, of course. Nothing is going to change.'

'Then live with it,' she fumed. 'And give me a cigarette. I forgot mine when I came out this evening.' As he held out his packet she went on: 'And, just in case I've given you wrong ideas, I don't find your beliefs that stupid. Exasperating, infuriating, excessive, even absurd, but not stupid. Is that clear?'

The teasing half bow he gave her as he lit her cigarette told her they were on speaking terms again. In the distance the drone of another approaching bomber squadron could be heard. It brought to her the young pilot's rumours about Sean's time at Lemington. Although sensing there were further risks in mentioning his involvement, she knew her questions had to be asked. 'What was it like at Lemington? Was there much action there?'

75

He nodded. 'Enough.'

'Does that mean you had losses?'

'Yes. We had our share.'

'It must be awful losing friends? Did you lose any?'

His almost imperceptible start told her she had touched a nerve end. 'We all did. That's what this filthy business is all about.' Then, as if her questions were cutting too near the bone, he ground out his cigarette and glanced at his watch. 'I'll have to be going soon. The transport will be coming early in the morning and I haven't packed yet.'

She knew she would get no more from him about Lemington. His words reminded her of his nearness to battle. The second bomber swarm was overhead now, shattering the silence with a hundred engines. His eyes rose to them. 'It's a bomber's moon tonight. Jerry's going to get another beating.'

The words broke from her without her permission. 'You are going to take care of yourself, aren't you?'

He looked at her in surprise, then laughed. 'Of course, I always do.'

'That's not what I've heard,' she said and then mentally kicked herself.

He was staring at her. 'Who told you that? Surely not your husband?'

'Douglas? Of course not. I've gathered it from everything you've said.'

76

He shrugged. 'It's true I don't exactly love the world. But that's nothing to do with taking care of myself.' He made a face, whether in disgust or indifference she couldn't decide. 'In any case we'll have a few weeks of peace and quiet soon. We're being converted to Mustangs.'

'What are Mustangs?'

'The latest American fighter. With long range tanks we'll be able to escort bombers right into Germany. It should help to cut down our bomber losses.'

'But doesn't that mean you'll be airborne longer?'

'Yes. We can give cover well beyond France. I suppose we're lucky to be getting them. We thought they'd all be kept for the Yanks.'

Although knowing the conversion would mean greater danger for the escorting fighters she felt that to dwell any further on his survival chances would earn either his curiosity or his impatience. In the event she chose humour. 'Anyway, don't do anything rash. The world's not over crowded with idealists.'

He laughed. 'You mean fruit cakes, don't you?'

Grateful for his riposte she laughed back. 'All right. Fruit cakes if you must. They're just as scarce in wartime, so keep it in mind.'

They chatted for a few more minutes while she wondered how she could arrange to see him again, for she had the feeling their talks were being helpful to him. The problem was how to keep contact without hinting there was a future in their relationship. She tried to keep her question casual. 'Will you get much time off when you're back on duty?'

He shrugged. 'It depends on the jobs we get. If we're on maximum effort the station's closed even for phone calls. At other times we get the odd night off. But I don't know how we'll be fixed on the conversion course. Why?'

'I wondered if you'd care to come again one night. Donnington isn't far away.'

'But what about your work?'

'I can stay until the doctor passes my father fit again.' She smiled. 'Being his daughter does confer a few privileges. As the doctor thinks it'll be some time before it's safe for him to be left alone I'm hoping for a few more weeks yet.' To avoid embarrassment she pointed at the sleeping dog. 'I have to ask you for Jason's sake. He's going to be very upset if he doesn't see you again. Here's our phone number.'

He took the piece of paper she handed him and gazed down at it. 'Are you sure you want to do this?'

Aware she was on dangerous ground she

trod carefully. 'Yes, why not. We've become friends, haven't we?'

He slid the paper into his tunic pocket. 'All right. But where should we meet? Here?'

Thinking of Charles she nodded. 'Why not?' Turning, she pointed at the old gazebo. 'If it's raining we can always take shelter in my log cabin.'

He smiled. 'All right. Make it here. I'll be in touch as soon as I can.'

She could not describe her feelings when at last they shook hands and he left her. She could only relate it to the emptiness she had felt when her brother had been sent into action. It had been a loss without relevance to sex or human desire but to the severance of minds that had found pleasure in pure companionship. When some small rebellious voice within her questioned the likeness she dismissed the doubt angrily. There was nothing in this arrangement that anyone could question. By chance she had encountered a human being in need of help and understanding and if she could supply those basic needs it was surely the least she should do. Opening her handbag she searched for the name of the officer her ardent young admirer had given her in the White Hart. Finding it with some relief, she spent the next hour writing and re-writing a letter.

EIGHT

There was only one couple in the tea room as Linda entered, two elderly women chatting over a pot of tea. Glancing at her watch and seeing she was early, Linda closed her umbrella and seated herself at a table near the window. A moment later a young girl not older than fifteen emerged from a curtained door and approached her. 'What can I get you, miss?'

'I'm waiting for someone,' Linda told her. 'Can I wait to order when he comes?'

The girl looked doubtful, then nodded. 'Yeah, I suppose it's all right. But don't you want something while you wait?'

Linda gave her a smile. 'No, thank you. I'll let you know when I'm ready.'

With another doubtful look the girl withdrew through the curtained doorway. Lighting a cigarette, Linda glanced through the window. It was raining in Lemington and pedestrians were hurrying past in coats and mackintoshes. As Linda watched them her thoughts went back to Smalloaks and her father's doubts of her mission. 'You're making too much of this, darling. He's only some bolshie pilot who's playing on your sympathies and good looks. You should forget about him instead of wasting any more of your leave.'

'No, Dad. He's not a bit like that.' She had paused, searching for the right words. 'He's so different it's difficult to describe him. He has a kind of fierce intelligence that's at odds with the world. It gives him views that must be hell to live with.'

Charles had looked amused at her verbal extravagance. 'If he's as bad as that, darling, I can't see how you can be of any help.'

She had felt vexed both by her own words and his inability to understand. 'It's not only his intelligence that's destroying him. Something else has happened to compound it. I just know it.'

'But what can you do, darling? Even if you find out his history, how is it going to help him?'

'I don't know,' she confessed. 'But because he came back to talk to me I feel I must be helping him in some way. And perhaps I could do more if I knew what had happened.'

Charles had gone silent for a moment. Then with a soldier's directness he looked her straight in the face. 'You haven't fallen in love with him, have you?'

This time his suspicion had angered her. 'Dad, that's ridiculous. He's an atheist and a revolutionary. Most of the time I've quarrelled with him and at times even disliked him. So please stop getting ideas like that.' When he had remained silent she had gone on: 'All that's happened is that I've met a person in need of help. A wounded man if you like. What's one supposed to do? Ignore him?'

His eyes had stayed on her a moment before he had nodded. 'You always were the girl who couldn't pass by a wounded animal. And you do like your mysteries, don't you? All right, then the thing to do is speak to Douglas about him. No one's in a better position to find out the man's problems.'

The suggestion had dismayed her. 'Douglas? I can't do that.'

'Why not?'

'This isn't a young airman finding the war's too tough to take. Just the opposite. He's a fully grown man with beliefs that clash with almost everything Douglas stands for. So how could Douglas help him? He'd probably see him as a man trying to get his ticket.'

Charles had given her a troubled look. 'You haven't much confidence in Douglas, have you?'

'No, Dad. It's not that. But Douglas is a professional solder, as you were. He sees everything in a wider context. He has to. He can't spend his time investigating the background of a single pilot with contrary beliefs and values.'

Charles had shaken his head. 'I still think you should tell Douglas instead of getting yourself involved like this.'

She had been alarmed now. 'You won't say anything to him, will you? Please, Dad. He really wouldn't understand.'

Charles had sighed. 'No, I won't say anything. But keep in mind you're married to a high ranking officer. Don't get so involved that it causes problems between the two of you. That could happen if the word gets around.'

Her thoughts broke off as she saw a smallish man in an RAF raincoat pause on the pavement outside. After peering through the rain streaked window he turned and made for the door. Relaxing, she waited while he entered the café. After gazing round, he approached her. 'Excuse me but are you Mrs Martin?'

She extended her hand. 'Hello, Squadron Leader Philips. How kind of you to come.'

His hand was chilly from the rain. Wearing spectacles he was barely as tall as she herself, a man in his forties with no pilot brevet and a somewhat featureless face. As he removed his cap she saw his black hair was receding, with a bald patch already showing beneath its thinning cover. It was not an inspiring face and yet in some way she drew comfort from its anonymity. 'Will you have tea, Squadron Leader? Or do you prefer coffee?'

'Tea, thank you.' She sensed embarrassment in him as he removed his raincoat. Realizing he was conscious both of her lineage and her marriage, she knew she must first put him at ease. 'Do sit down. Would you like a cake or anything with your tea?'

'No, just tea, thank you.'

She gave the order to the girl, then turned back to Phillips with a smile. 'Do you smoke, Squadron Leader?'

'Only a pipe,' he said. 'And I know they don't approve of pipe smokers in here.'

She thought she detected a trace of the north in his voice. 'Oh, dear. Have we picked the wrong cafe? I like pipes myself. My father's a great pipe smoker'

'How is he? You said in your letter he hadn't been well?'

Knowing it was unlikely she could gain an interview with him without influence, she had not neglected to make mention of Charles. 'He's getting better, thank you. Hopefully in another week or two he'll be pottering round the estate although because of his age the doctor thinks it'll be a long time before he's his old self again.'

'I'm sorry to hear it.' In the brief pause that followed she could feel him wondering how to broach the reason for her request. To assist him she gave an apologetic laugh. 'You must have wondered why I wanted to talk to you about Flight Lieutenant Hammond?'

He nodded. 'Yes, I did. Have you any complaint to make against him?'

'Oh no. Nothing like that. It has to do with my sister.'

'Your sister.' He looked puzzled. 'Might I ask in what way?'

After much thought she had decided to drop 'the friend' ploy she had used in Longbridge and use the more intimate one of her young sister living well away in Scotland. 'Yes. She met him somewhere at a social gathering when on holiday and was so impressed by him and his service record that she asked me if I'd get to know more about him from my husband. It seems she got the romantic idea that he'd had some tragedy in his life that has scarred him and wondered if my husband would find out details. But how could I bother Douglas with a young girl's romantic request? So I made a few enquiries elsewhere and when I found out he'd once served at Lemington I plucked up the courage to write you.' She broke off with a laugh. 'I know it's a silly request but you know what young girls are like and Susan's such a nice kid I do like to please her if I can.'

She found herself holding her breath when she finished. Knowing how thin her story was she was banking on her looks to carry the day. Although not conceited, Linda Martin knew she was good looking and like

85

beautiful women everywhere knew how good looks could often be more persuasive than words or argument. She had already noticed Phillips' interest at first seeing her and the admiration had not left his eyes during her explanation. 'Yes, I knew him very well,' Phillips told her. 'He was one of our best pilots. But that was some time ago when your husband was our C.O.'

She did not miss his unspoken question. 'Yes, I know Douglas was there but I'm sure he wouldn't know anything about Hammond's private life. But a young pilot I met the other day said you and he were friends and used to play chess together. So it struck me you might know him better than anyone.'

She feared for the moment that he was going to ask her the name of her informant. To prevent it she went on quickly: 'I'm afraid all this must seem very petty to you. But Susan seems to have taken a fancy to him, and for some reason is convinced he's had some disaster in his private life that has affected him.'

Behind his glasses, mixed with his admiration, she could now see curiosity and wondered if he was seeing through her deceit. Trying to imagine how Douglas would react if he learned about her ploy, she had a moment of panic. To her relief the girl arrived at that moment with the tea tray. To steady her nerves she gave it her attention. 'Do you take milk, Squadron Leader?'

'Yes, thank you. Just the usual.'

As she reached for the milk, she gave him a smile that begged forgiveness. 'I hope this doesn't sound like prying. I promise you that anything you tell me will go no further than Susan. But if you feel unable to give any secrets away I shall quite understand.'

Her smile seemed to win the day although he accepted his cup of tea before replying, 'Yes, he did have a hard time while he was here.'

'In what way?'

'He lost two people close to him. First one and then the other.'

Her heart gave a small thud of excitement. 'What friends were they? Male or female?'

His glance betrayed a sudden discomfort. Afraid of defeat at a moment of victory she took a risk by suggesting her own answer. 'Could one have been a girl, Squadron Leader? Someone he cared for very much?'

He hesitated, then sighed and adjusted his glasses. 'I suppose it doesn't matter to tell it now. Yes, it was a girl. He'd been up to Scarborough to see her.'

She could feel her heart beating faster now. 'Do you know who she was?'

'Oh yes. She was his sister.'

Her eyes widened. 'Sister?'

'Yes. Her name was Jacqueline. She worked in a military hospital up there. He and she must have been very close because he came back very distressed.'

Her curiosity was intense now. 'Why? What happened?'

He toyed with the spoon in his cup before answering. 'He never told me the details. Sean was never one to give anything away about his personal feelings although ready enough to talk about wider things.'

'What sort of things?' she broke in.

Phillips shrugged. 'Life, the world, people, religion –things that aren't usually discussed on a wartime fighter squadron. I think both Sean and I found it an escape to take the world to pieces now and then although we didn't do a very good job in putting it together again.'

Her mind had dropped on to the word religion like a falcon to a pigeon but she held her eagerness in check for the moment. 'You must miss those talks.'

His bespectacled eyes confirmed her impression that here was another lonely man. She also had the impression he was finding it a relief to talk about an absent friend. 'Yes, I do,' he admitted. 'Sean's a deep thinker. In fact in some ways he's a thousand years ahead of his time and people like that aren't exactly plentiful in the Services, But I sensed a change in him after that last trip to Scarborough.'

'In what way?'

'He seemed embittered. And more aggressive with it. Particularly against religion.'

She could not believe her luck. 'Had he been religious before?'

'Not that you'd notice. But he had never attacked it this way. Now he was saying things I wouldn't have wanted our padre to hear.'

'But what had religion to do with his sister?'

'I wondered that myself but when I tried to bring it up he would just give me a look and walk away.'

She was both elated and disappointed. 'Then you never found the reason?'

'No. But it must have been profound because it changed him. Mind you, so did the loss of Preston.'

'Preston? Was he the other person you mentioned?'

Phillip's expression changed as if he were suddenly regretting his last remark. Needing to know more she leaned forward and lowered her voice sympathetically. 'How did he lose Preston, Squadron Leader? In combat?'

As she was speaking she could see shutters closing behind his eyes.

'No, Mrs Martin. Although he was a pilot, Preston wasn't an operational casualty. At least not in the traditional sense.'

She tried to look innocent. 'You mean he

died from natural causes?'

He took a sip of tea before replying. 'I suppose you could call it that. But it did hit Sean hard. I understand they'd been friends from childhood days.'

'Did any of these incidents affect his combat behavior?' she asked. 'I mean did he start taking more risks?'

She could see his bespectacled eyes assessing her and wondered if she had gone too far. When it came his answer was guarded. 'He was always our best pilot. Any other man would have gained a much higher rank.' Then, as if allowing her beauty to overcome his caution, he went on: 'I suppose you could say he began taking more chances. But never without good purpose.'

It was enough to tell her what she believed already. She wanted to inquire more about Preston but felt Phillips' suspicions might then take shape. Instead she fell back on what she felt was safer ground. 'He did have a bad time at Lemington, didn't he? But on the other hand he had you as a friend and it's obvious you were a good one. How did you find his ideas and beliefs? Susan said he seemed so different to other men she knew. Is he so different?'

Phillips looked visibly relieved at her less contentious question. 'Totally different. That's why he's never got the promotion he deserves. The Services don't like thinkers like

Sean. They see them as disruptive elements, a threat to their regimental traditions and military history.'

'But you say he's an exceptional fighter pilot. So why would anyone see him as a threat to military traditions?'

Phillips smiled. 'You have to hear his beliefs and ideas to understand that. For one thing he sees war as the basest act of the human race. It disgusts him.'

She tried to look surprised. 'You make him sound like a conscientious objector. Yet my sister says he has the DFC.'

Phillips made an almost apologetic gesture. 'I know. It doesn't make sense, does it? A highly efficient fighting man who thinks war is a disgusting and demeaning practice and thinks regular soldiers ought to be consigned to museums.' He made a sound that sounded like a mischievous chuckle. 'He used to say they aren't flesh and blood but clockwork toys that click and salute when orders come through. Along with his other ideas it isn't a mixture that blends well in the Services.' Then he remembered who she was and made a grimace. 'Sorry, Mrs Martin. None of this is meant to be a crack at your father or husband.'

With Douglas intensely proud of his career and his unit's history, Linda was trying to imagine what he would think of such profanities. At the same time she found she was warming to this small Intelligence Officer. She laughed. 'What are you, Squadron Leader? The milk or the cream?'

'I'm just the milk, Mrs Martin, and skimmed milk at that. A bank manager in peace time. No war hero like Sean and yet perhaps that's been a help in understanding him better.'

'Why has he this thing against regular soldiers?' she asked.

Phillips hesitated. 'It's just prejudice. I can't altogether agree with it because I know some highly intelligent officers but I can see what he's getting at.'

'What is he getting at?' she asked. Then, seeing Phillips' embarrassment she went on: 'You can tell me. All this is in confidence between us.'

Phillips looked apologetic. 'Sean feels that any man who swears fealty to his country has sold his conscience with it. No matter how crooked its politicians turn out he has to obey them. That might include killing innocent people in unlawful wars. For that reason he thinks that no man who values his integrity can become a regular.'

Could this be the only reason he dislikes Douglas, she thought? Surely not. 'Then I take it Sean is a volunteer?' When Phillips nodded, she went on: 'He won't make himself very popular among regular officers if he goes around saying things like that.'

Phillips looked relieved she had taken his words so well. 'To be fair to him he doesn't say it aloud. But word gets around and it does explain why he's not popular in some quarters.'

She tried to look amused. 'What other unpopular ideas does he have?'

'Quite a few,' Phillips admitted. 'Patriotism is one of his bugbears. While most of us are proud of it, to Sean it's the very emotion that divides nations and often leads them into war.'

So these were his genuine beliefs she thought as she continued to show surprise. 'But doesn't he realize it's part of our nature to put our country first and to relish our military history. We all admire battle honours. I find my own feet tapping to regimental tunes and marches.'

He nodded. 'So do I. But to Hammond they are sacrifices that have to be made if we're ever going to stop national rivalries and get any kind of permanent peace. Moreover he has some highly intellectual belief that when people bond together in the way they have today it reduces their perception and general intelligence. Instead of being rational they act like football crowds or Germans at Hitler's rallies. He blames it on apathy.'

'Apathy?'

'Yes. It's so much easier to sit back and do

nothing than to stand up and protest. So although they might not like a tyrannical or terrorist regime their apathy sweeps them into becoming part of it. He believes that's why the Germans allowed Hitler and the Nazis to take over. They just sat back and allowed it to happen.'

She shook her head in disbelief. 'He does go deep, doesn't he?'

Phillips nodded. 'He's a complete misfit in the Services. He sees the entire concept of nation states, national rivalries, national armies, and the rest as tribal and adolescent. To him there's nothing more ridiculous than creatures that claim to be intelligent, arguing, fighting, and dying over pieces of a planet that in itself is nothing more than a speck of dust in an infinite universe. He saw the League of Nations as the first hope of a saner world and its demise as evidence of our permanent stupidity.'

She made herself laugh. 'He's a complete idealist, isn't he? He's attacking the human race for thousands of years of evolution and development. What makes him so different to the rest of us?'

Her question seemed to catch him off balance for the moment. 'I've asked myself the same question. I've sometimes wondered if that accident he had in France before the war when working over there has some bearing on it...' Then, as if punishing himself for the remark, his tone became impatient. 'No, that's ridiculous. Quite absurd.'

'What accident?' she asked curiously.

His curt hand dismissed her question. 'Sorry. It's a private thing. In any case it's not relevant.' He continued as if he had never made the remark. 'Sean might be an idealist but he's a realist with it. He knows the world he wants can't happen in a thousand years. But that doesn't stop him showing his contempt for the present one. Perhaps that's why religions disgust him for underwriting it.'

'You're saying it could be one reason for his atheism?'

Phillips gave a shrug. 'Perhaps. I don't know.'

'What are his other beliefs and dislikes?'

'He is quite certain that if we don't establish a world government after this war and give it the resources it needs, it won't be long before we wipe ourselves out.'

'A world government,' she repeated. 'When there has never been so much hatred and cruelty between nations. Doesn't he see how unlikely it is?'

'Oh, he knows his ideas are centuries ahead of his time. Perhaps that's part of his problem.'

'You're really saying he's an intellectual, aren't you?'

'Oh, yes. Very much so. But can you imagine how it sounds to high ranking officers when they hear his point about patriotism? It's a miracle he's kept his commission. In fact I doubt if he would have kept it if he wasn't such a damn good pilot.'

'It doesn't add up, does it,' she said. 'He despises patriotism and hates war and yet fights and kills with the best of them. It hardly matches up with a man who seems to believe in the brotherhood of man.'

Phillips nodded. 'No. At least not on the surface. But although he talks little about his childhood he once let out that he was badly bullied at school. I think that gave him a lifelong hatred of bullies and when you think of it bullies don't come much bigger than the Nazis. And as their main aim is to impose their creed and nationalism on the rest of us, there is some logic in his thinking.'

She wondered if Douglas had ever heard these views from one of his pilots. Before she could reply, Phillips' sudden question caught her attention. 'Do you know why I believe he has these dislikes and wishes? I think they come from pain.'

She gave a start. 'Pain?'

'Yes. Although he'd kill me for saying it, I think that deep down he's an over-sensitive man who suffers from the pain he sees in the world. And he believes nationalism and religion are among the main causes of that pain.'

'And yet he's still prepared to cause more pain by shooting men down.'

'Yes. But remember he loathes the aims and ambitions of the bullies that are causing pain all over Europe and the Far East.' Behind his glasses Phillips' eyes twinkled at her. 'I did say he is complicated. At the same time no man could have a better friend.'

She knew now that she liked this middle-aged officer. 'Tell me your first name. I can't go on calling you Squadron Leader. It's too stuffy and military. Mine's Linda.'

He looked startled by her familiarity. 'It's Peter. But are you sure you don't mind?'

'I wouldn't suggest it if I minded. But tell me. Do you think all the things you've told me about Sean are the reason he was posted from Lemington?'

'No, I can't think that. Those orders come from the very top: Extra air activity in one sector can cause it. No, his private beliefs wouldn't he an influence there.'

She wanted to know more about Sean's dead friend but instinct told her Phillips had told her as much as he dared. Instead she sat back and gave him a grateful smile. 'I do appreciate your telling me these things. They won't go any further than Susan. I promise that. Now will you have more tea? There's plenty in the pot.'

He shook his head. 'I'd like to but I'd better not. I've lots of reports to write when

97

I get back.'

'Then I suppose I'd better go too,' she said. 'I shouldn't leave my father for too long. But I have enjoyed meeting you and having our talk. It's been a real pleasure.'

The admiration was back in his eyes. 'I've enjoyed it too. The Group Captain is a very lucky man.' Then, as if afraid he had said too much, he held out his hand for the bill. 'Let me have it, please.'

She laughed. 'Nonsense. It was I who asked you to come. I just hope we'll meet again one day, Peter. In the meantime good luck and take care of yourself.'

He picked up his raincoat, shrugged it on, and then turned to her again.

'Goodbye. It's been such a pleasure meeting you.' He held her hand a few seconds more than was necessary. Then, giving her a last embarrassed smile, he left the café.

She paid the small bill and then hurried through the rain to the Bentley. As she drove away she tried to untangle her thoughts. While she had initially guessed a woman might have a major part in Sean's bitterness the possibility it might be his sister had never crossed her mind. What on earth could a sister have done to stir up such emotion, she wondered? And what was there about Preston's death that had made Phillips, so open in other aspects, clam up so quickly in the way he had?

But although both mysteries fascinated her, there were other questions puzzling her as the old Bentley covered the miles to Smalloaks. Was Phillips right in believing it was Sean's sensitivity that shaped his eccentric views on life and religion, or could the mild Intelligence Officer's interpretation be biased by the friendship and admiration he obviously felt for the decorated pilot? And what was the accident Sean had suffered in France that had made Phillips so cautious and tight lipped? Well before Linda reached home she knew she would not rest until the mysteries surrounding Sean were solved.

NINE

The following morning when returning from the local shops Linda found Charles sitting in a deckchair on the terrace reading his newspaper. 'Hello. What are you doing out here?'

Charles lowered his newspaper. 'I've been for a walk. And now I'm enjoying the sun. Why?'

'You're feeling better, aren't you?' she said.

'There never was much wrong with me before. I told you that weeks ago. Where have you been?'

'Just to the shops. I need a new pullover but found I didn't have enough coupons for the one I want.'

'That's a pity. Why don't you use my coupons? I don't need any new clothes these days.'

She kissed his cheek and then sat on the terrace wall before him. 'I wonder if I can. I'll ring the shop later to find out.' She turned and gazed across the forecourt and lawn to the wood beyond. 'What a beautiful day. I suppose Jason will be wanting a walk now I'm back?'

He nodded. 'I heard him barking at Mrs Griffiths a couple of minutes ago when she was hanging the washing out. By the way Douglas phoned this morning. He said he's hoping to get here this Sunday.'

'Just for the day?' she asked.

'He couldn't say yet. Does it matter?'

'Not really. Although now you're frisky again I want to get up to Scarborough for a couple of days.'

Charles looked curious. 'Scarborough? Who are you seeing in Scarborough? Nothing to do with this chap Hammond, I hope.'

Although hating to tell yet another lie she could see no alternative. 'No. It's an old school friend of mine who's working up there these days. I thought this was a chance to see her while I'm off work.'

Charles looked relieved. 'Thank God for

that. You've asked quite enough questions already about this Hammond chap. Particularly when all you've found out is that he's a revolutionary, as I said he would be in the beginning.'

Not wanting to add anything to the brief and incomplete sketch of her meeting with Phillips that she had given Charles, she changed the subject. 'I shan't want the car this time. I'll take the train.'

'You've no other option,' Charles said, nodding at the old Bentley parked on the forecourt below. 'I'm not getting my patrol ration for another two weeks.'

The sound of aero engines saved her a reply. Turning and shading her eyes she saw a cluster of Bl7s silhouetted against the bright morning sky. Lowering his spectacles, Charles followed her gaze. 'Another Yankie daylight raid. But where's the fighter escort?'

'They'll rendezvous with them later,' she told him. 'According to Douglas it's usually over the Channel.'

Charles replaced his glasses. 'Isn't that one of the jobs your boy friend does?'

Although she knew he was only teasing her she still bit her lip. 'Dad, he's not my boy friend. So don't say such things.'

He gave her another mischievous grin. 'I'm sorry, darling. But what do I call him?'

'Call him by his name. Only don't tell it to Douglas. I don't want Sean getting into trouble on my account.'

'Has he contacted you since he left hospital?'

'No. And I don't expect he will now that he's back in action again.'

The B17s heading south, were disappearing over the trees. Charles gave them a nod. 'I preferred my feet on the ground during my war.' His eyes moved to her. 'Douglas says Jerry's fighter defences are still strong. Has he told you that?'

She nodded. 'Yes. It shows in our losses.'

The thunder of the B17s was dying in the distance. 'I wonder what percentage of casualties survive to be prisoners,' Charles mused.

For a moment she felt chilled. 'God knows. Not that many I shouldn't think.'

The sight of the bombers had turned Charles reflective. 'I hope prisoners get better treatment than our lot got in the Great War. They had a hell of a time when Jerry got short of food. That was when the thoughts of those back home could be life savers.'

She did not answer. The appearance of B17s over the estate usually signified the build up of a daylight raid on German targets and she was wondering if Charles could be right and that Sean's squadron might be involved. It was only when she heard the words 'life savers' that she interrupted Charles. 'What did you say?'

Charles feigned indignation. 'You weren't listening, were you?'

'Yes, I was. You were talking about prisoners of war. And then you said something about life savers. What did that mean?'

Charles pulled his pipe and tobacco pouch from his jacket pocket. 'I was pointing out how in wartime the memories of home can sometimes be the difference between life or death to a man. When there's nothing but mud, death and bullets around you or just plain misery, the thought of a fireplace and a woman can make the difference between wanting to end it all and wanting to live.' Charles' reflective voice ran on as he packed tobacco into his pipe. 'It's a pity more women don't think of that before they write those Dear John letters to their sweethearts or husbands.'

She missed nothing of his words this time and was reminded of her earlier thoughts that a girl might be responsible for Sean's undoubted bitterness. But now she had learned Jacqueline was his sister the possibility made no sense, although Phillips had been positive that after Sean had seen her he had returned upset and distressed. At least, she thought, as she left her father and entered the house, with the name of the girl and her workplace in her possession, she now had an excellent chance of solving one of the mysteries that surrounded Sean.

Had Linda known it, at that moment Sean was sitting in the cockpit of his Spitfire on Donnington airfield. The orders had come through only an hour ago. Another bomber escort operation. A mission always disliked by fighter pilots because if detailed to give close support they were not allowed to break away to engage the enemy. However in this case Sean and his fellow pilots were the other section of the escort, the escort-cover wing whose task was to fly at high altitude and give cover to both the force of Bl7s and the fighters defending them.

Like the rest of his squadron he was waiting for their Controller's all clear. It came a few seconds later together with a green Very light that arched over the runway. As Spitfires ahead of him began moving away he eased his throttle forward to four pounds of boost. As the aircraft accelerated he eased the stick forward to lower the nose and give his elevators control. He was running at speed now and correcting the Spitfire tendency to swing on her narrow undercarriage by use of the rudder. As he saw the ground falling away he retracted the undercarriage, eased his pitch control back, and set his throttle to keep pace with the aircraft climbing ahead of him. Then, in an act as significant as the closing of a visor, he slid his perspex hood closed. Like the rest of his squadron, Sean Hammond was ready for battle.

As planned the Spitfires sighted their charge over the Channel. By this time the B17s Linda had seen flying over Smalloaks had been augmented by more American squadrons and from the high escort wing, now flying at 29,000 feet, they looked like a massive armada of ships with their condensation trails reaching back for miles. Milling around them, like miniature corvettes, were the Spitfires and Thunderbolts of the close escort squadrons.

Sean, with oxygen mask in place, was flying as second leader in a fingers Four formation. A voice sounded in his earphones. 'Red One to Squadron. Enemy coast ahead. Test your guns.'

Spitfires swung from side to side as pilots turned on their fire and safe buttons and pressed them. Bursts of smoke, instantly torn away by slipstreams, appeared on the leading edges of wings. On every pilot's windshield illuminated circles appeared as reflector sights were switched on.

Below the Spitfires, B17 gunners and their escort were obeying the same order. Although careful pains had been taken that the enemy should not know their target, and Allied spoof attacks to cause confusion were already in progress, few pilots and gunners of the main force believed they would escape attack before their target was reached. German defences always seemed prepared and their fighters to know by instinct the route that each attack would take. Most men attributed it to German efficiency, others gave it little thought at all. It had been that way since their first mission and was now accepted as a way of life. What few, if any, men were told was that the enemy could not only follow their route across the Channel but often received advance warning of their aircraft taking off from their airfields.

The secret was the large radar complex on the Norwegian coast called Freya. Far ranging, it could spot air activity over Britain and when enough heavy bombers were seen converging into its air space warnings were sent to German controllers to alert their squadrons. With the enemy observer corps and the Kamhuber radar line in Germany also alerted, there was now little or no chance of a heavy force reaching its objective unnoticed.

As the minutes passed, sooty black blobs began bursting among the packed B17s. The dreaded 88mms guns were now in action and more than one stricken B17 reeled away and vanished into the mist below. The firing continued and although every explosion hurled out shards of red hot steel, the flak bursts gave ironic comfort to both the bombers and their escort. While the firing continued the aircraft were spared an even greater danger.

Ten minutes later that danger arrived. The sooty black bursts ceased and for a moment red marker explosions took their place. An American voice was heard over the crackle of static. 'Watch out, you guys. They're signalling our position to their fighters.' Gunners on the B17 adjusted their chewing gum, cocked their .5 Brownings, and waited.

The first attack came from the front: 109s and Focke Wulfs firing rockets and cannon before veering away and finding individual targets. Now the radio static was drowned by shouts and curses as captains called orders to their crews and men yelled warnings to one another.

To Sean and the rest of his escort the scene resembled a herd of huge animals being harried by wolves trying to separate the pack into vulnerable members. In other sections of the sky the wolves were in combat as the close support Spitfires and Thunderbolts strove to keep them from attacking the B17s. As Sean gazed down, the Controller's voice sounded over the din in his earphones. 'Keep a sharp look out, Red Leader. They might have sent a high level cover.'

Sean knew the Controller was right a minute later as an urgent warning sounded. 'Red Four to Red One. They're coming out of the sun, skipper. Dozens of them.'

Spitfires banked and turned as wingmen followed their leaders. The high sky, which had seemed to belong to them earlier, was suddenly filled with spitting aircraft as friend and enemy fought for position. Tracer bullets traced deadly patterns and a 109 with a wing blown away went spinning down like a falling leaf.

In the way of aerial combat the sky so full of aircraft at one moment went suddenly empty as the engagement spread out in all directions. A voice sounded in Sean's helmet. 'Red 1. You all OK?'

Two voices gave the affirmative. Red 1 came again. 'Red 3. You OK?'

Sean took no notice. His eyes were fixed on a single B17 below. Detached and well away from the main force, with one engine smoking and another feathered, it was being attacked by two 109s. With bursts of tracer coming from only its starboard gunner, it was clear the bomber was near to destruction. Sean addressed his microphone. 'Red 3 to Red 4. I'm going down. Cover me.'

With that he dropped a wing and went down like a gannet. An angry voice followed him. 'Red 3. Get back in formation!'

Sean ignored the order. The angry voice came again, now addressed at his wingman. 'Red 4. Ignore Red 3 and get back into formation. Immediately!'

A momentary hesitation and then Red 4's

108

apologetic voice. 'Sorry, Sean. You heard the order.'

Sean had no time to reply although with his wingman climbing away he was now unprotected from the rear. The first of the two 109s was already swimming into his gun sight and growing larger by the second. As the pilot sighted him and swung away Sean followed him, the speed from his dive taking him less than a hundred yards from the startled pilot. As the 109 swung back into his range bars, Sean opened fire. At such close range his cone of fire covered the 109 and it disintegrated like a child's toy. Even so a parachute blossomed out from the falling wreckage and drifted down into the mist below.

The second enemy pilot, although shaken by the devastating attack, was fully prepared to take on the mad Englishman. Within seconds both aircraft were involved in a deadly ring of roses with each pilot fighting to turn inside the other to get in his first burst of fire.

Death or survival now depended on the turning ability of each aircraft and the skill of each pilot. As Sean gripped his stick with both hand and 'g' forces dragged at his belly and legs, he began to see the tail of the 109 creeping into his windshield and then into the outer circle of his reflector sight. He waited, waited, and then as the desperate

German pilot tried to drop a wing and dive away he jabbed his thumb on his firing button.

His tracer and armour piercing bullets shot out like as many lances, ripping along the 109's fuselage and then smashing into its engine. Sparks flew in all directions and then suddenly a sheet of flame leapt up and swept back over the fuselage.

Pulling away Sean saw the enemy pilot struggling to free himself from the damaged cockpit. But bullets had jammed his canopy and the flames were in full command, hissing into the cockpit like a blow torch and turning the 109 into a furnace. As the flaming wreckage went spinning down with a man suffering the agonies of hell inside it, a jumble of voices entered the airwaves, one carrying thanks from the survivors of the crippled B17, another reprimanding Sean for his disobedience, a third giving a report that the Spitfires had reached the limit of their range and the second escort of Mustangs would take over. But Sean neither answered nor indeed heard any of them. With his face mask removed and his head bowed, he was retching violently in his cockpit.

TEN

The phone rang late that afternoon when Linda was making coffee for her father. At first she had difficulty in recognizing the voice that addressed her. 'Is that Mrs Linda Martin?'

'Yes. Who is that?'

'Hammond. Sean Hammond.'

She lowered her voice. 'Hello, Sean. What can I do for you?'

'I can get away tonight. Some time after seven. Do you want me to come or not?'

'Yes, of course I do. I can be there after dinner. Say around eight thirty. Will that be all right?'

'Yes. OK. See you then.'

As she was replacing the phone she heard her father call from the sitting room. 'Who was that, darling?'

She felt she must lie again. 'It was this friend of mine in Scarborough. She wants to know the date when I'm going up.'

'What did you say?'

'I said I wasn't sure yet but that I'd phone later.'

'You'd better check with Douglas first, darling. You don't want to clash with a day

111

when he can come.'

She made no answer. She was wondering why Sean's voice had sounded so changed.

She took a bottle from her father's fast diminishing wine cellar later that afternoon. Knowing he would guess immediately her reason she planted the bottle and two glasses in a carrier bag in a kitchen cupboard so they could be taken away later without notice. When she carried out the operation successfully that evening she realized what a proficient deceiver she was becoming. It was not a thought that filled her with pride.

She left the house early so that Jason could have his walk before her rendezvous. As a result the summer sun was still visible when she entered the wood and made her way to the lake. As it came into sight Jason gave a bark and began wagging his tail. Guessing the reason she watched the dog ignore the water and scamper instead towards the gazebo. As she drew nearer to it she saw Hammond seated on the bench inside, patting the dog but taking no notice of her approach. 'Hello,' she said. 'Have you been here long?'

He answered without lifting his head from Jason. 'Only a few minutes.'

'How did you get here?'

'I borrowed a van from the transport department.'

She lowered the basket to the ground and dropped on the bench alongside him. 'Why are you sitting in here tonight?' When he gave a shrug but no reply, she went on. 'The wind is a little chilly, isn't it? I put on a cardigan myself.'

The sudden lift of his head and his abrupt question put an end to her chatter. 'Why did you go to see Peter Phillips?'

Believing she could trust the small Intelligence Officer she felt dismay and disappointment. Then she realized she never extracted a promise of confidentiality from him. Moreover Sean was his friend so mention of their talk could hardly be called treachery.

She struggled to answer the question. 'I suppose I want to help. And knew I couldn't until I understood your problems.'

His hostility frightened her. 'What problems? And who the hell asked for your help?'

Unable to think of any reply that would appease him she felt her heart hammering. 'I know you didn't ask for help. But everything you said suggested it. I'm sorry if I seem a busybody but I was brought up to take notice of such things.'

He cursed. 'Because of that damned religion of yours, I suppose.'

She was close to tears now. 'Perhaps it has something to do with it. I don't know. But I am sorry if I've upset you.'

His aggressive stare seemed to probe into her mind and search every protesting cell. Then he muttered something and, ignoring her, slipped a cigarette into his mouth and struck a match. Giving both of them time to recover she opened the bottle of wine and handed him a filled glass. As he took it from her she gave a start. 'Why are you trembling like that?'

Ignoring her he lifted the glass and drank deeply from it. Alerted now by his condition, she noticed he was looking drawn and haunted. She laid a hand on his arm. 'Sean, what's wrong? Has something happened?'

Ignoring her he bent down to pat Jason again. As she repeated her question he exhaled smoke, then shook his head angrily. 'Leave it, for Christ's sake. Tell me what went on between you and Phillips? What did he say about me?'

She knew he was stalling her by asking about Phillips but for the moment knew she had to play along with him. 'He thought you a deep thinker and someone far ahead of his time.' She tried to laugh. 'Not a description that came as a great surprise. He also let out that you had worked in France before the war.'

His sudden start was a betrayal in itself. 'What else did he say about that?'

Puzzled by his concern she trod carefully. 'Nothing else. Did you work there long?'

His eyes were intent on her as if assessing her honesty. 'Just over a year. Why?'

She hid her curiosity with a shrug. 'Nothing. Then you must speak French? Do you?'

He seemed to relax. 'A little. What else did he say about my private life?'

'He didn't volunteer any information. He just answered my questions, that was all.'

He ignored her sophistry. 'He told you about Jacqueline and Preston, didn't he?'

Realizing Phillips had been more frank with him than she thought, she felt a little more secure. 'Yes. He mentioned you had problems with two people close to you while you were at Lemington.'

His question had the sharpness of a spear. 'Did he give you the reasons?'

'No. Perhaps he didn't know them or felt they were too personal. Certainly he gave nothing away about them.'

He gave her a look and then seemed to relax. Growing in confidence she decided to ask a question herself. Jacqueline she felt could wait. Instinct told her the dangers there were too great and in any case she might soon be seeing the girl. Preston she felt was a safer bet. 'Sean, what happened to Preston? Phillips said the two of you grew up together. And he did say he wasn't killed in combat.'

She held her breath but to her relief he only sucked in smoke at her question. When he did not reply, she went on: 'Then how did he die, Sean? Was it some kind of accident?'

The sudden directness of his stare puzzled her. 'Do you really want to know?'

'Yes. That is if it doesn't hurt too much to tell.'

He took another long swallow of wine before turning back to her. 'It's not a pretty story although the details might not surprise you.'

'Not surprise me? I don't understand.'

'You're in the Air Force too, aren't you? Or at least you're married to it.'

'I'm married to Douglas, yes. But he doesn't talk much about the service. He prefers to keep it apart from our private lives.'

She could not determine the look he gave her. Bitterness, mockery, resentment, all seemed there and more. 'Perhaps you'll think him wise when you hear about Preston,' he said. 'Do you still want to know what happened to him?'

She wondered why her mouth had suddenly gone dry. 'Yes. I've just said so.'

'Then here it is. A story about one of our country's more endearing ways.'

When he had finished she felt she had been given a harsh blow across the face. 'Are you sure about this?'

'Of course I'm sure. He was my friend, wasn't he?'

116

She was feeling shocked and chilled. 'But couldn't the news about him have leaked out by accident? I can't believe it was deliberate.'

His laugh had the bitterness of acid. 'It was no accident. It's standard procedure.'

'Are you certain of that?'

'Of course I'm certain. All of us in aircrew live under the threat.'

'Then I agree it's awful,' she confessed. 'Cruel beyond words.'

His laugh came again. 'It's not a pretty world, is it, Mrs Martin? Is there any wonder some of us want to change it?'

'Who was responsible for all this?' she asked.

'The MO., the Station Commander, the Military Police, Group Headquarters, everyone involved in administration and discipline.'

She had heard only one post named, the Station Commander. 'I can understand how you must feel about it. I truly can.'

He exhaled smoke. 'It wasn't his courage that ran out, although it would have been no disgrace if it had. It was his will to live. But to them it made no difference.' His voice changed and mocked her.

'Don't look so shocked. It's all part of the colourful tapestry of this wonderful world. Designed by the same people who believe patriotism is the keyword to integrity and

117

that any dissident or misfit should be stamped on with jackboots.'

His bitterness chilled her further. She wanted to ask the reason for his friend's breakdown but instinct told her it wasn't the moment. In the silence that followed, a breeze rustled the trees and she heard the far off sound of a train. Needing to break the silence that she felt was isolating them she reached for Sean's glass and re-filled it. As she handed it back she noticed again how his hands were trembling. 'You still haven't told me what happened today. Were you involved in that daylight raid?'

He took the glass from her, holding it in both hands. 'How do you know there was a raid today? Did your husband mention it?'

'I've told you – he doesn't often discuss service matters with me. As you know there are British and American heavy bomber bases north of us. When a squadron of them pass overhead we know it usually means a heavy raid is on. We've checked it time and again with the evening news.'

He nodded but made no further comment. As he took a sip of wine she tried again. 'That's why I wondered if you were involved. Or were you on some other operation? You can tell me, can't you? I think I'm a safe security risk.'

He gave her a look but then lowered his eyes to Jason who was curled up at his feet.

'You don't want to hear the grisly details of a fighter pilot's day.'

'You're quite wrong,' she said. 'I do. Please tell me what happened.'

He was stroking Jason's head and for a second she thought what gentle hands he had for such a man. Then, suddenly, to her alarm, his shoulders began shaking. Before she could speak his voice came, choked and strangled. 'Leave it, for God's sake. Can't you understand? I can't talk about it.'

In her urgency to help him she chose her words badly. 'Why not? It isn't something you're ashamed of is it? If it is, you can still tell me.'

At that he jerked upright and she knew she would never forget the look he gave her. 'Ashamed? Of course I'm ashamed. In God's name, what else could I be? Only what choice have we got in the filthy world He's given us?'

His outburst chilled her further. 'I'm sorry. I shouldn't have asked you.'

His bloodshot eyes stared at her for a few seconds more, then he gave an exclamation and turned away. At that moment a loud scream came from the woods behind them. As it rose and then died into a series of agonised cries she knew it was a rabbit being killed by a stoat or weasel. As the sobbing cries died away she heard his voice again, changed beyond recognition this time. 'It was a nightmare. Hellish. Something I'll never forget.'

Certain he intended not to tell her, she realized later it was the death cries of the animal with its connotations that had betrayed him. 'A nightmare? What happened, Sean?'

His voice might have come from a man under physical torture. 'I burned a man alive today.'

She gave a violent start. 'What on earth are you talking about?'

Now his memory was released it spared neither of them. 'I set an enemy plane on fire and watched its pilot burn to death. Trapped and going through the torments of hell.' His bloodshot eyes glanced up and punished her. 'All in the name of my country. Isn't that patriotic? Isn't it something to be proud of?'

She could find no words to answer him. At that moment his glass of wine fell to the ground, causing Jason to start and jump up. At the same moment he dropped his face into his hands, his entire body shaking in torment. Unable to help herself, she threw her arms around him. 'Sean! You didn't mean his aircraft to burn. You couldn't help that. These things happen in wartime.'

He did not hear her in his outburst of shame. 'I saw him burning, Linda. His canopy was jammed so he couldn't escape. God, it was horrible. Yet the Yanks sent a message of thanks when we got back. They

120

thanked me! Can you believe that?'

She tried to lift his bowed head. 'You mustn't punish yourself like this. Sean, do you hear me? Look at me!'

His face, blinded with pain, lifted slowly. Without thought, she drew him towards her and kissed his wet cheeks and haunted eyes. Her words, born of compassion, came without thought of her status. She was a woman confronted with a suffering human being and at that moment they were the only two people in the world. 'My poor darling. You mustn't blame yourself like this. You're not to blame for this war. Are you listening to me?'

His response was equally instinctive. His arms tightened around her and his tormented face crushed against her own. For a full minute they were locked together as if they were lovers.

She never knew who recovered first. All she remembered was Sean releasing her and turning away. 'I'm sorry. I don't know what happened to me.'

At that moment her only emotion was relief at his recovery. 'What are you sorry about? You're a sensitive man who's had a horrible experience. I wish more men were like you.'

His laugh was like the scraping of rusty metal. 'I'm a bloody fighter pilot. I'm supposed to crow like a cockerel when I shoot an enemy down.'

'You're a human being with human feelings,' she said. 'Instead of being ashamed, you should thank God you have them.'

He took a deep, shuddering breath. Unsure of her next move she filled her own glass with wine and passed it to him. As his swollen eyes met hers, with a look she could not analyse, she knew he had recovered and felt able to ask her question. 'Why did the Americans thank you, Sean?'

He winced and then shook his head. 'God knows. Ask them.'

'I don't need to. You saved one of their B17s, didn't you? And probably risked your life in doing it.'

When he gave no answer she knew she was right. 'You know you're going to kill yourself one of these days if you go on like this, don't you?'

His self-disparaging laugh told her he was his bitter self again. 'I've a feeling two or three Americans might argue it would be a fair swop. And a certain German pilot too.'

'You know what I mean. Doing your duty is one thing. Going miles past it is something else.'

His sarcasm told her of her mistake. 'You've got the wrong man. It's your family and friends who act out of duty. I'm one of those warped characters who do it for different reasons.'

'I know your reasons but getting yourself killed isn't going to help them. Nor is it going to help those who care about you.'

He took a glance at her before he took a sip of wine. In the silence that followed she wondered if she had gone too far. Yet since her father's words about the value of a woman's loyalty it had seemed the only ploy available to her that might save this man's life. It was deceit, she felt, but if it saved him from self-destruction did that matter? As the long seconds passed by she tried to imagine what thoughts her words had given him. To ease the suspense she broke the silence herself. 'You called me Linda a moment ago. Until then it was always Mrs Martin. Why haven't you used Linda before? I prefer it.'

He shrugged. 'Perhaps it was to keep reminding myself you're a married woman.'

'What has that to do with it? We can still be friends, can't we?'

The look he gave her convinced her it was a gamble she could take without appearing flirtatious. 'If we are friends then I want you to promise me something. Come and see me at your next opportunity. Will you do that?'

His glance and the unspoken vibrations that exist between male and female told her the invitation was welcome. Yet to her disappointment he shook his head. 'I can't make any promises. When we're converted to Mustangs our base could be anywhere.'

It was a contingency she had not considered. 'But you'll still get leave, won't you?'

'A day or two maybe. But not enough to travel very far.'

Then she remembered her birthday. 'How long is the war going to last, Sean?'

He showed surprise at the question. 'God knows. Forever the way it seems at the moment.'

'But people still make arrangements. Life still goes on.'

'So?'

'If we can't meet before, meet me on my next birthday.'

He looked curious. 'When is that?'

'The 2nd of December. So your conversion course will be long over. Will you do that for me?'

Knowing the absurdity of her request to a wartime serviceman she wondered at the temerity of it. It was not the first time she had invited him back and yet it was behavior so unlike her that she could hardly believe it came from the same person. She was half expecting sarcasm but instead he gave an amused laugh.

'That far off? How can I promise a thing like that?'

'It's easy. Just say it. It won't hurt.'

She found she was holding her breath as

he hesitated. Then he laughed again and lifted his glass. 'All right. It's a date. The 2 December. But where shall we meet? In Trafalgar Square?'

Although she knew he was only appeasing her she had a ridiculous sense of triumph as she feigned indignation. 'Good heavens no. Why give London the pleasure?' She motioned at the lake and trees around them. 'This is where our friendship began. Why look elsewhere?'

'Of course,' he said 'In your haven. Where else?'

Knowing she might not see him for months, if ever, she was dreading their parting but now she had extracted his absurd promise she had the fear something might be said that dispelled its strange comfort. It came as a relief when he glanced at his watch. 'I'll have to get back. I shouldn't have been out this long.'

He did not shake her hand this time. Instead he took it, held it a moment, and then lifted it to his lips. At the glance he gave her she had an odd sensation of being in another place and time, a sensation that seemed to blur her perceptions and deny her hearing his last words and her reply to them. She became herself only after he had left her, with Jason following him to the woodland path that took him away. Standing by the lake, on which the lilies were flowering, she tried to make sense of her behaviour. What was the driving force that seemed to govern her conduct towards a man with whom she seemed to share few sentiments and even fewer beliefs? Did she find some perverted attraction in his viewpoints or was her religious faith giving her a belief that her influence would in some way save him from his passionate atheism? Did it also give her a childish belief that their promised assignation would keep him safe in a world that was killing the dreams of thousands like them every week that passed?

She could find no answer to any question as the shadows of the evening closed in around her. It was only when Jason returned and nuzzled against her impatiently that she stirred and moved away, leaving her haven to the shadows and the approaching night.

ELEVEN

She made her first mention of it to Douglas the following Sunday when Charles had retired upstairs for his afternoon nap. They were both sitting on the sitting room sofa enjoying a cup of tea she had just made, with Douglas looking relaxed with his tunic unbuttoned and a cigarette in his hand. She had postponed putting the question since his arrival that morning but not wanting her father involved and knowing Douglas had to return to Group Headquarters after dinner that evening she knew it could wait no longer. At the same time, knowing the hidden dangers behind the question, she felt nervous making it. 'Doug, tell me something about LMF.'

At first, Douglas appeared not to take in her question. Then he gave a start. 'LMF? What do you want to know about that for?'

To cover herself she knew she had to tell yet another lie. 'I was in a shop the other day and I heard a group of airmen talking about it. I'd heard the expression before, of course, but never given it much thought. But from what I could gather someone these men knew had suffered it and it made me curious.'

Douglas grimaced. 'Suffered is hardly the word. LMF means Lack of Moral Fibre. Someone they knew must have been in aircrew and tried to dodge combat. Become a coward in other words.'

She pretended ignorance. 'Do they get punished for it?'

'Of course they get punished. It costs thousands of pounds to train aircrews. They can't be allowed to quit if they find they don't like its risks or dangers.'

'But aren't aircrews volunteers in the first place?'

'Yes, and that's the point. It can take well over a year to train a pilot and nearly as long to train observers. If there were no punishment for avoiding action, some men would volunteer just to escape the war for that time. So how can that be allowed?'

'But surely not many would do that.'

Douglas shrugged. 'Who can tell. It isn't a risk anyone dare take.'

She could see that. 'But what about the men who volunteer only to find their nerves won't take it when they're put to the test? Is it right to punish them?'

'What choice do we have? We can't let 'em escape scot free or any man who has a near escape might refuse to fly again.'

'But, Doug, they aren't all like you. You never seem afraid of anything. But what about some kid who didn't know he wasn't cut out to be a fighting man until he's put to the test? Is it right to punish him for something he can't help?'

'How can we know one from the other? We can't read their minds or evaluate their courage before they're sent for training. Whether we like it or not we have to treat them all the same way. Otherwise we'd be accused of bias or favouritism.'

To her surprise she could not fault his argument. 'What is their punishment? I've never been sure.'

'They're cashiered and reduced in rank to a general duties airman, which means in their case they get all the dirty and unpleasant jobs. Some are sent to an Aircrew Refresher Centre where they have a pretty tough time. Either way, they're disgraced before their friends and comrades.'

Aware of its dangers she had to steady herself before asking her key question. 'Is that all?'

He gave a slight start, then turned and stared at her. 'Isn't that enough?'

'Not from what these airmen were saying. They made it sound as if worse was to come.'

To her dismay his tone changed and he moved along the settee towards her. 'Who were these airmen?'

'I don't know. Just men I heard talking. Why?'

'Why? They were talking about things that are still classified. Do you know which airfield they came from?'

'Of course I don't.' His expression was alarming her. 'Why are you looking like that?'

'Because those airmen were talking about things in public that would put them in the glasshouse if I could get their names. Haven't you any idea what airfield they came from?'

'I've told you I haven't. But what's the mystery? Why is the rest of it classified?'

Her distress seemed to placate him. 'Darling, some things in wartime can't be told to the general public. They wouldn't understand the need for them.'

'You mean they'd find them too unpleasant?'

He gave a reluctant nod. 'Yes.'

She braced herself. 'Can't you tell me what it is? I'm not likely to spread it around and get anyone into trouble. But I would like to know what happens to men whose nerves break down.'

'Who become cowards,' he corrected.

She bit her lip. 'If that's how you want to put it, yes. What else happens to them? They're not imprisoned, are they?'

He reflected a moment, tapping ash from his cigarette into a tray. Then, making up his mind, he turned back to her. 'No, they aren't given any further military punishment. But if you must know, their local press is usually informed of their cowardice. That's been found to be the most effective deterrent of all and the part that's classified. Satisfied now?'

Although, after Sean's revelation, the news came as no surprise she could still not hide her disgust. 'That's awful, Douglas. That's sadistic.'

He drew in smoke before replying. 'I can't say I like it myself. Nor do some of my colleagues. But don't forget what used to happen to such men in the last war. They were tied to a stake and shot. At least our cowards live to tell the tale.'

'All of them?' she asked.

He frowned. 'What do you mean – all of them?'

She was only too aware of the dangerous ground on which she was now treading. 'I was thinking of the effect it could have on some men.'

His frown deepened. 'What are you getting at?'

Although she felt she was in a minefield she could see no way of retreating now. 'If LMF is made public like that, a man might find his wife, his girl friend, or even his family turn against him. Some men might find that too much to bear?'

'So what's your point?'

She steadied herself. 'Don't some go completely to pieces?'

She could see him debating his reply before he answered her. 'If men aren't brave enough to fight they're not usually the type to punish themselves afterwards.'

'But it must happen sometimes,' she argued. Her question came out before she could prevent it. 'Has anything like that ever happened to you? Did you ever have to punish a man for LMF?'

She held her breath in the long silence that followed. Then he nodded although his expression betrayed his resentment at the question. 'Yes. Once.'

She feigned innocence. 'I'm sorry, darling. That can't have been pleasant for you.'

'It wasn't,' he admitted. 'Particularly as once he'd been a good pilot.'

'How did he take it? Well or badly?'

'Badly, I'm afraid.' He exhaled smoke before turning to her in a way that suggested he was punishing her for her curiosity. 'If you must know, this chap hanged himself.'

She feigned shock at his words. 'How awful. Did it upset you?'

'Of course it did. It upset most of us. But what was the alternative? Slap his wrist and give him a nice safe office job? We have a war to win and if we lose it by going soft it won't be only cowards who'll get punished. Decent men and women will be put against the wall by the Nazis and shot simply because they believe in fair play and democracy. So what choice do we have? One bad apple in a barrel can turn the lot sour. That's the way the world is and the way it's always been.'

Although she knew his case was self justification she could still find no weakness in it when she took Jason for a walk that afternoon. She could almost hear Sean saying the same thing only from an entirely adverse viewpoint. And just as his arguments always seemed logical in their own terms, so Douglas was logical in his. In fact at that moment she felt nothing but sympathy for Douglas at having to instigate a military process which could lead to such cruel consequences. In terms of a war in which civilization was in danger, would she or any other patriot have behaved differently? She knew they would not.

It was one of those cases where there was no right or wrong, she thought. Nationhood, democracy, patriotism and perhaps the modern version of Christianity could not allow dissidents to endanger the status quo and the outcome of the war. Sean's brief with its accent on universal co-operation at the cost of nationhood was an enemy of the system that demanded strength for its survival. Even his hatred of religion clashed with Christianity's modern version although perhaps not with its earlier teachings.

Not with its earlier teachings. Her mind which had produced the phrase from nowhere, paused in surprise and then in excitement as she considered it. Had he, Sean, with his hatred of religion, ever given thought that his ideas of tolerance, forgiveness and the unity of brotherhood ran in perfect parallel to the early teachings of Christ?

She wondered what Sean would make of the notion and for a moment longed to discuss it with him. Along with the wish came another thought. What was Sean's complaint

133

about the role required by anyone who enlisted in the armed forces of his country? – that he surrendered his conscience as well as his body to its laws and customs. Knowing what had happened to Len Preston before his breakdown, would Douglas, by nature a just man, have ordered the humiliation and ultimate destruction of Len Preston if the choice had been his own to make? She believed not. Medical help, yes. A period of rest. An admonishment, perhaps. But nothing as brutal as LMF. In having to inflict that, Douglas had been a victim himself.

Then the pendulum of her thoughts swung again. Sean had confused her enough with his criticisms and far fetched ideas to the point that she was beginning to see faults in her marriage, in her friends, and in a world that until then, in spite of its problems, had seemed based firmly enough on the laws of God and nature. Helping Sean to overcome his bitterness was one thing. Changing her own beliefs and life style was another. In an effort to make amends for her near apostasy she gave Jason only a brief walk and on her return was quick to respond to Douglas's suggestion that they spent the rest of the time before dinner in her bedroom.

TWELVE

The train was hot, stuffy, and crowded. To catch it she'd had to change at Southampton because of enemy damage to the track, then at London, and finally at York. At York she had been lucky. From London she had been forced to stand in one of the crowded corridors but at York a sailor had given her a seat in one of the packed compartments. It had meant sitting beside an old man whose cough suggested incipient bronchitis and a woman nursing a baby but, remembering her father's adage that beggers can't be choosers, she had gladly accepted it although with the baby having to be burped every few minutes and once bringing up a few blobs of half-digested milk onto her shoulder, doubts of her acceptance were creeping in.

She kept having other doubts too. Why was she taking this long and tiring journey? What benefit to Sean could come from it? Whatever had happened between him and Jacqueline, the separation seemed to have been permanent and so her intervention could hardly bring about a reconciliation. While she had been seeing Sean there had seemed a purpose in finding a reason but now, sitting in the stuffy compartment with her skirt riding up her legs as she tried to escape the retching baby, and with a stout middle-aged man opposite making the most of her exposed legs, the only purpose seemed female curiosity and she had always been one to despise tittle tattle and the prying into others' personal affairs.

She wondered how Sean was faring. He had made no further contact with her since his last visit, which she could only hope meant he had experienced no further ordeals. At the same time she knew it could be diffidence, for she could well believe that a man of his character would feel shame at his breakdown in front of her. A third possibility was that the conversion of his squadron to Mustangs was already taking place and on an airfield too far away from Smalloaks to make a visit possible. She had been tempted to ask Phillips if he knew or would find out if the conversion was already in progress but decided it would make her interest in Sean seem too personal.

The jolt of the train broke into her thoughts. As it came to a halt a loud voice outside told her she had reached Scarborough. With instinct telling her the stout character opposite would make a pass at her if she left the compartment with the other passengers, she kept her seat while they rose and collected their luggage. When they

136

began filing out and he was compelled to follow them, she waited a few seconds more, then made her way on to the platform.

She stood a moment taking her bearings. She had no time schedule to keep. Unsure what to say if she phoned the hospital beforehand, her only option had been to establish its location in Scarborough in case no taxis were available and to leave the rest to chance. Relieved to find a few taxis were operating, she lined up behind a queue of passengers outside the station and waited her turn.

With taxis as sparse as everything else at this time, it was twenty minutes before her turn came. 'Where to, Miss?'

'I want the hospital, please. The military one.'

To her relief the driver knew his way but his chatter made it difficult for her to string her thoughts together and by the time the cab pulled up at the hospital entrance she was still uncertain how to make her approach. Pulling herself together she pushed through the doors into the foyer. Seeing an elderly male clerk sitting inside a small office she approached him. 'Good afternoon. I wonder if you can help me? I've come on behalf of an Air Force pilot who has a sister here, a nurse called Jacqueline Hammond. He asked if I would look her up while I'm in these parts. Would you let her know I'm here? My name is Mrs Martin.'

Although clearly impressed by her looks and voice, the clerk shook his head. A man with a large mole on his left cheek he had a pronounced Northern accent. 'I'm sorry, luv, but I've only been here a few weeks and so don't know all the names.'

Linda motioned at a couple of books stacked inside the small office. 'Couldn't you look in one of your registers? I could do it for you if you're busy.'

'I can't do that without permission, luv. And the matron's doing her wards at the moment. If you'd like to wait half an hour or so I'll give her a buzz. She's the one best likely to help.'

Aware that a harassed matron might want substantial reasons before her nurses were called off duty, Linda was reviewing her options when a staff nurse came out of a side door. Without thinking, Linda hurried across to her. 'Excuse me but I'm trying to find a nurse called Jacqueline Hammond. Do you happen to know her?'

The woman paused. 'I did once. But she left the hospital over nine months ago.'

'Does that mean she resigned?'

'I don't know. Possibly.'

'Do you know where I can find her?'

The staff nurse was moving away. 'I'm sorry. I didn't know her very well.'

Linda made a last desperate try. 'Is there

anyone who did know her that I can talk to? It's rather urgent.'

The woman hesitated a moment, then went over to the desk. 'Try to get hold of Nurse Duncan and ask her to come and see this lady.' As she moved away she nodded at Linda. 'This nurse knew her well. They were friends.' Before Linda could thank her she was on her way with the quick strides of her profession.

With renewed hope Linda moved back to the desk as the clerk picked up his phone. A minute later he lowered it and turned to her. 'I've left a message on her ward, luv. She should be here soon.'

The girl arrived ten minutes later. Even in her uniform, with a blue cape thrown over her shoulders, she was attractive with blond hair and pleasant features. 'I'm Paula Duncan. Are you the person who wants to know about Jacqueline?'

'Yes. I'm Mrs Martin. Linda Martin. Have you time to talk now?'

'We're not busy at the moment so the sister says I can take my break. I've got half an hour. Do you want to talk here or would you prefer the tea room down the road?'

'Let's use the tea room,' Linda said.

They were settled in the cafe five minutes later with a pot of tea on the table. When Linda offered the girl a cigarette and she refused, she lit one herself to gather her thoughts. 'You must wonder why I'm so curious about Jacqueline. But first I'd better check she is the one I came to see. Did she have a brother called Sean?'

The girl's expression gave her an immediate answer even if her words did not. 'I'm sorry but why do you want to know? Jackie was a good friend of mine and I can't talk about her private life without a reason.'

Liking her immediately, Linda realized there was going to be no way of getting the truth without telling it herself. 'A couple of weeks ago I met Sean Hammond and I've never met a man more at war with himself. Since then I've learned he has a sister called Jacqueline who worked in your hospital. As a friend hinted his black moods might have something to do with Jacqueline I thought I'd make a few inquiries while I'm up in these parts. Am I right she could be the reason?'

The girl was toying with her teaspoon and for a moment it seemed she would not answer. Then her eyes lifted. 'I don't accept Jackie was responsible, Mrs Martin. That's putting the blame on her. I don't think she deserves that.'

Mixed with her curiosity at the girl's words, Linda was relieved she was not wasting her time. 'I'm not blaming her, Paula. How can I? I don't know what happened. But I am hoping you'll tell me. I promise it'll go no further.'

Once again there was a short silence. This time Linda saw the girl's eyes were on her left hand which was resting on the table. The question that followed gave the reason. 'Are you still married, Mrs Martin?'

'Yes, I am. Why?'

'I'm sorry but I can't help wondering why you are so interested in what happened between Jackie and Sean.'

It was a question Linda least wanted. To save a few seconds she gave the girl a smile. 'Call me Linda. Please.' When the girl nodded, she went on: 'I find that hard to explain. As I told you, I met Sean by accident and got the impression he was the loneliest man on earth. He never said that to me, nor did he ever mention Jackie, but I could tell that something was wrong and I made inquiries. When I was told a girl was involved I thought at first he'd had a broken love affair but then discovered Jacqueline had been his sister. Puzzled by that and finding out she worked up here I decided to see her. What I intended to say I can't even imagine.' She attempted a laugh. 'I know it sounds stupid but that's about all there is to it.'

The girl's eyes were on her face now. 'Then you are doing this entirely for Sean? Might I ask why?'

'I don't know. I truly don't. He just seems

someone in need of help or at least understanding. And as he is a man fighting for his country, I felt he deserves a little of someone's time.'

She could see another question in the girl's blue eyes and was relieved when it was not asked. Reaching for the teapot and refilling their cups, she went on: 'You're probably wondering what help I can give him if I find out the facts. Quite honestly I don't know. But it does help to talk and from what I have seen of him he'll never talk about such things to his fellow airmen. So I thought if I could find out what had happened he might find relief in talking to me. I know it might not help but I'd be a poor human being if I didn't try.'

The suspicion in the girl's attitude seemed to die. 'My problem is that I don't want to say anything against Jackie. She was a lovely person and the best friend I ever had. Although she's gone I still care about her.'

'I appreciate that. I don't want you to run her down either. I just want to know what could have happened between two people that affected one of them so much. Did Jackie fall in love with somebody Sean didn't like?'

Again the girl hesitated. 'Yes, I suppose she did. But not in the way you mean.'

Linda leaned forward. 'I don't follow.'

'It was a different kind of love. Something

so powerful she said it was impossible to fight.'

'What kind of a man could do that, Paula? Who was it?'

The girl shook her head, her voice embarrassed. 'It wasn't a man, Linda. It was God.'

THIRTEEN

Linda felt as if a lightening bolt had struck her. 'God! What on earth do you mean?'

'It was God who took Jackie away from Sean, Linda. Not a man.'

'But how? How did religion come into it? Was Jackie religious? Did Sean say or do something to offend her?'

Paula shook her head. 'She became religious but what happened had nothing to do with Sean. It was Jackie's new priest who did the damage.'

'Her new priest? Why? Didn't he like Sean?'

'I don't know whether he liked him or not. In any case that didn't come into it.' A frown marred the girl's pleasant face. 'It's not an easy thing to explain. When I first met Jackie in our training hospital she loved music, theatres, dancing, parties, games, boy friends ... she was the centre of every party she went to. She played the piano and had a beautiful singing voice. God, how I used to envy her. And yet you couldn't be jealous because with it all she was unselfish and generous.'

'Are you saying she changed later?'

'Not right away. The change came after she was engaged.'

'Then she was engaged?' Linda interrupted.

'Yes. That was before the two of us were transferred to Scarborough. It was here it all happened.'

'Go on,' Linda urged.

'It began when Jackie and Sean's mother lost her home. She lived in Leeds and during the heavy raids of '41 her house was hit and she was buried beneath it. From what I could gather she was saved by a wooden beam that kept her from being crushed but she would still have died from suffocation if some First Aid man hadn't returned to the wreckage and started digging again. As far as I could make out it was that unexpected act that triggered off everything that happened later.'

Linda was fascinated. 'How?'

'It seemed their mother was highly religious and had always hoped that one day Jackie would enter the church in one role or other. Now that she believed her prayers had been answered and God had saved her life, she felt both of them should show gratitude.'

Linda showed disbelief. 'You mean she used it as a kind of blackmail?'

'I don't think Jackie saw it that way. Although she'd never shown religious tendencies before, I suppose her mother's faith must have had a subconscious influence on her when she was a child and this near miracle must have convinced her that her mother had been right all along.'

'You're saying this incident made Jackie religious too?'

'Yes. She became a different girl after seeing her mother. She stopped going to parties, dances, the theatre ... you wouldn't believe the change in her. She told me she'd moved to another church and met a marvellous new priest. I began worrying about her but physically she seemed fit enough. The change was in her mind. Sean must have picked it up from her letters because he kept coming up to see her at every opportunity. The crisis came when one day she broke off her engagement, telling her fiancé she couldn't marry him because she intended to become a bride of Christ.'

Linda's bewilderment grew. 'But why did this affect Sean? Couldn't he bear this change in her?'

'No, it wasn't that or at least I don't think so. It was because her fiancé was a great friend of his. I only met him twice but liked him very much. To make it easier for him

Jackie had said her new religion wouldn't allow her to marry anyone but she told me something quite different. It had been her priest who had forbidden it.'

The suspicion that had entered Linda's mind had turned her mouth dry. 'Forbidden it! Why?'

'Apparently it was because Len was Jewish by birth and the priest convinced her it would be an irreligious union.'

It took a moment for Linda to find her voice. 'I think I know his name. It was Len Preston, wasn't it?'

There was a sudden silence in the café. Paula was gazing at Linda in surprise. 'Did you know Len?'

'No. But I heard about him the other week. He was an RAF pilot in Sean's squadron.' Her voice hardened. 'How could Jackie do such a thing to a decent man? Particularly in wartime.'

Paula flinched. 'I know how it sounds. But don't blame her too harshly. I've never seen a woman so upset after they broke off the engagement. She sobbed for days. At times I thought she would have a nervous breakdown.'

'Then why did she do it? Why did she let a prejudiced priest determine her life like that?'

'I don't know, Linda. He had gained some influence over her that she couldn't throw off.' As Paula paused Linda saw there were tears in her eyes. Reaching out she took the girl's hand and found it ice cold. 'I'm sorry. You're finding this painful, aren't you? Would you rather wait and tell me the rest later?'

Paula brushed her eyes. 'No. It's all right. Only I felt so sorry for them both. From everything Jackie told me she was helpless to change her mind. She said that although she still loved Len, God was speaking to her through the priest and she had to obey. It was like being torn apart. I've never seen anyone suffer the way she did.'

'And what about Len?'

A shudder ran through the girl. 'That was awful. Two days after she broke off their engagement he came back to the hospital to see Jackie again and was told by matron that Jackie had been on night duty and couldn't be disturbed. When she wouldn't give way he went berserk and started throwing doors open to find her. It took three male orderlies to stop him and throw him outside. They still talk about it in the hospital. God, how that man must have loved her.'

In her mind Linda could see it happening and winced. 'What happened after that? Do you know?'

'None of us saw Len again but Sean came up again to see Jackie to try and change her mind. But it was hopeless. The priest had convinced her she belonged to Christ and she handed in her resignation to the matron.' Paula's voice broke. 'A week later she was dead.'

Linda gave a gasp of shock. 'Dead?'

'Yes. It happened one night during the blackout. It seems the priest or one of his followers was taking her up to Scotland to some religious centre when their car crashed into an Army lorry. She was killed instantly.'

Linda was stunned. 'My God!'

The girl brushed her eyes again. 'I believe Sean was shattered. He and Jackie had always been close. What it did to Len I can't imagine. Has Sean ever mentioned what he's doing now?'

Linda, still recovering from the news, almost told her, then checked herself. She had brought enough unhappy memories back, she thought. There seemed little point in adding more weight to them. Instead she shook her head and sat back. 'I'm grateful to you, Paula. I understand things much better now.'

The girl's voice was curious. 'What will you do about Sean? Tell him you've found out what happened?'

Linda realized she did not know. 'I'm not likely to see him for some time. He's on operations at the moment.' She attempted a laugh. 'I know. You must be wondering what's the point of all this. To be honest I don't know myself.'

Paula hesitated, then glanced at her watch. 'I'll have to get back or I'll be in trouble with the sister.'

Linda placed a hand on her sleeve to restrain her. 'Just one thing before you go. I gather that for a couple of years before the war Sean worked in France. Did Jackie ever say anything about his work over there?'

The girl paused. 'Yes. I think he worked for a timber firm. But that was all. Except for the accident he had.'

'Accident? What kind of accident?'

'I think it was a car or a van hitting him when he was crossing a road. They thought he was badly hurt for a time but he soon recovered and went back to work.'

Linda's excitement died into disappointment. 'And that was all? Nothing else?'

Paula shook her head. 'That was all Jackie said about it. Probably it was all Sean had told her.' Her tone changed. 'Are you coming back with me or going back home?'

'No, I've got what I wanted, thanks to you. So I'll start making my way home.'

The girl nodded. 'OK. Good luck, whatever happens.'

Thanking her again Linda watched her making for the door. Then to her surprise Paula ran back to her. A moment later she heard a whisper in her ear. 'I can tell you why you're doing all this, Linda. You're in love with Sean. That's your reason.' Then she was gone, leaving Linda sitting at the table as if frozen into stone.

The journey back to Smalloaks was as hot, stuffy and uncomfortable as the outward one but Linda remembered few of its details. The questions, answers, and further questions that kept pouring into her mind allowed her no thought of physical comfort. One question at least had received an answer, she thought. Until then she had found it difficult to understand why a man of Sean's mental strength had allowed his sister to play such a negative part in his religious beliefs. Now, with a bigoted priest being the cause of his sister's death and his friend's disgrace and suicide, the picture became only too obvious.

But it was not the only thought that dominated her mind during the long journey. What would she say to Sean if he were to visit her again? What purpose would it serve to let him know she knew his secret? Would talking about it help him or would it only drive it further into his mind?

The questions came and went but brought with them no answers. One came more and more often, sometimes between the others and sometimes overriding them. Was it possible that Paula was right? Was it possible she was lying to herself in believing her wish to help Sean was altruistic and was not borne of physical attraction and self interest?

With its implications for Douglas and her marriage, the thought began to dominate all others and by the time she finished with trains that day she had a throbbing headache. It took her another fifteen minutes to find a taxi and it was well past midnight before she reached the blacked-out Smalloaks. Glad that her father had long retired and she did not have to face his questions she tiptoed quietly up to her room. Although she sank into bed with relief, it was almost dawn before she was able to sleep.

FOURTEEN

The parachute was descending with painful slowness. A Mustang was circling round as if intending at any moment to attack the small figure that dangled below it. On the ground below, villagers were staring and pointing up at the drama. Higher above in the dazzling blue sky, like shoals of fish in mortal combat, boxes of B17s and their accompanying escort were engaged by Focke Wulf and Me 109 fighters, but the blinding sun and their height made them little more than an impersonal backdrop to the nearness of the helpless parachutist and his circling enemy.

Seconds seemed like minutes as the drama unfolded. A light breeze was carrying the parachutist to the far side of a hill crest on which stood a small church but at the moment he was in full view of the village and its people. Men digging in the fields that led up the hillside rested their sweating arms on their shovels and turned their weather-beaten faces upwards. Some watched in pained silence. Others could be seen swearing to themselves. One, a huge middle-aged man in a sleeveless shirt, was gripping his spade handle as if it were the throat of the Mustang pilot. As the parachutist dropped lower and the circles of the enemy fighter tightened round him the tension became almost unbearable.

Then the unforeseen happened. An Me 109 came diving from the dazzling sky like a gannet. Dropping on the tail of the Mustang it opened fire with both cannon and machine guns. The Mustang pilot, intent on the German parachutist, saw his danger too late. Before he could escape, the cone of fire streaking towards him tore off his port elevator and severed his controls. Reeling drunkenly, the Mustang lurched over the hill crest and crashed into a field beyond. Giving a shout of delight and triumph, the huge man yelled to his colleagues and, shovel in hand, raced towards the crash site. Above, the Me 109 made one pass over his stricken enemy and then climbed to help his comrades in their battle against the B17s.

Although not on fire, the Mustang was a crumpled and smoking wreck when the peasants cleared the hill ridge. Some of the village women and a few children were also running up the hillside and all were showing varying degrees of hostility towards its pilot. He had survived the crash but looked unconscious in the crumpled cockpit.

The huge peasant was the first to reach the wreck. Grabbing a panel that was trapping the pilot he struggled to break it clear. When he failed he smashed his shovel against the panel while yelling to the other men to help him. They were only too willing and a few minutes later the pilot was dragged out, pulled away from the smoking wreck, and then thrown to the ground.

It proved no act of mercy as men crowded round the unconscious man. Muttering something to the others, the big peasant spat down at him, then drove a huge boot into his body. Egged on by the act, other men followed suit, rolling the pilot over with the impact of their kicks. Nor did the violence stop there. A woman, panting from her exertions, pushed forward, bent down, and ran her nails down the man's face as if to blind him. As blood from the scratches welled out, the huge man grabbed one of the pilot's arms and motioned one of his friends to stretch it out. When the arm was securely held, the man raised his spade with the intention of breaking or even severing the arm. But before he could bring the spade down an authoritative voice rang out. 'Nein, Johann. Halten sie nun!'

For a second the uplifted spade quivered as if Johann were about to disobey. Then he turned in anger to the elderly priest who had pushed through the vengeful crowd. 'He deserves it, Father. He tried to kill one of our pilots. When our man was coming down helpless in his parachute.'

'You are wrong, Johann. He was protecting our pilot until he was safe.'

Cries of protest came from the surrounding men and women. The priest turned to them. 'Did any of you see him open fire?' When no one replied, he went on: 'He could have killed our pilot half a dozen times but he did not. He shot him down, it is true. But once he was helpless he protected him.'

Johann was still shaking with rage. 'How do you know this?'

The priest pointed back at the church on the hill crest. 'Because I could see what you could not.' His eyes moved down to the unconscious pilot. 'This man might be an enemy but he is a merciful one. Our duty is to care for him now he is helpless.'

A cry came from the woman who had scratched the pilot's face. 'Do you know the orphanage at Beinvaden was bombed two nights ago and twenty children were killed? These are terror flyers, Father. They don't deserve mercy.'

The priest turned to her. 'Our airmen over England will be hated the same way, Beate. Bombs fall on the innocent as well as the guilty. But this man showed mercy to his enemy. For that reason alone we should offer it to him.'

Johann had not finished yet. 'How do we know you are right? You are the only one who doesn't think he was trying to kill our man.'

'I have told you why. I saw his behaviour long before you did. He had a dozen opportunities to kill our pilot but did not. He was protecting him until he was safe. If you do not believe me, find our pilot and ask his opinion. He will tell you the same.'

His final words appeared to convince even the sullen Johann. 'Then what do you want us to do with him? We haven't any Army or police units around here.'

'Our first task is to cure the injuries you have inflicted on him.' The priest turned to the group who were now looking either confused or ashamed. 'I want some of you to carry him to the church where Martha will find out how badly hurt he is. Until then I want you all to say nothing about him. It might kill him to be carried away in an Army truck.'

Johann looked startled. 'You are going to report him, aren't you?'

The priest showed impatience. 'Don't be a fool. Of course I am. Once he is fit to travel we shall take him ourselves to the Army garrison in Weishaven.'

'But is that safe?' Johann argued. 'He looks a strong man. What if he recovers quickly? You and Martha wouldn't be able to stop him.'

The priest pointed scornfully at the unconscious pilot. 'Does he look like a threat? After the way you've treated him it'll be days before he is fit to walk and by that time he will be in a prisoner-of-war hospital. Now stop arguing and get him up to the church. I want to find out how badly hurt he is.'

Sean's eyes opened slowly and painfully. At first the figures and the room around him were blurred and indistinct. Then, as he saw one of the figures move, he tried to speak. At first he heard only a croak. As he tried again, he managed a hoarse question. 'Where am I?'

He felt a hand on his forehead and heard a low accented voice. 'You are quite safe, Flight Lieutenant. No, don't try to move.

Wait until you are stronger.'

The advice was not necessary. The sea of darkness that had allowed Sean a glimpse of life was closing over him again. A moment later the accented voice died away as he sank once more into unconsciousness.

The blurred scene appeared again. 'What is this place?' Sean managed.

The accented voice replied once more. 'You are in a church, Flight Lieutenant. You are quite safe.'

'Why am I in a church? Am I dying?'

'No, my son. You are receiving medical attention. You are in God's hands.'

Delirium distorted the pilot's reply. 'I don't believe in God. So why are you wasting your time?'

'Close your eyes and sleep, my son. We will talk later.'

The blurred scene faded, the darkness swooped back, and all was silence again.

'Flight Lieutenant. Can you hear me?'

Sean opened his eyes. Slowly the man sitting at his bedside came into focus, a white-haired man whose elderly, lined face was oddly solicitous. Behind him was a small room with whitewashed stone walls and a few pieces of simple furniture. Sean swallowed, coughed, then managed to speak. 'Yes. Who are you?'

'I'm Father Libermann. You are in my church. You were shot down very close to it? Do you remember being shot down?'

Outlines began appearing on Sean's memory. As their details became harsher, he gave a violent start. 'Yes. I was watching a pilot I had shot down. But what am I doing in a church?'

'You were in great danger, Flight Lieutenant. The local people thought you intended to shoot that pilot. So it was safer to bring you here until you were fit to travel. You were badly concussed when you crashed. But before we talk any more you must have something to drink.'

Sean felt his head lifted and a cup placed to his mouth. He managed to sip a few spoonfuls but then broke into a bout of coughing. As he sank back exhausted the priest withdrew the cup. 'You can have more later when your throat is less sore. Do you want to ask any questions now or wait until you are stronger?'

As he was speaking Sean noticed a woman entering the vestry. Big boned but elderly, wearing a black dress and shawl, she said something in German to the priest, who replied in the same language. Nodding, she cast a glance at Sean, then began attending to a wood stove at the far end of the vestry. Sean's eyes moved back to the priest. 'Why haven't the Luftwaffe picked me up?'

'They don't know about you yet, Flight Lieutenant. I told the local villagers to say nothing until you had received decent medical attention.'

Sean was trying to clear his confused thoughts. 'But why? I'd just shot down one of your aircraft.'

'You also protected its pilot afterwards. Why did you do that, Flight Lieutenant?'

'I don't know,' Sean confessed. 'But he had fought well and I suddenly felt a need to see he landed safely.'

Libermann smiled. 'And I felt a need to protect you from angry peasants. Perhaps we both allowed our humanity to escape from the madness of war.'

Sean stared up at him. 'How do you come to speak English so well?'

'My father married an Englishwoman and she made me learn English. As she was quite strict about it and only died two years ago I was never allowed to lose it.'

'Do your parishioners know this?'

'Perhaps some do. But it doesn't matter. They know I am a good German.'

Sean did not answer. Conscious of his stiffness he drew back the blankets that covered him and saw his upper body was strapped in bandages. 'Have you done this?' he asked.

The priest shook his head and nodded at the woman by the stove. 'No. Martha has been looking after you. She is my housekeeper but was a nurse in her early days. But we tell no one or she would be conscripted into the Army Nursing Corps.'

'Does she speak English too?'

'No.'

'Then tell her I'm grateful, will you?'

He received a smile from the woman as the priest passed on his message. Sean's eyes moved back to Libermann. 'How long have I been here?'

'Three days, my son.'

Sean gave a start. 'Three days! Isn't this going to get you into trouble?'

Libermann smiled. 'Perhaps a little. But I'm sure it will be put down to our peasant stupidity.'

'From all I hear about your Gestapo, I wouldn't bank on that. What about the pilot I shot down? He's sure to tell the authorities.'

'No. I spoke to him and he was grateful for your protection. He'll only talk when we are ready.'

'He's not going to wait more than three days or he'll get into trouble himself. You'd better get the word out, Father. I wouldn't want either of you punished for your kindness.'

The priest's expression held his eyes. On a woman it could have been described as affection. 'You will stay here until you are fit to travel, Flight Lieutenant. My church takes its orders from God, not from soldiers or policemen.'

'But there's no point in getting yourself into trouble when I'm going to be a prisoner whatever happens,' Sean argued. 'Help me up and send Martha with a message.'

Libermann gazed round at the woman, then bent over the pilot. A moment later Sean heard a whisper in his ear. 'When Martha leaves I have something very important to tell you. So please lie there quietly until we are alone.'

FIFTEEN

Martha wrapped a shawl around her shoulders, then said something in German to Libermann, who shook his head. 'No. You go to Hermann and your son and get a good night's rest. The Flight Lieutenant is much better today. We can manage now.'

The woman cast a glance at Sean who was propped up by a pillow. 'Is she going home?' Sean asked.

'Ja. She slept here in a chair last night in case you needed attention. Martha is a good woman.'

'Thank her for me,' Sean said. 'Tell her I'm grateful.'

Libermann turned back to the women and passed on his message. Martha gave Sean a half smile, then crossed to an outside door. 'Don't come in early tomorrow,' Libermann told her. 'I'll see to our breakfasts. Stay in bed and catch up with your sleep.'

The woman nodded, then closed the door behind her. Libermann waited a few seconds, then crossed over to the door and opened it a few inches. Satisfied, he closed the door and turned to Sean. 'It isn't that I don't trust her. But the less she knows the safer it is for her.'

Sean frowned. 'Safer? I don't understand.'

Libermann went to a second door that led into the small church and gazed into its darkened interior. Unable to be sure it was empty, he walked the full length between the aisles before returning to the vestry. By this time, puzzled by his behaviour, Sean was sitting up in bed. 'What's worrying you? Are you expecting someone?'

Libermann closed the door. 'Sometimes one or two of the villagers come up and sit in the church when the bombers fly over. Perhaps they feel safer here. But it is quiet tonight.'

When Sean did not answer he drew up a chair to the pilot's bedside. 'I am right, am I not? You are feeling stronger?'

Sean nodded. 'I've lost the headache. And it's less painful when move. But my face feels sore and stiff. Did I damage it in the crash?'

Libermann rose and brought him a mirror. Sean winced at the scratched face that stared back at him. 'How did that happen?'

Libermann dropped back into his chair. 'As I said, the villagers were angry because of the children's bombed orphanage. One of the women lost control. Don't blame her, Flight Lieutenant. The bombing is causing many deaths and much suffering.'

Sean lowered the mirror. 'I'm not blaming her. And it's easier to understand what you saved me from. But don't leave it any longer or you'll pay too heavy a price for it.'

Libermann nodded. 'It's true you've made a quick recovery. Two days ago you were delirious. Even last night you talked a great deal. I thought it would be at least another two days before you were fit to move.'

'It must be that soup Martha's been giving me,' Sean said. He handed back the mirror. 'But surely you weren't prepared to wait that long before turning me in. That would have been crazy.'

Libermann did not answer. His expression was puzzling Sean. It suggested a conflict of emotions that were still not fully resolved. 'Something is troubling you, isn't it?' Sean said. 'If it has anything to do with me, stop worrying about it. You've given me over three days of peace and medical attention.

What happens next is something no one can help. One thing is certain. I'll always be grateful.'

Libermann shook his head. 'I did nothing no other priest wouldn't have done. I couldn't let the villagers murder you, for their sakes as well as your own. That was my duty as a man and a priest.'

'You still didn't need to bring me up here and take care of me. Stop running yourself down, Father. In my book you're quite a man.'

Libermann spoke as if he had not been listening. 'You talked a great deal in your sleep. I have never known a man talk so much.'

'What did I say? What a damn awful war it is?'

'You talked of many things. But mostly about the war you have within yourself.'

'War within myself? What does that mean?'

'I was puzzled myself at first. But then, as you gave away your ideas and beliefs, I began to understand. You are an atheist who believes in everything the great prophets taught to men thousands of years ago. You have taken notice of the things our Christ said, not the Nicene interpretation that gives us Christianity without its message.'

Sean stared up at him. 'Nicene interpretation? What does that mean?'

'It was the Roman way of introducing Christianity without its politics and responsibilities. And because it suited emperors, kings and the rich and powerful, we have been brainwashed with it for seventeen centuries.'

'I don't follow you. What have the Romans to do with it?'

'Constantine couldn't introduce a religion that denounced might and power to an empire that dominated half the known world. So he emphasised Christ's humble birth and agonising sacrifice but said little if anything about Christ's politics. It was all too revolutionary. And hasn't it stayed there ever since? Whenever have you heard priests or parsons denouncing warlike leaders or telling the rich they have less chance of getting into heaven than a camel getting through the eye of a needle? Usury, once a mortal sin, now governs our banks and our economies. And yet to make profit out of another man's needs is the very opposite of Christ's message.'

Sean was staring at the priest in disbelief. 'You do realise what you're saying?'

'Yes. Since 325AD we've been taught to worship the man but less and less of his principles. Constantine knew human nature well. He knew it needed a supreme power to worship but would go its own venial way if its guidelines were blurred or indistinct.'

Sean broke free from the spell of the priest's words. 'I'm sorry, Father, but you've got the wrong man. I've nothing but contempt for religion, as everyone who knows me will tell you.'

The priest gave a half smile. 'Like the woman Linda?'

Sean started. 'Did I talk about her too?'

'Many times. And your sister too. That was a terrible loss for you but do not blame God for it. The sinner was the priest who advised against her marriage. His prejudice betrayed his cloth. We are all brothers under God, although over the centuries we have forgotten it.'

'What did I say about Linda?' Sean interrupted.

'You said she could not understand you because she is religious and you are not. But you are wrong about her, Flight Lieutenant. God has not yet told me the reason but it is vital that you see her again.'

Sean stared up at the man's lined face. 'Vital? Why?'

'It is your destiny. That is why the two of you met in the first place.'

'Father, I met her by accident. I took a short cut through a wood and there she was. It was nothing to do with destiny or anything supernatural. You often meet people that way and some of them stay in your mind although you may never see them again.'

'But you saw this woman again, Flight Lieutenant. You went back to her three more times. That wasn't by chance, was it?'

Sean had the odd feeling that in another dimension he was losing a sacerdotal argument. 'Father, she was intelligent and attractive. That's why I went back.'

'Are you quite sure of that?'

Sarcasm began to stain Sean's voice. 'Are you saying God sent me back? Come off it, Father. I'm a normal man and she's a very beautiful woman. Don't tell me God works through our glands.'

Libermann took no offence. 'Some would say yes if it serves His purpose. And there is a purpose here. A vital one.'

'I can't think what it is. She's married and also seems a traditionalist. All we did was argue. What was the purpose of that?'

'Perhaps it was to loosen your minds. Until you met her you were almost proud of your atheism while she was deeply embedded in the soul of her culture. Perhaps your arguments began the process of preparation.'

Sean frowned. 'Preparation? What are you talking about?'

'Perhaps Linda had to hear your beliefs and you needed to trust her.'

'Trust her? Why would I need to do that?'

'Because God tells me that meeting you had with this woman is going to have consequences beyond anything you or I can ever imagine.'

This time Sean could not hold back laughter. 'I must have been more than delirious. What else did I talk about?'

'As I've said, you talked about your beliefs. Your dislike of national armies, your disgust of religious and racial prejudice, your scorn of patriotism and how divisive it is.' A smile crossed Libermann's face. 'Martha found that hard to understand when I translated it for her. She could not understand why you killed Germans for your country when you felt no patriotic commitment to it.'

Sean examined the priest's lined face. 'Does it make sense to you?'

'In one way yes. I deplore the killing but I understand the motive. I dislike bullies too. If we must have enemies it is better they are bullies than men with whom we have no quarrel. We were meant to share this world, not claim small pieces of it and fight over them like dogs over a bone.'

'Does that mean you see Hitler's armies as bullies?'

'Yes. I see all aggressive nations as bullies.' Libermann's smile was a mixture of humour and regret. 'That's why my good bishop sent me out here into the wilderness to save my skin. I saw the anomalies in our current religious beliefs and began to speak of them aloud. Luckily for me my bishop saw the danger and posted me out here to save me from the Gestapo.' Then his tone changed again. 'The world suffers because we quickly forgot the divine messages given to us so many years ago.'

'Tell me those messages,' Sean said.

'Tell you? You know them better than any of us. That all men are brothers and mercy, tolerance, and forgiveness should rule our lives. That we should love our neighbours as ourselves. That we should forgo our national pride and love our enemy. That to seek riches when millions are starving is the very reversal of Christ's life and teaching. The message is much the same in all of the great religions. You, who claim to have no God, are one of the few who remember those messages. You have been given a great gift, Flight Lieutenant. So why don't you show God more gratitude?'

Sean, who had been listening in fascination, now found his voice again. 'You've got the wrong man, Father. I'm a fighter pilot and I hate bullies like hell. Have you forgotten that?'

'I know what you are. You're a human being and you have your failings. But I know your hatred of bullies is born of your hatred of cruelty. Most men hate for far less.'

Sean cleared his throat. 'One thing is certain. Your bishop is right. You're no ordinary priest. So why are we enemies?'

'We are enemies because of man's iniquity.

But in the eyes of God we are brothers.'

Sean dropped back on his pillow. 'I wish I could share your faith. But I've seen too much killing and done too much myself to believe a merciful God runs this world.'

Libermann shook his head. 'Unlike my fellow priests I don't believe it either. Otherwise how could we exercise free will? We humans run this world, which means we should accept our responsibility for its cruelty and its wars. But being hypocrites we are only too quick to reinstate God when we need someone to blame.'

Sean made a humorous gesture. 'I hope I never meet you in debate, Father. They don't come any better.'

He received a smile in return. 'I have one big advantage, my son. I have a good lawyer behind me.' Then Libermann's tone changed as he leaned forward. 'Tell me something. From your heart, not from your head. Do you want to believe in God?'

The question caught Sean by surprise. 'Me? No. I find the world too disgusting. Sinners like me only keep sane by accepting we are semi-intelligent animals in an uncaring universe. Perhaps if one could believe it had a purpose it might be different. But I can't believe that.'

The loneliness implicit in the pilot's words sent a slight shiver through Libermann. 'But life has a purpose. A massive one. We are here to work for God. To serve and strengthen Him.'

'Strengthen? Are you saying He needs our help?'

The priest sighed. 'Again I am in conflict with my teachings. I believe he does. I believe good and evil are in eternal conflict and God needs our support. Can you doubt it when you look around and see all this hatred and conflict?'

Sean could not believe what he was hearing. 'Are you telling me you're a priest who doesn't believe God runs this world?'

Libermann shrugged. 'How can I believe it if I believe in free will? How can I believe it when I witness so much cruelty? As the tenants of this world, we carry the responsibility of caring for it and who is better equipped than you with your thoughts and beliefs? They are a fire within you. They come out like the blows of a heavyweight boxer. They make people listen and think, as they did Linda. Whereas cowards like myself have given up the fight and talk only about sowing seeds, gathering in the harvest, and giving blessing to newly born babies.'

Sean gazed at him a moment longer, then sank back again on his pillow. 'You're wasting your time, Father. There's too big a difference between us. I kill men and send their souls to hell or wherever they go. You take care of them and save them from

171

themselves. I'd call that quite a difference, wouldn't you?'

'Not necessarily. We all have roles to play and often don't recognise that path we are treading or where it will lead us.'

Sean's scratched face grinned back at him. 'I know where mine is leading me. To stale bread and ersatz coffee in a prisoner of war camp.'

Libermann's quiet voice sank even lower. 'Are you quite sure of that?'

Sean frowned. 'What do you mean?'

'This woman Linda. Didn't she ask you to return to her sanctuary whenever you could? And particularly on her birthday?'

Sean nodded. 'She's that kind of woman. She felt if I had a woman to write to and return to it might help to save my skin.'

Libermann shook his greying head. 'No. Although she did not know it herself, she was asking much more than that. God had told her she must see you again for His own purposes. That was the real reason behind her request.'

'What purposes?'

'I haven't been told them yet but I know they are divine ones.'

Sean smiled. 'You see God in everything, don't you?'

'God is in everything, my son. God was in your reply when you said yes to please her.'

Glancing round the small vestry Sean

made a wry gesture. 'Maybe, but I didn't keep my promise very well did I? Who gets the blame for that? My flight controller, my shoddy flying, or did God send down that Me 109 to prang me?'

Ignoring his sarcasm Libermann lowered his voice. 'What would you have done if you'd survived your mission? Would you have kept your promise?'

Sean stirred impatiently. 'Yes, I suppose so. But what's the point of all this?'

Libermann's voice sank even lower. 'Because I want a solemn promise from you. If I allow you to escape, will you make straight for that woman and that sanctuary?'

SIXTEEN

Sean gave a start of disbelief. 'You're not serious.'

Libermann shook his head. 'I've never been more serious in my life. I've listened to your secrets for three nights and the feeling has grown that this is my duty.'

'Duty? Good God, man, your duty is to turn me in. If you don't, the Gestapo will hang you on fish hooks. With everyone in the village knowing about me, you won't have a leg to stand on. Don't even think

173

about it?'

'Perhaps I've no choice, Flight Lieutenant. Perhaps it is something I must do.'

'Don't give me that God's stuff again, Father. That's bullshit. You've just talked about free will and personal choice. That's how the Gestapo will see it when they sharpen their knives. In any case how far would I get in this condition? They'd capture me in half an hour and you would die for nothing.'

Libermann shook his head. 'I don't think they would capture you. Not with the help I believe you will get.'

'You're saying God would help me? Me, the guy who gave Him up for dead years ago? Father, I respect your beliefs but now we're talking about the real world of war, guns and bullets. I'm a shot-down English pilot in Germany and every man I meet is my enemy. I'm also not in the best of physical shape. So you are offering to risk your life on odds that are no better than ten to one against. Those are lousy odds, Father.'

'That's for God to decide, my friend. For some reason I do not understand, He needs you to live for His own very special reasons.'

'I will live. Your prison camps feed their captives, don't they?' Even as he argued a part of Sean's mind was ridiculing the situation. A man to whom imprisonment would be an abhorrence was arguing against an offer of freedom. The world was madder than even he had believed. 'I'll survive and when the damned war is over I'll see Linda again. So where's the need for the big gesture?'

Libermann leaned forward, 'You are not the only one who has had dreams these last three nights. Shall I tell you mine?' As Sean nodded he went on: 'Last night I saw myself standing beside an oak tree and saw a single acorn fall to the ground and roll a few yards down a hillside. Then a tractor came, ploughing up the ground. As it was heading towards the acorn I felt certain it would be crushed or destroyed. But as the tractor passed by I saw the acorn fall into a furrow and the ground close over it. Then time came and went and one day a tiny green sprig appeared in the brown earth. Defying all the tractors that had kept coming over the years it continued to grow and I knew that one day it would be a massive tree that would dominate the land.'

Sean showed his scepticism. 'And you see that as a message?'

'Yes. Perhaps it means that you and a few others like you contain seeds that must not be allowed to shrivel and die in imprisonment. Those ideas of yours that even Linda could not at first accept are those seeds. They will grow as more and more men see their need. You will not live to see them flower nor perhaps will your grandchildren. But they will flower one day and that is why those precious seeds must never be lost or endangered.'

Sean's amused smile spread. 'And you are saying my meeting with Linda will begin all this? How?'

'I don't know. God hasn't told me. But in some way it will be the beginning. That is why it must happen.'

'You're forgetting one thing, Father. My atheism that goes with me. Do you want that to flower too?'

To his surprise Libermann gave a vigorous nod. 'Yes. Modern religion is corrupt. It is impregnated with jingoism, nationalism, self-pride, and self-interest. As I keep on telling you, your beliefs are the ones taught to man thousands of years ago.'

Sean could not longer hold back his laughter. 'If I didn't know you better, I'd say you were the world's best flatterer, Father. I'm both an atheist and an idiot whose ideas are so far fetched they could never be accepted in ten thousand years. Linda herself said that. So why is it so important I see her again?'

'I don't know. I only wish I did. All I have been told is its importance to this unhappy world.'

'Father, Linda is a happily married woman. There's no way she can strike up a meaningful relationship with me. I don't know what I said in my delirium but it's given you the wrong picture.'

'No. It is her destiny and yours. I know it.'

'But how do you know? Where have you got this crazy idea from?'

'I've told you. It comes from God himself. Who else could make me release you?'

Sean's tolerance turned into impatience. 'Don't even think about it. It would be plain suicide. And what about Martha? Do you want her to be punished too.'

'That is why Martha has not been told about this. She will arrive late tomorrow morning to find me bound and gagged with a head wound. The villagers will not be surprised. More than one of them warned me you might try to escape.'

Sean did not answer for a moment. Then he shook his head. 'It's an old trick and your cloth won't help you either. Didn't you say you were the only one who understood why I was circling your Me 109 pilot?' When Libermann did not answer, he went on: 'When the Gestapo hear that they'll put two and two together and get the right answer. You'll be giving your life for mine and when I'm re-captured it'll be a sacrifice for nothing. Which makes no sense at all.'

Libermann's smile was whimsical. 'It may not make sense to you or me but which of us can see into the future? I have been told it is my duty to let you escape and I have made my plans accordingly.'

'Duty? Your duty is to your country. Aren't you forgetting that?'

'I think I am a good German, Flight Lieutenant, but my duty to God must come first.'

Sean made a gesture of disgust. 'This is all in your mind. God doesn't care about me or he wouldn't have had me shot down. Face it, Father. It's a crazy idea and I want no part in it. In fact I shan't go even if you throw me out.'

'You will have to go,' the priest said. 'Or you will get me into trouble.'

'In what way?'

'Because of the preparations I've made. I've been collecting food for you and I've obtained clothes and written a letter for you to take. If the Gestapo found it in a search it would compromise me.'

'Letter? What kind of letter?'

'You cannot speak German so you will travel as a Swiss civilian who was in a traffic accident and been in hospital and is now trying to return home. Can you speak any foreign language?'

'Reasonable French. I once worked a year over there. But why?'

'Because being Swiss gives you a choice of language that makes you less suspicious to an interrogator. The letter explains in

German what has happened to you and asks for things like train or bus tickets. As you will also have a map and money, it should help you to reach Switzerland or even Spain.'

Sean was fascinated in spite of himself. 'And how am I supposed to take care of you before I go?'

'We'll use the sheets to gag and tie me with. Then you will make that large bruise on my head and be on your way. You must leave at least an hour before sunrise to escape being seen by any of the labourers.'

Sean eyed him, saw his determination, and made his decision. 'All right. Let me see the letter and we'll play it from there.'

Libermann's smile was quizzical. 'Only when you promise you will go, Flight Lieutenant. Not before.'

Muttering a curse, Sean began climbing out of bed. Libermann moved his chair to block him 'You won't find the letter. I learned much about you in your delirium, so you won't see it until you have given me your promise.'

Sean tried to push the chair away. 'It's an insane idea. You'll be arrested and I'll either be shot or captured again. I'm not going, Father. As soon as it's daylight I'll walk down to the village and give myself up.'

Libermann's eyes met his own and there was no compromise in them. 'If you do that I shall tell the police of my intention and show them the letter. So your refusal will cause the very thing you fear'

Sean cursed. 'That's pure blackmail. What the hell's the matter with you? Do you want to die a traitor to your country?'

The priest's quiet voice had never been more steady or more certain. 'I do not believe I am failing my country. I am obeying a voice that says I must free you to follow the path you have been given. Why won't you grant me my wish?'

'And you believe this voice comes from God?'

'I know it does. That is why I must obey it.'

Unable to think of a reply, Sean motioned Libermann to remove the chair and lowered himself to the floor. Wincing at the pain in his ribs, he took a few steps round the vestry before pausing by the priest, his voice still angry with defeat. 'I think you're wrong. Criminally wrong. You're going to regret it only a few hours after I've gone. Are you listening to me?'

He received a smile of extraordinary sweetness. 'No, my friend. A man never regrets obeying his conscience and his God. Now please hurry and do as I say because you must be on your way before daybreak.'

The telephone rang as Linda was making morning tea for her father who was still in bed. Hoping it might be from Sean she ran into the hall. 'Hello. Who is that?'

'Is that Mrs Martin?'

She recognised the voice but to her disappointment it was Phillips and not Sean. 'Yes. What is it, Peter?'

The pause before Phillips replied made her heart miss a beat. The slight cough that preceded it heightened her apprehension. 'I'm afraid I have bad news for you, Mrs Martin.'

She had to take a deep breath to steady herself. 'Is it about Sean?'

'Yes. It seems he didn't return from an operation two days ago.'

Her legs suddenly went weak and she had to support herself against the phone table. Phillips' voice came again. 'Are you still there, Mrs Martin?'

With an effort she lifted the receiver again. 'Yes, I'm here. What happened? Was he killed?'

'No one is sure. The operation was escort duty over Germany and he was missing after an attack by enemy fighters. No one saw his Mustang go down so he's reported missing.'

She wished her mind would clear and her hands stop shaking. 'So his conversion course was over. How did you hear this?'

'I have a colleague on his squadron who knows we were friends. He phoned me this morning.'

She pulled herself together. 'If no one saw

181

him shot down, then couldn't he have crash-landed and be a prisoner?'

'That's what I'm hoping. Eventually the Red Cross might find out and let us know.'

'How long does that take?'

'It's impossible to say. It depends where he crashed and how soon the enemy found his plane.'

'Will enquiries be made?'

'Of course. And as soon as anything is heard my colleague will let me know. I'm sorry to give you this news. I know it's going to be painful news for your sister. But tell her not to give up hope yet.'

In her shock at the news it took Linda a moment to remember the excuse she had given Phillips. 'Yes. Yes, of course I'll tell her. She will be upset. But you will let us know if you get any more news, won't you?'

'I'll phone you right away, Linda. There's still hope he might be a prisoner.'

She did not hear Phillips' final words. She was still supporting herself with the table when Charles, wearing a dressing gown, appeared in the sitting room doorway. 'Who was it? Was it Douglas?' Then he noticed her expression and gave a start. 'What's the matter, girl? You're as white as a sheet.'

With an effort she turned towards him. 'It was a call from Lemington Airfield. Do you remember that airman I found on our estate? The one I told you about?'

182

Charles frowned. 'Who can forget him? Was it he on the phone?'

She found her lips were quivering and had to fight to steady her voice. 'No. He's been shot down. They don't know if he's dead or a prisoner of war.'

Whatever his private feelings, Charles knew when sympathy was appropriate. He approached Linda and put an arm round her shoulders. 'I'm sorry, darling. Who phoned you about him? Douglas?'

She longed to throw her arms around him and sob her grief but knew she must not. Instead she used impatience to fight off her distress. 'No, of course it wasn't. As I've told you before Douglas knows nothing about him. Nor do I want him to.'

Knowing his daughter well, Charles took no offence. 'Didn't anyone see him go down?'

She brushed a hand across her eyes, a gesture almost angry in its resentment and impotence. 'No. I suppose he was doing one of his crazy stunts again and lost contact with his wingman. I always had the belief he would kill himself sooner or later.'

Charles's arm tightened comfortingly around her. 'You don't yet know he's dead, darling. From what you told me he seemed a tough character. He might have survived the crash and be a prisoner. Don't give up hope yet.'

She wondered at her anger when she wanted only to cry. 'He doesn't fly as if he wants to live. Squadron Leader Phillips told me that.'

Charles was too wise to ask any further questions at that moment. 'All you can do, darling, is wait until you get further news. Now come and have a drink. I think you need one.'

She pulled herself together, countering his concern with impatient concern of her own. 'Why did you come downstairs? You've just had one setback and you'll have another if you don't do what the doctor says and take more rest. Go back to bed and I'll bring your breakfast up. Please, Dad.'

Charles, old and experienced enough about the working of the human mind to know how one worry could moderate another, played his part admirably. 'You're right, darling. I do feel a bit wobbly this morning. All right. I'll go back and stay in bed until lunch time. How's that?'

She kissed him. 'Much better. Now off you go while I finish making your breakfast.'

SEVENTEEN

Sean lowered his case to the ground, lifted his raincoat collar, and drew his hat farther down over his eyes. A chilling wind was gusting down the road and bringing with it a shower of rain. Although the civilian clothes Libermann had found for him were adequate for his role, he knew that if they were once allowed to become too wet or soiled they would no longer serve as a disguise, particularly once the news of his escape had been circulated.

He gazed back down the country road. There was now enough daylight for him to see the small row of houses he had passed a few minutes ago. The road was still free of traffic but with the sky lightening by the moment he knew it would not stay that way much longer.

Not for the first time he wondered if he were making the right choice. On leaving the church his first instinct had been to take to the fields where the likelihood of encountering German military units had seemed less likely but he had soon realised this could contain its own dangers. A Swiss civilian with nothing to fear from the German populace would surely create suspicion by his very avoidance of them. Moreover it had rained the previous day and in no time his shoes and trouser cuffs were brown with clay. If he continued trudging across the fields his appearance in itself would give him away. Taken in the round it had seemed safer to encounter his enemy than to avoid him and so he had made his way down to the country road which, according to Libermann, ran to Weinfeld where he might catch a train.

As he had left before daybreak he had felt reasonably safe for the first two hours. Only one man on a bicycle had passed him on the dark road and although he received a stare from the cyclist, who was no doubt surprised to see a lone civilian at that time in the morning, there had been no suspicion in the greeting given him. With Libermann not expecting Martha back at the church before nine a.m. the chances were good that Sean would be well away from the village before the alarm was raised.

At least that had been their hope, Sean thought ruefully as he picked up his case again in which Libermann had packed all the food he could spare. What neither man had considered were the shoes the priest had obtained for him. Although Libermann had obtained the right size, like new footwear everywhere they gripped in the wrong places, and it had not taken Sean long to wish he had never made the change. While on a close inspection his RAF shoes would have betrayed him, the compensation would have been less pain and greater progress.

He wished he knew the time. With his watch having an English hallmark it could not be kept and a replacement was something Libermann had not been able to obtain. With the sky bright now from horizon to horizon, he could only guess it was between six and seven. If he were right he still had time before his escape was discovered and broadcast.

The sound of an engine broke his thoughts. Glancing back he saw an Army truck heading towards him. Knowing any attempt to hide would draw immediate suspicion, he knew he must continue walking and pretend unconcern of the truck and its passing. Then in time he remembered his role and his letter. If Libermann's plan was feasible, it might be better to find out now rather than later. So, bracing himself, he turned to face the oncoming truck. When it was fifty yards from him he took a deep breath, raised his arm, and thumbed its driver for a lift.

As the truck began slowing down, he saw there were two uniformed men inside the cab. As it drew up alongside him, the driver leaned from the side window. 'Was möchten Sie?'

Shaking his head Sean handed up his letter. 'Je suis Suisse. If you read this you will understand.'

The driver stared down at him. 'Sprechen Sie kein Deutsch?'

'Nein. Je parle francais, seulement.'

The driver, a sergeant, gave him another stare, then passed the letter to his passenger. As the man took it Sean saw with alarm he was a Wehrmacht officer. For a full thirty seconds the officer read the letter, his expression betraying surprise and not a little suspicion. Then he raised his head and tersely waved Sean round to his side of the cab. To Sean's relief he addressed him in French. 'You say you are Swiss?'

'Ya. I'm trying to get to Weinfeld. I wondered if you would give me a lift?'

'Why are you walking at this time in the morning?'

Fervently hoping his French would pass the test, Sean was relieved to hear the German's French was no better. 'I was hoping to get a lift from a friend but his car would not start. So as I have to catch a train I had no option but to walk.'

'But Weinfeld is twenty miles away.'

'I know. That is why I was hoping I could get a lift.'

The officer, full of the haughty arrogance of his kind, gazed again at the letter. 'What are you doing in this country?'

Sean was about to say he was on business and then realised he knew of no business that justified a Swiss citizen walking down an empty road a couple of hours after dawn. 'I came to see a friend in Uberlaten. The one who was going to drive me to my train this morning.'

The officer glanced back at the letter, then unexpectedly threw open the cab door. 'All right. We are going to Weinfeld. But another time do not stop an army vehicle. We have other things to do but give lifts to civilian hitch hikers.'

Sean passed up his case then climbed in, hiding with some difficulty the pain from his bruised ribs. 'My name is Meyer Heinrich,' the officer told him. Then he motioned at Sean's scratched cheeks. 'What happened to your face?'

Sean managed a laugh. 'It's a ridiculous story. But you know how unpredictable cats are. My friend in Uberlaten has one. I was playing with it the other day and it suddenly turned on me. I think I must have trapped its tail.' Only too aware how thin his story was he held his breath as he lowered his case into the well of the cab.

Heinrich's dry but amused voice told him the story's very lack of plausibility made it credible. 'Are you sure it wasn't a tiger instead of a cat?' As Sean relaxed, the officer turned and nodded to his driver. As the truck pulled away Heinrich motioned at the letter he was still holding. 'This friend in Uberlaten? Did he write this letter for you?'

'Yes. Knowing I can't speak German he felt it would make it easier for me to buy tickets on buses and trains.'

'Who is he? You have not said.'

Sean took a chance on the officer not knowing the inhabitants of the small village. 'He is a chemist. I've known him for many years.'

'Is he German?' When Sean nodded Heinrich went on: 'If you cannot speak German, how is it you could talk with him?'

Realising he had not been given a lift out of goodwill alone, Sean had to think fast. As he searched for an excuse he noticed a radio and transmitter bolted below the cab dashboard. Apprehension gave him the lie he needed. 'He speaks French like you do. He picked it up in Switzerland when he worked there many years ago.'

The look he received turned his mouth dry. 'But you did not pick up your French in Switzerland, did you, Herr Schmidt. Your French is as bad as my French, as even I can tell. So why are you telling me these stories?'

Believing his escape was over before it had properly begun, Sean could do no more than simulate offence. 'My friend and I communicated in French because it was a common language to us both. The reason

190

my French isn't too good is because I was brought up in an Italian speaking canton. What's so odd about that?'

Expecting a challenge Sean saw Heinrich frown instead. 'Do you carry proof of this?'

Heartened by the unexpected reaction and remembering the cynical platitude that the bigger the lie the more likely it is to be believed, Sean went for broke. 'I did have my Swiss passport. But it was kept by your immigration officials to be picked up in two weeks, the maximum time I'm allowed to stay. That's why I need to get back in a hurry. I don't want to be arrested or kept in Germany.'

As Sean had hoped, it was clear Heinrich knew nothing about his country's immigration procedures. 'You say the immigration people kept your passport? Haven't you needed it while you've been here?'

'No. You're the first who's asked to see it. Can I have my letter back, please? I might need it when we reach Weinfeld.'

Hardly able to believe his ploy had worked Sean held his breath as the officer gazed once more at the letter in his hand. Then, frowning, he handed it back. 'My country is at war, Herr Schmidt, and the task of all good Germans is to watch out for enemies of the state. A man walking alone at night causes suspicion. That is why I had to interrogate you.'

Sean was only too ready to accept the veiled apology. 'I understand that. You were only doing your duty. For my part I can't get home soon enough. If I'd known you were being bombed so much I'd never have made the journey.'

Feeling contempt was taking the place of suspicion in the officer, Sean was content enough to relax in the silence that followed. He had no illusions about the dangers that lay ahead. Even if he succeeded in catching a train in Weinfeld there was always the possibility this officer might make enquiries about his country's immigration service and radio ahead for his arrest. However, as it seemed he had successfully crossed his first hurdle, there was little profit in dwelling on the perils ahead. Surprised by his optimism but comforted by it, Sean turned to his window and paid interest in the country outside.

In the few miles the truck had travelled, the agricultural fields had given way to grass covered hillsides and clumps of trees. A small village swept into sight with housewives and children waving at the Army truck. Whatever the mood of city dwellers after their months of night and day bombing, the morale in the countryside seemed unaffected, Sean thought. The war had a long way to go yet.

A sudden buzzing caught his attention as the village fell away. As the officer reached forward and took the two-way microphone from the dashboard Sean felt a sudden pang of apprehension. Tense again, he listened to the officer speaking in German and imagined a tone of triumph and self-satisfaction entering his voice. Whatever the subject of the conversation, it lasted over a couple of minutes before the officer replaced the microphone and spoke to the sergeant driver. Seeing the man start and glance at him, Sean thought the worst for the moment but when the truck picked up speed and the officer made no immediate comment he decided his nerves were seeing danger where none existed.

His relief lasted less than fifteen seconds. Suddenly he felt a jab of pain in his bruised ribs and heard a sharp order. 'Open your coat and your shirt.'

Turning, Sean saw the officer's Luger was dug into his side. As he hesitated, the pistol jabbed again. 'Do as I say?'

Knowing the game was over, Sean unbuttoned his raincoat and his shirt, revealing the bandages still strapped round his ribs. Heinrich's voice was exultant. 'So I was right about you, Flight Lieutenant. That is your rank, is it not?'

Sean replaced his shirt and raincoat and sank back. His first thought was of Libermann. 'How did your people find out I'd escaped? I thought it would take them two more hours at least.'

'One of the villagers was worried about the priest and came to check on him before going to work. When he saw you'd escaped he phoned the police.'

Sean was wondering what his capture would do to Libermann's religious faith. 'I hope the priest is all right? I couldn't help hitting him when he tried to stop me.'

The haughty voice that answered him had a sadistic note. 'You didn't hit him hard enough, Flight Lieutenant.'

Sean turned to see Heinrich's expression. 'What does that mean?'

'It means your priest will live to face a traitor's death. He has been arrested and will be handed to the Gestapo.'

Sean suddenly felt sick. 'That's ridiculous. All he did was nurse me. Is that a sin in Nazi Germany?'

'He did more than nurse you, Flight Lieutenant. He helped an enemy of the Reich to escape. He obtained those very clothes for you. A shopkeeper in Uberlaten has confirmed it.'

'That's a lie. I found them in his vestry.' At that moment, resigned to his capture, Sean's only thought was to save Libermann. 'This is crazy. They've arrested an innocent man.'

Ignoring his protest Heinrich switched his pistol to his other hand and, reaching for the radio, dialled a number. When he finished making his call Sean addressed him again.

'What are you going to do with me now? Turn me over to the police?'

Heinrich pointed to a signpost ahead. 'No. We're taking you to a military unit a few miles from here. They will take good care of you.'

'Can I contact your people in Uberlaten from there? That priest was kind to me. I can't let him be punished for my escape.'

He received a mocking smile. 'Very altruistic, Flight Lieutenant. You can try your lies on my colleagues, although I doubt they will believe you any more than I do.'

Through the windshield Sean could see the signpost approaching. The road to which it pointed led across a shallow valley and then towards a series of wooded hills. As the truck slowed down in preparation to making the turn, the jab of the pistol into his side told him Heinrich was reading his thoughts. 'Don't even think about jumping out, Flight Lieutenant. You would not run five yards before I killed you. Like the villagers in Uberlaten I have no love of terror flyers.'

The truck made the turning and built up speed again. On both sides of the road Sean could see a drop of fifteen to twenty feet as it spanned the descending hillside. The road itself, clearly rarely used, was uneven and the truck began rocking and dipping into pot holes. With his bruised ribs protesting,

Sean found himself hoping the military unit was not far away. As one deep pot hole shuddered the truck and brought an involuntary grunt of pain from him, he heard Heinrich's sarcastic laugh. 'What's the matter, Flight Lieutenant? Are our country roads too punishing for you?'

Too busy clinging to his seat to think of a fitting reply, Sean saw the road ahead was swinging into a series of S bends. As the truck approached them the driver, seeing a large pot hole half filled with water almost under his wheels, pulled sharply on his steering wheel to avoid it.

His act was half a second too late. Instead of missing the pot hole his right front wheel caught its edge and dropped into it. With the water contents hiding the true depth of the hole, the wheel thudded down with an impact that tore and burst the tyre. Before anyone in the cab could react, the truck lurched violently to the right and a second later plunged off the road and rolled down the shallow embankment.

Sean remembered little of the fall. Like Heinrich and the driver he was hurled violently about in the cab and it was seconds after the truck lay at the base of the embankment that he realised what had happened.

At first the pain of his ribs occupied all his attention. Then he realised that at some time during the fall he had been pitched out of the truck, which was lying on its side some twenty feet away. Seeing or hearing nothing from it and realising he had received no injuries other than the violence his ribs had suffered, he drew himself toward the truck and peered inside.

One look sufficed to tell him he had nothing more to fear from its occupants. Heinrich, with his head twisted grotesquely towards his shoulders, was clearly dead from a broken neck. The unconscious sergeant was lying on top of him with a head wound that was soaking his hair with blood. Hearing hissing from the engine Sean reached in and cut the ignition. Then, fearing fire, he tried to drag both men away from the vehicle.

With the effort torturing his ribs he managed to pull the unconscious sergeant away although the effort nearly exhausted him. With the truck no longer a fire risk he was tempted to leave the dead Heinrich where he was but then changed his mind and laid him beside the driver. His last tasks were to retrieve his case, which had survived the accident, and to lay a folded tunic from Heinrich under the driver's head.

Aware this was his chance to escape he knew every moment counted but both his mind and body needed rest. To his relief he found cigarettes in Heinrich's tunic pocket and lit one while he sat on a clump of turf and tried to put his thoughts together.

He could make no sense of what had happened. That would have to wait for another time. All he could do at the moment was assess his situation. With the news of his escape now broadcast and perhaps the details of his clothes given too, dare he continue in his present role? Beside him there were two uniforms that would probably fit him. The thought was tempting but he was only too aware that in Hitler's brutal regime it would provide the excuse to have him shot as a spy.

Yet wasn't it a risk worth taking? In all likelihood it would make things easier for him, particularly if he used Heinrich's officer's credentials. For a man who valued his life as little as Sean Hammond, he was puzzled how quickly he rejected the temptation. No, he had been given a role. It had served him well so far. It would be wiser to see it through to the end.

With his decision made he realised how lucky he had been that no traffic had passed on the road above to complicate his situation, although it was luck that could not last forever. Wincing at the pain in his ribs he rose to his feet and took all the money he could find in the pockets of the two Germans. Then, picking up his suitcase, he began limping back to the Weinfeld road.

EIGHTEEN

The old man alongside Sean shifted and muttered something in German. Sean stared at him, then guessed his request. Picking up the case at his feet, he rose and allowed the man to push past him. Sitting back he watched the man make his unsteady way down the aisle to the toilet. As the train ran over a set of points and swayed, the man lurched against a uniformed woman sitting next to the carriage door. Although she betrayed momentary irritation at the incident she nevertheless caught hold of the old man's arm to steady him. Thanking her he disappeared behind the adjoining door.

The train had been crowded when Sean had boarded it and he had been lucky to find the spare seat beside the old man. At the same time he had taken note of the rest of the passengers. Although most of them were elderly civilians, among them was a German officer of a unit he did not recognise and sitting alongside him a civilian in his middle thirties. Whether they had entered the carriage together or met by chance he did not know but he had noticed both men's eyes turn on him as he moved down the aisle to take his seat. The rest of the passengers were young soldiers, men whose appearance suggested they were returning to their units after a few days leave. Although one or two of them had shown mild curiosity at seeing a man little older than themselves in civilian clothes, their expressions suggested they were more occupied with what awaited them on their return than with a civilian with a small suitcase.

It was the officer seated on the opposite side of the aisle and in direct view of Sean that held his attention. Middle-aged, of average build, he had the features and bearing of an academic rather than an officer of the Third Reich. Nevertheless Sean was only too aware he represented as big a threat to his liberty as the late Heinrich and although he was chatting amicably to the civilian alongside him, the occasional glances he gave Sean had made him wonder if it might be wise to leave the train at some convenient station in the hope the officer might decide he was only a civilian making a routine journey. But as the minutes slipped past and the officer made no move, Sean began wondering if getting off the train might seem more suspicious than remaining on it. After all there was always the possibility that the officer's curiosity might simply be that of the young soldiers. Moreover, although his facial scratches were beginning to heal and Liber-

mann had treated them with a masking oint-
ment, they were still visible enough to
engender some curiosity. In his insecure
position, Sean reminded himself, it was too
easy to see danger everywhere.

After all, he thought, he had been lucky so
far. After his escape from Heinrich he had
been picked up by a farmer who had
accepted his letter without suspicion and
cheerfully offered him a lift into Weinfeld.
Inevitably, with the news of his escape now
broadcast, there had been a checkpoint
along the road and when the farmer's truck
was halted Sean had believed his recent
escape had been only a reprieve. Instead, to
his surprise, his letter had been accepted at
face value and the farmer had been allowed
to continue. It could mean only one thing,
Sean realised. Whatever had happened to
Libermann, no mention of the help he had
given or of the letter he had written can
have passed his lips.

Until this reprieve Sean had been undecided on his next move. If checkpoints were
already set up, obvious escape routes like
railway stations would be certain to have
their quota of police and military units. At
the same time checkpoints would also exist
on all roads radiating west from Weinfeld, so
would their usage be any less dangerous? It
was unlikely that every checkpoint would be
as accommodating as the one he had just

passed and with many miles to travel the risks could only grow in number.

It was reasoning that led to only one conclusion. Risk the railways. If his letter was accepted, in a few hours he could be a hundred miles or more away from his point of escape. If his letter failed it would almost certainly have failed sooner or later and he would be no worse off.

To his surprise it did not fail. Although it was scrutinised at the station gates by a sergeant and a second soldier who was called in to answer Sean's French, the second soldier's interpretation of the language was so atrocious that the sergeant grew impatient at the muddled conversation and eventually waved Sean through.

A similar farce had occurred at the ticket office. With no colleague who could speak French to assist her, the middle-aged woman who took Sean's letter kept questioning him in German to which he could only repeat Stuttgart and put money on her desk. Finally, no doubt influenced by his mimicked Gallic gestures, she handed him a ticket, his change, and threw in a girlish smile for good measure.

Sean's luck had continued to hold when, on boarding the busy Stuttgart train, he had found the empty seat beside a man too old and tired to engage in any embarrassing conversation. Lowering his small suitcase to the floor, he had hoped the train would soon pull away. When it did ten minutes later he shared a sense of triumph and the whimsical thought that perhaps the popular belief in German efficiency was just another of those national myths.

The sight of the old man returning from the toilet broke into his thoughts. As he rose to give the man access to his seat he saw the officer down the aisle gaze at him again. Avoiding a clash of eyes that he felt might encourage suspicion, Sean re-seated himself and reviewed his limited options. On boarding the train he had congratulated himself on his good fortune. Now he was realising how the train limited one's possibilities of escape.

Trying to look as casual as possible he drew his folded map from his inner pocket and tried to estimate the train's progress. As they had drawn out of a station only a couple of minutes ago he estimated the next one was approximately forty kilometres away At the speed they were travelling he had a good fifteen or more minutes to make up his mind.

He returned the map to his pocket. As he lifted his head a railway inspector with a limp entered the carriage. Instead of asking to see tickets, the man went to the German officer and whispered something to him. The officer glanced at Sean, then sat listening to the railwayman who seemed to be passing on some urgent message. Beside him the civilian was also listening. With all three men occasionally glancing at him, Sean became certain he was the object of their attention.

Needing time to think, he rose and put his suitcase on his seat to indicate an intention of returning. Then he turned and began walking down the aisle away from the three men. Although he made himself walk in a leisurely fashion he could feel goose pimples on his neck as he imagined the men staring after him.

He reached a toilet, entered it, and bolted the door after him. If he were right he had only a few seconds of freedom left before his recapture. Standing there he could feel the carriage wheels clattering on the steel rails below. As the carriage rocked, forcing him to grab the door handle for support, his quirkish sense of humour came to his aid. If he were going to be re-captured what the hell was he doing in a train toilet? Couldn't he have found a place more dignified? The thought had no sooner been and gone when he heard footsteps outside the door and saw the door handle turn. Bracing himself he waited for an order to open the door but instead he could hear nothing but the clattering of the wheels. Could he be wrong about the three men, he wondered. Was his imagination seeing danger where none existed and had the door been tried only by another passenger who had now gone off to find another toilet?

He decided to wait five minutes before returning to his seat. Remembering the cigarettes he had obtained from Heinrich, he lit one and drew in smoke. He wondered what the time was. From the light coming through the frosted window there were still a few hours of daylight left. Which meant, if he were fortunate enough to reach Stuttgart a free man, there should be time to find some kind of accommodation. He would need sleep because with the priest and himself making escape preparations, no rest had been possible the previous night.

A sudden deceleration of the train threw him off balance. At first he wondered if they were approaching a station. But as the carriage swayed and then picked up speed again he knew it had only been crossing a series of points. As he reached the end of his cigarette and tossed the stub into the toilet, he decided to return to his seat. Better to find out his fate one way or the other than fool around like this. As he reached for the door knob he heard footsteps approaching. They paused outside and the door knob turned again. Knowing it might be the impatient passenger again Sean was about to slide back the bolt when an authoritative voice sounded: 'Öffnen Sie die Tuer sofort!'

Unsure of its origin or its meaning Sean paused for a moment. Then, knowing it made no difference either way, he drew back the lock and pulled the door open.

It was not a fellow passenger standing there but the German officer with the railway inspector and four young soldiers standing alongside him. Playing his role to the last Sean asked his question aggressively, 'Qu'est ce que votre dépêche?'

The officer's reply was in impeccable English. 'Good afternoon, Flight Lieutenant. I am Colonel Bauer. Please be so kind as to come with us quietly.'

Sean decided it was worth one last try. 'Je ne parle pas Anglais. Je suis Suisse.'

'It's no use, Flight Lieutenant. News of you has come through the railway radio network. It has given us all details of your escape since you left Uberlaten. So, as you English say, the game is up.'

With the young soldiers staring at him aggressively Sean knew it was true. At the same time he found amusement in his thought that at least Bauer wasn't an arrogant bastard like Heinrich. He replied in English. 'I hope they don't still believe the priest was guilty. All he did was attend to my injuries. He had every intention of surrendering me to you people as soon as I was fit to walk again.'

Bauer gave a shrug of regret. 'I know nothing about that, Flight Lieutenant, but I am sure our people will give it their full attention. Now let us go back to your seat where you have left your suitcase.'

Before Sean could say more the officer nodded to the young soldiers who caught hold of Sean and roughly bundled him back to his seat where the adjacent seats had all been cleared of passengers. Almost subconsciously Sean noticed that the civilian who had been talking earlier to Bauer had now moved to a seat at the opposite side of the aisle where he could hear the conversation between Bauer and his captive.

Pushed into his earlier seat Sean found himself sitting between two of the young soldiers with Bauer and the other two soldiers facing him. It was the officer who broke the silence. 'Don't be disconsolate, Flight Lieutenant. You have done very well so far. But tell me. How did you get those facial scratches?' When Sean told him, Bauer made a face. 'Our interrogators can't be as efficient as we are told. There was no mention of scratches in the report we received.'

Sean realised it explained one mystery: why he had not been recognised at the road block or at the station. 'Perhaps the woman who attacked me didn't like making the admission.'

Bauer nodded. 'It's possible although with

terror flyers so unpopular no one would have blamed her. But tell me what happened to the officer and the Army truck that gave you a lift? How did you arrange that accident?'

Sean stared at him. 'Arrange it? The driver struck a pot hole and we turned over.'

The officer's intelligent eyes were studying him. 'Are you saying you were not responsible for what happened?'

'Of course I'm not. How could I turn a truck over?' Then Sean gave a start. 'They're not saying I killed that officer, are they?'

Bauer nodded. 'That is what they said over the radio. As I have just said, terror flyers are not popular in Germany.'

Through the train window houses were appearing. As the train began slowing down Sean indicated the houses. 'Do you take me off here?'

'No. We're taking you to Stuttgart. We've arranged for your escort to be waiting there.'

'Who will it be?' Sean asked. 'The Luftwaffe?'

Bauer shook his head and Sean believed he saw sympathy in his eyes. 'I'm afraid not, Flight Lieutenant. I did my best but people of higher rank than I have decided otherwise. One way and another they seem to have their knives in you. I truly am sorry but it seems our Gestapo have been ordered to interrogate you.'

Sean felt his spine cringe. 'The Gestapo? Why?'

Bauer lifted his shoulders. 'They believe you somehow persuaded a German priest to release you and aid your escape. They also believe you killed a German officer. More than enough to interest our Gestapo colleagues, don't you think?'

At that moment the train jerked to a halt. The civilian across the aisle picked up his suitcase and made for the exit. Too occupied to notice him, Sean gazed at Bauer. 'They're setting me up, aren't they? Why? Is it because of Libermann?'

NINETEEN

The following day Charles took a turn for the worse. He had complained of not feeling well the previous evening and when he showed no improvement after a night's sleep Linda took no chances and called for medical advice. After an examination Dr Rudston called Linda aside. Elderly and reliable he had served the family for many years and knew most of their secrets. 'I'm not too happy with his condition, Linda. It might just be a minor setback but I'm going to play safe and keep him in bed for a few days. How are things with you? Didn't you say you were due back at the Ration Office next week?'

'I was, yes, but I've got permission to stay with him until he's fully recovered. If you verify he's had a setback I'm sure there'll be no problem. But I'll check with them right away.'

Rudston nodded. 'Let me know as soon as you can. If you can't manage it we'll have to bring in a nurse.'

'I will,' she promised. 'I'll phone them this morning.'

She did and to her relief was told she could stay until her doctor gave her clearance. There were benefits being the daughter of an ex-member of the General Staff she thought as she replaced the receiver. She was just leaving the hall when the phone rang and drew her back. 'Hello. Linda Martin here.'

'Hello, Mrs Martin. This is Peter Phillips. I wonder if I could see you for a few minutes?'

The implications of his call set her heart hammering. 'See me? Do you mean come to Lemington?'

'No. I'm in Longbridge today. I can't get away for long but if you could drive out here I could see you in the local pub. It's called the White Hart.'

Her question could wait no longer. 'Has it

anything to do with Sean?'

'Yes, it has. That's why I'd like to see you.'

It took all of her courage to ask the question. 'Is it bad news?'

Phillips' hesitation was slow torture. 'No. Not really. He survived the crash and is still alive.'

Still alive! The two words were the only ones she heard at that moment. 'Is he injured?'

'No, I don't think so.'

'Then what else have you to tell me? This is wonderful news, isn't it?'

'I'd still like to see you, Linda. It is important.'

'But something you can't tell me over the phone?'

Again that hesitation. 'I'd rather see you in person. Couldn't you manage just a few minutes?'

'I'll have to see our helper, Mrs Griffiths. My father isn't well this morning. If she can stay I'll come right away. Is that OK?'

'Yes. Do try to come. I can be in the pub in half an hour.'

Slamming down the receiver she ran into the kitchen where Mrs Griffiths was preparing lunch. Receiving her assurance she would remain in Smalloaks until her return, Linda then ran back into Charles's bedroom. 'Will you be all right for an hour or two, Dad? I have to go into Longbridge.'

Charles, looking pale but curious, raised his head from his pillow. 'Why? What's happened?'

'I'll explain when I get back. I can use the car, can't I?'

'Yes but watch the petrol. It must be getting low.'

'Never mind. I'll have to risk it. If you want anything, call Mrs Griffiths. She's staying until I get back.' With that she ran out to the Bentley.

To Linda's relief she found only civilians in the White Hart's lounge. She had been afraid her young pilot admirer, Jack Etherington, might be there and cause her embarrassment. Instead there were only three middle-aged couples seated at the tables and none paid her any attention when she ordered a glass of wine and then took a seat by the window. Phillips' absence did not surprise her. Only twenty minutes had passed since she had run out to the car and accelerated down the road to Longbridge.

At the same time her urgency to hear his news was stretching her imagination to the limit. If Sean were still alive, what could have happened that Phillips did not want to tell her over the telephone? She tried to calm herself by lighting a cigarette but found her eyes straying every few seconds to the road that led from the airfield.

Her nerves were tightly strung when a staff car drove down the road and entered the car park. A few seconds later Phillips appeared in the doorway. Coming out of bright sunlight and with his eyesight suspect, he did not see her immediately. About to rise and give him a wave she saw his face lighten and a moment later he was hurrying towards her. She tried to read his expression but it only betrayed the admiration he had showed for her at Lemington, which at that moment irritated her. He was breathing hard when he reached her table. 'Hello, Linda. I'm sorry I'm a few minutes late but I was held up at the last moment.'

She motioned him to sit down. 'Don't worry about it. I've only been here a few minutes myself.' Before she could ask the question that was burning her mind he motioned at the bar. 'Let me get you a drink.'

She tried to stop him. 'No, I have one here.'

He waved aside her protest and a couple of minutes later brought her back another glass of wine. Her impatience grew as he drew out his pipe and pouch. 'Do you mind if I smoke? They allow pipes in here.'

Feeling she had to play up to him she shook her head. 'No, I don't mind. As I told you my father smokes a pipe all the time.'

He began pressing tobacco into the pipe bowl. 'I'm sorry to hear he isn't well. Nothing serious, I hope.'

Why was he stalling like this, she wondered. 'Dad's not a young man so I'm hoping it's just old age. The doctor thinks he'll be able to make a better judgement in a day or two. But why are you here today? You're not moving to Donnington, are you?'

'No. It's because Donnington was Sean's old squadron and so news about him is sent here. I know the officer who handles that side of things and asked him to let me know if anything came through about Sean. As it's hush hush information he couldn't risk giving it to me over the phone. So I drove over to see him.'

He was coming to it at last, she thought. 'And that's why you wanted to see me in person?'

His eyes fell down to his pipe where his fingers were packing down the tobacco. Then they rose to hers. 'That was one reason?'

'What was the other?'

He hesitated again. 'Telephones are such impersonal things, aren't they? One can't express one's feelings over them. At least I never can.'

His ambiguity brought back her apprehension. 'Feelings? I don't understand. You said Sean was alive and not badly hurt. Doesn't that mean he is a prisoner-of-war and relatively safe?'

'Yes, he was a prisoner. Although he was

fortunate because it seems a local priest had to save him from some local villagers.'

Her eyes widened. 'Save him? What does that mean?'

'I'm not sure of the details but aircrews can be in danger these days if they fall into the hands of civilians. Particularly in rural areas. They see our crews as killers of women and children.'

A shiver ran through her. 'But you say a priest saved him?'

'So we are told. But the incredible thing is this priest allowed him to escape.'

She stared at him, unable to believe what she was hearing. 'A German priest let Sean escape? Sean, who dislikes religion. In heaven's name why?'

Phillips shook his head. 'I can't possibly imagine. But it happened.'

'How do you know all this?'

'By luck. It seems a Swiss Red Cross representative heard the entire story on a train before and after Sean was recaptured. He radioed Sean's name back to his headquarters and they let us know right away. I've never known this happen before so in one sense we're very lucky.'

She did not know whether to feel relief or disappointment. 'So he is a prisoner again? Is that the news you had for me?'

When he did not answer she thought at first he was preparing to light his pipe. Instead she caught his expression. 'There's something else, isn't there?'

He sighed. 'I'm afraid so. That's one reason I felt it better to see you than talk on the phone.'

Something about his eyes, his tone, his expression, and something she could not define told her as clearly as words that this middle-aged anonymous squadron leader had seen through her earlier deception. Uncertain whether to bluff it out or continue the lie, she gave herself time by taking out a cigarette. As Phillips reached for a match, she made her decision. 'You know that story about my sister wasn't true, don't you?'

If anything he looked more embarrassed than she. 'Yes. I guessed from your interest that it was personal. But no one else will know. You need have no fears of that.'

She accepted the light he gave her and drew in smoke. 'Thank you. But tell me the rest of it. What couldn't you tell me over the phone?'

She could not analyse the look he was giving her. It was a mixture of disbelief, hope, scepticism, embarrassment – a host of conflicting emotions that made no sense to her and yet warned her to brace herself for a shock. Her mouth felt bone dry as she asked the question again. 'What else haven't you told me, Peter?'

He took a deep breath as if he were

216

bracing himself too. 'I never told you what happened to Sean in France before the war, did I?'

'I knew he'd been over there,' she told him. 'Jacqueline's friend told me. But what has that to do with his escape and recapture?'

He glanced away as if seeking help. 'Perhaps nothing. And yet it could explain why the priest let him go.'

Her temper broke at his behaviour. 'For God's sake come out with it, Peter. What happened to him when he was in France? I know he had an accident but what's so peculiar about that?'

Her anger seemed to help him. 'It wasn't that simple, Linda. He didn't just have an accident. For a brief time he was clinically dead.'

The lounge suddenly went deathly quiet. Her huge eyes gazing at him as if he had lost his mind. 'Dead? What in God's name are you talking about?'

His gesture was both apologetic and vulnerable. 'I know how it sounds. But it's true. His head struck a pavement and when an ambulance reached him his heart had stopped. It was over five minutes before it responded to resuscitation. The French doctors were amazed at his recovery. Although it seems it has happened before, it's extremely rare and few people have recovered so quickly.'

Her astonished voice seemed to be coming from far away. 'But who told you this?'

'Sean himself. I'm the only person that knows. If the Services had found out he'd never have been accepted as a pilot. So he's kept it a secret ever since.'

With her head swimming she hardly knew what questions to ask. 'You think this is why the priest released him? Because he believed Sean is special in some way?'

'It's only a guess because I wouldn't have expected Sean to tell him. But it's the only reason I can offer.'

Questions, some logical, some irrational, were now flooding into her mind. 'You don't think these extreme ideas of his are related in some way to this accident, do you? That his mind was affected and the other things that happened to him since, like his sister and Len Preston, have compounded the trauma?'

Phillips shook his head. 'If I'm certain of one thing it's that his brain wasn't damaged. I've never met a man with a clearer and more logical mind.'

'And yet his views are extreme. You've said that yourself.'

'I've never found his views illogical. And I don't think you have either.'

She knew he was right. Before she could ask another question his next words checked her. 'I'm afraid that isn't all, Linda.'

Her short laugh seemed to come from a stranger. 'There's more?'

'I'm afraid so. Although the Swiss representative left the train before Sean was taken off, it seems he had heard all the details of Sean's adventures and what the Germans intended to do with him. Their plans must have startled him. No doubt that's why he sent in his report so quickly.'

Her mouth had gone dry again. 'What sort of plans?'

'It seems the Germans are blaming Sean for the death of an officer who was killed after giving Sean a lift in his transport. As this death wasn't caused in combat and because Hitler has recently given orders that prisoners who cause trouble can be shot, the Swiss representative says that Sean will be handed over to the Gestapo instead of the more responsible Luftwaffe.'

The peace and quiet of the lounge suddenly seemed unreal. 'Gestapo! Are you saying he will be murdered?'

Phillips's expression betrayed his distress at being the bearer of the news. 'They may not go that far. But as things have turned out it might have been far better if he had not been released by the priest.'

'But can't anything be done? Can't our people protest and offer an exchange or something?'

Even as she spoke she knew the absurd

impracticality of the suggestion. Phillips' reply confirmed it. 'If he were a high ranking officer I suppose such a thing might just be possible. But with the Nazis the brutes they are, it wouldn't have a chance.' Then he hesitated and met her eyes again. 'Unless our Staff people could work through the Red Cross and let the enemy know we are on to them.'

A name flashed into her mind. Douglas. For a split second it brought a ray of hope. 'Could it work?'

'I don't know. I've not heard of it tried before. But if they thought it could affect how their own captured airmen are treated, it might have a chance. But it would need Swiss help to put such a deal across.'

It was very clear to her now why Phillips had wanted to talk to her in person. Yet with the complexity of her relationship with Sean known to him, was he really hoping she took the problem to Douglas? 'Couldn't you or your Donnington contact bring it up to the General Staff? After all, Sean has an excellent combat record.'

Phillips grimaced. 'I'm only a squadron leader, Linda. As things stand I'm lucky to have a contact who gives me such classified news. But neither of us has the clout to move mountains and that's what it would need in this case.'

She took a deep breath to brace herself.

'Would my husband have that clout?'

The sudden glimmer in his eyes told her he had hoped for the question. It also reminded her she was not the only one suffering from the latest news. 'Not in himself, I wouldn't think. But he mixes with the people who might have.' Phillips lowered his eyes to his pipe before continuing. 'Why? Are you thinking of asking him?'

Knowing he was aware of her deception about her sister, she was conscious of his dilemma. As if guessing her thoughts he spoke again without looking up. 'I do understand how difficult it might be for you as things stand. But he will never hear the details. You need have no fears of that.'

She wished herself in a dimension where time never moved and decisions were never required. She accepted the light he gave her and drew in smoke before answering him. 'I suppose I ought to ask him if it will help Sean. But will it? It all sounds so unlikely.'

'I can't say, Linda. But it seems the only chance we have.'

'How long have we got?'

'Not long. He might already be in their hands.'

She swallowed. 'I'll have to think about it. In the meantime will you keep me posted if you hear anything more?'

'Of course. I'll keep in touch with my contact here and ask him to find out all he can, although I should point out that the Swiss representative got his news in an unusual way and we're not likely to be so lucky again.'

She nodded dully. 'Never mind. Tell me whatever you can.'

As they both rose, Phillips betrayed his true distress for the first time. 'I am sorry, Linda. Sean was a good friend of mine so I know how you feel. But try not to worry too much. The worst might not happen.'

Questions poured into her mind as she drove back to Smalloaks. Why had the German priest allowed Sean to escape? Could it really be because of his bizarre experience in France? If so, what did the priest believe had happened in those few minutes of death? Did he believe Sean carried some message that must not be lost to the world? Could this explain why she herself had often felt Sean's beliefs had a validity in spite of their conflict with her own?

The thought turned her mind into a battleground. One half of her scoffed at the superstitious idea that a few minutes of heart arrest could imbue a man with such extreme ideas. The other half, her religious self, asked questions that staggered her with their implications.

It took the memory of Sean's danger to bring her mind back to the war and its brutality. If Sean had killed a German officer what would happen to him when he was passed over to the Gestapo? Could he possibly be saved if she spoke to Douglas about his case or would it only stir up a hornet's nest of recriminations without sense or purpose? On her arrival home, when she climbed the stairs to check on her father, she was no nearer making a decision than she had been in Longbridge with Phillips.

TWENTY

The train jerked to a halt. At the end of the aisle the civilian who had been chatting to Bauer disappeared and a moment later was seen walking away down the platform. As other passengers disembarked from the train, Bauer left his seat and, leaving Sean guarded by the four soldiers, followed them outside. By the time he returned to his seat the train was on the move again. He offered Sean a cigarette before asking his question. 'I'm still intrigued, Flight Lieutenant. How did you kill that Army officer of ours?'

'I didn't,' Sean said tersely. 'How could I when both he and his driver were armed?'

Bauer nodded. 'That's what makes me believe you. But your problem will be to convince the Gestapo.'

With no means of escape left, Sean felt he had nothing to lose. 'Your country puzzles me. It was once civilised. So how do you justify scum like the Gestapo.'

Instead of the anger he expected he received a patient smile. 'Perhaps you should ask that question of the Treaty of Versailles. If a country is left without means of sustenance it follows the first Pied Piper that offers it aid.'

'Is that what you call Hitler? A Pied Piper?'

Bauer smiled again. 'It is as good a name as any.'

'It's true in one sense. He's leading you right over the cliff edge.'

To his surprise Bauer nodded. 'Without any doubt. That has been obvious for many months.'

Sean motioned at the expressionless soldiers seated around them. 'Aren't you afraid of saying that? Isn't it treason?'

Bauer shrugged. 'They can't speak any English. But yes, of course it is treason. Almost any truth is treason in Germany these days.'

Puzzled, Sean studied his unit and rank badges. 'I know you're a colonel. But what unit do you belong to?'

'I'm in the Abwahr, Flight Lieutenant. What you would call the Army Intelligence service. Drafted into it from happier days when I taught philosophy at Heidelberg.'

Sean nodded. 'I thought you were a different breed from the character who picked me up in the truck. So you're saying it was Versailles that bred Hitler?'

'Yes.'

'Yet there had been a war with Germany long before Hitler came into power.'

'Yes, but that had been like many wars. Over domination and power. This one is over ideology. A very different thing and in many ways a more dangerous one.'

'Aren't all wars dangerous?'

'Of course. Wars are symptoms of man's wretched and painful evolution. Until one nation conquers all the others they will continue.'

'Unless we devolve a world government instead.'

Bauer studied Sean's scratched face with amusement. 'Is that why Father Libermann released you, Flight Lieutenant? Because he saw in you an idealist?'

Realising with some guilt he had been enjoying his discussion with the German, Sean remembered his duty to the priest. 'He didn't release me, Colonel. You must impress that on your people. I just took advantage of his kindness. You must make them believe that.'

'I can tell them until the cows come home, as you English say, but it will do no good. Do you know what he told our interrogators?'

Fearing the worse Sean shook his head as Bauer continued. 'He said he had found a man whom God needed for this misguided world. Do you think anyone who knows Father Libermann is going to believe he did not release you after such a remark? It is an admission in itself.'

Sean was feeling chilled. 'How do you know this?'

'I was given more news of you and Libermann by the signalman at the last station. Father Libermann released you, Flight Lieutenant, for some reason known only to himself. For my personal interest I would like to know that reason. You see, Father Libermann is not just any old Catholic priest. He was once known nationally, and certainly by my university, for his many disparate and unorthodox opinions. That was why his Church moved him to a distant, rural parish.'

Puzzled, Sean stared at Bauer's sensitive, intelligent face. 'What sort of opinions?'

'Highly non Catholic ones, Flight Lieutenant. Father Libermann does not see God as a lovable old man with white hair and beard. To him that is the only image our immature minds can visualise, although it is true that some religions do not postulate a god. Libermann believes God is a positive power that embraces the entire universe and is enriched or impoverished by every thought or deed within it.'

Sean frowned. 'A positive power? Is that supposed to mean a power that can influence or affect living events?'

Bauer nodded. 'Very much so. Just as evil can create the reverse effects.'

'As Hitler is proving,' Sean added.

Bauer's sensitive mouth twitched humorously. 'Yes. As you point out, in Father Libermann's eyes Hitler and his cronies are not doing our universe a great service.'

Although Sean was only too conscious Bauer might be setting a clever trap, at the same time the German's words were making sense of Libermann's behaviour. He cleared his throat. 'I'm not surprised he has such ideas. Even an atheist like myself could see he is no ordinary priest.'

At that Bauer showed surprise. 'You are an atheist, Flight Lieutenant? Did you confess this to the good Father?'

Sean did not miss his opportunity. 'Yes. It came out when we talked. So you see he had every reason to keep me a prisoner.'

Bauer's reaction both surprised and disappointed him. 'This is fascinating, Flight Lieutenant. As you say, why would a man like Libermann release a non believer.'

At that Sean lost his temper. 'He didn't release me. How many times have I have to tell you that?'

As one of the soldiers grabbed his arm

threateningly, Bauer waved the man back. 'Nein. Handeln ihm nicht.' His eyes returned to Sean. 'Forgive me, Flight Lieutenant. You have given Libermann your word and so cannot break it. I accept that. My problem is that I am fascinated by the man and believe he would make no such move without a very powerful reason.'

Although placated by Bauer's words, Sean chose his lie with care. 'Father Libermann did nothing but save me from having my eyes clawed out. You should be proud of Germans like him.'

Bauer shrugged. 'I couldn't agree with you more. Like some of my colleagues I find him a remarkable man.'

Sean snatched at the chance to change the conversation. 'If you respect him, how can a man like you stay involved with sadists like the Nazis?'

Bauer's expression changed. 'Are you married, Flight Lieutenant?'

'No, thank God.'

'You are right to be grateful. You have no hostages to fate. I have three, a young wife and two beautiful children. They are the answer to your question. In Father Libermann's terms and beliefs, Hitler uses the power of evil against us. And how successful it is.'

A sudden deceleration of the train made all of them turn to the window. Seeing nothing of note, one of the soldiers addressed Bauer. The officer nodded, then turned to Sean. 'It's probably an air raid. Possibly aimed at the rail junction ahead.'

'So what happens? Do we stop?'

Bauer shrugged. 'We'll soon find out.'

The train continued to run forward but slower as if the driver was unsure of his next move. Nodding at Sean and giving the soldiers instructions Bauer rose and vanished down the carriage aisle. Gazing through the side window Sean saw buildings were appearing among the fields as if the train were approaching another town. As he listened he heard a dull thud followed immediately by a second that seemed to shudder the lines beneath the carriage. Glancing at one another the young soldiers grabbed their rifles and the one alongside Sean tightened his grip on his arm.

The thuds grew louder and the train halted as if an order had been received. As Sean strained to see out of the window a sudden shadow swept over the field outside. A moment later he heard the familiar chatter of machine gun fire and the scream of bullets ricocheting from metal. It was followed by shouts from the startled soldiers and passengers as the train started forward again and then halted as if the driver were again undecided about the right move.

Although realising the train had come

under attack Sean had no time to speculate further before a huge explosion rocked the carriage on its rails. It was followed half a second later by an explosion on the opposite side that shattered the windows and showered glass over the frightened passengers. Beside Sean the soldiers seem to have forgotten his existence in the shock of the attack, giving him brief thoughts of escape until he realised the chances were still non-existent.

But then it happened. Firstly a massive roar of engines travelling the length of the train that had everyone crouching in their seats with hands protecting their heads. A few seconds of silence and then an explosion like the gates of hell blowing open. Time bomb was Sean's spontaneous thought, followed instantly by a sense of weightlessness, a blow of immense power and a black wall that swept over and buried him.

Sean recovered to a scene of total panic. Around him men and women were shouting and screaming and alongside him, with one side blown away, was his shattered carriage. Lifting his head he could see none of the German soldiers and guessed they were either casualties or too shocked for the moment to care about a prisoner of war. As an injured man staggered past him, Sean tried to assess his own injuries.

To his relief his hips and legs, while badly bruised, seemed intact and his ribs little worse than before. But when he tried to push himself up from the railway sleeper across which he was lying, his left shoulder gave a spasm of pain and gave his arm no support. Broken or dislocated he could not decide but it compelled him to roll over and use his right arm to push himself up. He sat on his knees for a moment and then managed to climb to his feet.

He knew he had no time to waste. Among the screams around him he could hear shouts and whistles and knew the train crew and its assortment of soldiers were struggling to bring order back from chaos. Moreover the attack on the train seemed to have ceased although heavy thuds in the distance suggested the rail junction was still under attack. Although every aching muscle in his body protested, Sean knew he had been given a reprieve and must take it. An instinct of survival made him glance around for an item of assistance. Seeing an empty overcoat lying on the track he reached for it with his good arm and hung it round his throbbing shoulder. Then he stumbled away.

He remembered little of his flight from the train. The pain in his shoulder was intense and his mind fuddled from the explosion. It was only when his breath and his legs could take him no further and he collapsed into a ditch that total clarity began to return. As the fire left his exhausted lungs and his eyes cleared he could see the stationary smoking train was a good mile away and he was among fields and not the buildings he had seen earlier. In his escape from the train, instinct had guided him in the safest direction. By this time the attack on the tail junction appeared to be over although flames and smoke were still rising from its buildings,

As his mind cleared further he wondered which unit had carried out the operation and whether Donnington had been involved. The thought alerted him to his situation. By this time patrols might be out searching for him although he could see none in the fields back as far as the damaged train. Was it possible that only Bauer, the train inspector, and the soldiers had known of his presence and the bomb had left none of them in a position to talk, he wondered? Or was everyone too injured or shocked to think about him?

Without an answer to either question and with his physical condition poor, Sean knew his options of escape were limited. Should he first try to put more space between himself and the stricken train or should he give himself the rest he clearly needed so he could face later problems with a fitter body and mind? It was not Sean Hammond's way to pamper himself but with his shoulder crying for rest and with the thick warm overcoat lying temptingly beside him, he made the decision that was to have profound effects on his future and the future of others. Drawing the overcoat around him he settled down in the ditch and closed his eyes.

TWENTY-ONE

It was Charles' announcement after lunch that he was feeling better that precipitated Linda's decision. She had wrestled with her problem all night and had found some relief in realising that her father, if no longer in a position to offer practical help, should at least be able to offer advice based on his one-time military eminence. In fact, the more she had thought about it, the more optimistic she had become. Many of her father's contemporaries were still alive. Why, then, had she been so certain he could not help? Old boy networks were influential factors, particularly in Britain, and their lobbying power might be far greater than she had realised.

By allowing her thoughts to progress this way she had become excited by them and, bitterly aware of the urgency of the situation, had decided to talk to him first thing that morning. But on seeing him she had suffered a setback. He had looked particularly pale and wan and when he refused his breakfast and asked to be left alone to sleep she knew she could not confront him with such a request. She knew how concerned he was about her involvement with Sean Hammond and to bring up the latest dramatic turns in the saga without any guarantee of success seemed too dangerous in his state of health. At the same time it threw her back into the state of distress and indecision she had suffered the previous day.

As a consequence her change of mood was dramatic when, after eating a substantial lunch, Charles made the surprise announcement he was tired of lying in bed and wanted to spend the afternoon in his favourite armchair beside the radio. Afraid he was taking a risk, Linda had firstly objected but Charles could be his own man when his mind was made up and by 3.20, with his only concession his dressing gown instead of his smoking jacket, he was back in his armchair twiddling with the dials on the radio.

Although conscious that her judgement was influenced by her wishes, Linda did a volte-farce and decided that after all he was well enough to hear her request. She waited until he had found the radio station he wanted and then, when he settled back his armchair to a Mozart concerto, she took her courage in both hands. 'Dad, there's somehing I have to ask you. It comes from something I was told yesterday.'

Charles turned to her. 'Yesterday? What happened yesterday?'

'I went into Longbridge. You lent me the car.'

Charles toned down the music. 'That's right. I did. But you didn't give me a reason.'

'Someone had phoned and asked to see me.' She braced herself. 'It was about Sean Hammond.'

If Charles felt surprise he did not show it. 'He was shot down, wasn't he?'

'Yes. That was the last I heard. But it seems he survived and became a prisoner of war.'

Charles made a moué of approbation. 'Good. I'm glad to hear he survived.'

'Yes, but there's more to it than that. It seems he was attacked by civilians and a priest rescued him.'

One of Charles's bushy eyebrows lifted. 'A priest?'

'Yes. I don't know the details but the priest must have taken care of him until he recovered from his crash.'

Charles was looking bewildered. 'Who told you all this?'

'I don't think I'm allowed to tell you that, Dad. But I believe it's all true.'

Charles stared at her, then accepted her evasion. 'All right. Go on. A priest took care of him. What happened next?'

'That's the astonishing thing. For some reason we don't know the priest organised Sean's escape.'

This time Charles did start. 'Escape? With the priest's help?'

'Yes. And afterwards while Sean was escaping a German officer was killed. Later Sean managed to board a train but was captured again and this time he is being sent to the Gestapo.'

Charles was all attention now. 'Why?'

'Because they are saying he killed the German officer. Apparently Hitler has made it a capital offence if any escaping prisoner harms a German soldier or civilian.'

Charles switched the radio right off He was showing disbelief as he turned back to Linda. 'I'm sorry, darling, but this sounds like a fairy story to me. Where has it come from?'

She shook her head. 'It's no fairy story, Dad. It came from the Swiss Red Cross. Apparently a representative of theirs saw Sean when he was on the train and in the hands of an officer and a party of soldiers.'

'But who is it over here who's obtained this news from the Swiss?'

'I don't know,' she confessed. 'And it wouldn't be fair to tell you who's passed the news over to me. But I'm sure it's all true and unless something is done quickly Sean is going into the hands of the Gestapo and we all know what sadists they are.'

For a moment Charles looked lost for words. Then he rose from his armchair, sat on the settee beside her, and put an arm round her shoulders. 'I'm sorry, darling. I really am.'

Knowing his disapproval of her friendship with Sean, his sympathy seemed the more moving because of it. As her tears came, she buried her face in his dressing gown. 'It's all so wrong, Dad. He's had nothing but bad luck and yet he's given everything for this country. And now he's going to be tortured and perhaps killed.'

Charles made no reply, only tightening his arm around her. She waited a moment longer, then lifted her head. 'Is there anything that can be done for him, Dad? Can't some kind of protest be made?'

Charles did his best to be gentle. 'I don't see what, darling. Not while we're still at war with Germany?'

'But, Dad, they're breaking the Geneva Convention if they punish him. Can't we threaten them in some way? Or offer the exchange of one of their prisoners?'

'Darling, this isn't a war like the last one. Although I was never involved myself I believe a few exchanges were made but even then it was only for high ranking officers. Junior officers were always expendable. In any case we're talking about Nazis now, a totally different breed of men. From all I gather, they don't give a fig for military traditions, and Geneva Conventions are just a joke to them.'

Although hearing what she had already feared she could not leave it there. 'But couldn't you bring it up yourself? Couldn't you mention it to your old colleagues and get them to approach the War Office?'

Charles did his best not to make her plea seem as absurd as it was. 'Darling, I'm sorry for the lad and it does seem a gross injustice. If I thought it would have the slightest chance I'd be on the phone this minute. But who is going to listen to an old man like me pleading for a mere flight lieutenant when the war is raging and there are probably hundreds of similar cases happening every day?'

Although in her heart she knew he was right, his certainty still shocked her. 'You're saying that a pilot with a DFC can be tortured and killed without anyone over here raising a hand in protest?'

It was her brimming eyes and pale cheeks that made Charles say the thing that both his military knowledge and his fears for his daughter's marriage were to regret a minute later. 'If you feel so badly about this, darling, then you should speak to Douglas. He's in the RAF and although his rank isn't enough to carry any international weight, he might have access to someone that has. It's the only move you can make. He'll be here on Sunday. Talk to him then.'

'But, Dad, he's never liked my association with Sean. He thinks he's some kind of a revolutionary. And you know how jealous he can be.'

Charles sighed. 'I know all that, darling. That's why I didn't want you to go on seeing Sean. But unless you feel it better to leave it all to fate, what other choice do you have?'

She desperately needed reassurance while knowing all the time Charles could give her none. 'Will Douglas be able to help him, Dad? That's what I need to know.'

Charles sighed again. 'Personally I don't think so. But then I could be wrong. I'm sorry, darling, but I've never run into anything like this before.'

She knew she had upset him when he asked to be helped upstairs half an hour later. Split between her concern for him and for Sean she had a sense of fatalism when she made Charles comfortable and retired downstairs. Perhaps our lives are written in the stars, she thought, but hope and human frailty make us try to circumvent them. Now it seemed she had no choice but to follow her star all the way.

TWENTY-TWO

It was the crash of the shot-down aircraft that awakened Sean. He had been sleeping the sleep of the exhausted and even the heavy drone of the second wave of approaching aircraft and the flak that greeted them had not disturbed him. But the crash and subsequent explosion of the stricken bomber, near enough to send a shock wave through the ground, made him open his eyes, and when he saw it came from a second wave of bombers he was wide awake and squinting up into the late afternoon sky to see the nature of the attacking force.

Flying at medium level, he saw it was a second squadron of B17s. The first one had softened up the target, the second was intending to destroy it. For a moment he wondered why the railhead was so important. His curiosity died as the flak bursts around the circling bombers ceased. To Sean it meant one thing. German fighters, no doubt led astray by spoof raids, had now found their main target and were about to attack.

Sean wondered how long he had slept. Not long was his guess. The afternoon light had not perceptibly faded and the interval between bomber strikes of this kind were seldom lengthy. Nor could he see any sign of police or troops searching for him when he peered over the edge of the ditch. Comforting himself that it was unlikely any would be sent out looking for him while the raid was in progress he lay back to watch its outcome.

He could see the B17s more clearly now. As if to ensure better targeting they were now below 15,000 feet and the battle between them and the enemy fighters was in full view. With no escort of Mustangs visible Sean could only conclude some error in timing had been made. As bomb doors opened in preparation of the forthcoming attack, telltail traces from cannon and rockets could be seen lancing towards them. Another B17 on the outside of the group exploded and dropped like a huge flaming torch. Another lurched away with a smoking engine. A few seconds later a dozen .5 Brownings latched on to an Me. 109 which had penetrated into a box of B17s and the fighter literally disintegrated into a dozen fragments.

Sean, who had been involved in a dozen such battles himself, was fascinated by the spectacle. His eyes moved and clung to a B17 that had become detached from its box and was being driven in his direction by two German fighters. As they followed him, their bursts of cannon fire preventing the aircraft from circling back to his comrades before they administered the coup de grace, Sean found himself rising to his feet as if to aid the harried pilot.

Although its gunners were putting up a courageous fight the odds were stacked against the B17. Although tracer from the B17's Brownings made more than one fighter take evasive action, the pursuers were as determined as wild dogs after a crippled wildebeest and, as burst after burst of cannon fire struck the B17, its side and belly guns ceased firing. As Sean gave a groan of disappointment, the massive aircraft began to reel as a fire broke out on its port wing. As an explosion followed and the aircraft over-turned, a single parachute appeared in the smoke-streaked sky. As the parachute drifted down, the stricken B17 plunged past it and struck the ground in an explosion that en-sured a fiery cremation for the rest of its crew.

Above, the two fighters were returning to the main fight above the rail head. When the Germans returned to their base, Sean thought, in the way of fighter pilots every-where, the arguments as to who gained credit for the kill would commence. Sean found he was sweating as he lowered himself into the ditch again. In combat a man's aggressive instincts hid from himself the true nature of his murderous role. From an objective viewpoint its savagery was only too apparent.

Remembering the single survivor of the B17, Sean glanced back at the parachute. At first he had thought it was drifting well away from him but either he had been wrong or the wind at low level was from a different direction because now he saw it was floating towards the field alongside him.

At first he felt alarm. If German observers had witnessed the destruction of the B17 it was certain they would send out troops or police to capture the surviving airman, which made it likely they would find him too. Intent now on the falling parachute he saw it was heading not only towards the adjacent field but perilously close to the ditch itself.

While there was still time he wondered if he ought to move away before the parachutist landed. Yet observers might already have binoculars on the airman and if he, Sean, made himself visible he might bring about his own recapture. Better to wait and play it by ear, he thought, as the swinging figure drew ever closer.

Sean could now see he was a burly man wearing the uniform and equipment of a B17 gunner. He landed no more than forty metres from the ditch, stumbling for a moment as his forward speed threw him off balance, then grabbing the underneath cords of his parachute to begin hauling it in. As a gust of wind inflated the fabric for a moment and the gunner threw himself forward to deflate it, Sean gave a muted shout. 'Drag it over to this ditch. We can hide it here.'

The gunner gave a start and swung round. Knowing he had to risk being seen by others, Sean crawled along the ditch until he was opposite the startled parachutist, then raised his head. 'It's OK. I'm on your side. Get your chute out of sight quickly.'

A helmeted, disbelieving face stared back at him. The startled voice had an American accent. 'Who the hell are you?'

'I'm British. I got shot down like you. Hurry with that parachute.'

The American's face was a study of shock and bewilderment as Sean drew himself from the ditch and crawled towards him. Grabbing a panel of the parachute with his good arm Sean tried to drag it towards the ditch. His cry added urgency to his act. 'They'll pinpoint the bloody thing's position if you don't get your finger out. Get moving, for Christ's sake.'

His words awoke the astonished American who grabbed the remaining silken panels and followed Sean to the ditch. A minute later, with the parachute buried beneath a bush torn from the side of the ditch, the two men had time to gaze at one another. The American, panting from his exertions, spoke first. 'What do you mean, you were shot down! Why the hell are you dressed like that?'

Sean, also breathless, managed only a few words. 'It's OK. I'll explain it all in a minute.'

The nearness of his escape from death, his plunge into the enemy heartland, and now his encounter with a man claiming to be his ally were proving too much for the American's credibility. 'I don't know what your game is, buddy, but this is crazy. Who the hell are you?'

Lifting himself painfully Sean pointed at the distant, still smoking train. 'That's what I escaped from when your first attack came. The guards holding me were either killed or knocked unconscious. I got this far when your second attack came.'

The American's expression was changing. 'You sure speak like a Limey. What outfit were you from?'

'Donnington was my last base.' Sean told him.

The American gave a start. 'Spitfire IVs and then Mustangs? You the guys who ride shotgun for us?'

'That's right. It was during one of those missions I got shot down.'

The burly American took a deep breath, then held out a hand. 'My daddy always said it was a small world. I'm Bill McNeil, waist gunner.'

'Sean Hammond,' Sean told him. 'Ex-Mustang pilot and now a dogsbody with a busted shoulder trying to get back to England.'

'Yeah. I thought you were carrying that left arm. Let me look. I've had a course in first aid.'

Sean allowed the American to examine his shoulder, noticing at the same time the size and strength of the man's arms and hands. 'What do you think? Is it broken?'

McNeil released him. 'It's hard to tell without an X ray. But one thing's for sure. It's not going to be your friend when you're trying to escape.'

Sean eased himself back into his jacket. 'I've had that thought myself.'

The American's big, oil-streaked, good-natured face grinned back at him. 'On the other hand three shoulders are better than one. What do you say? Shall we try it together?'

Sean smiled back. 'I thought you'd never ask. And that overcoat will hide your uniform, at least to laymen. But won't I slow you down?'

McNeil's grin spread. 'If you do I'll leave you to the Heinies. But my guess is you know more about this escape racket than I do. So what's our first move?'

TWENTY-THREE

It took nothing more on Sunday than the sound of a car on the courtyard to start Linda's heart pounding. Having lived her confrontation with Douglas a dozen times since discussing its likelihood with Charles, she had believed the imaginary scenes had exhausted all her fears and forebodings. Now she realised they had only served to sharpen and tighten her nerves as she made her way to the door.

Douglas, running up the steps, caught her and kissed her as she stepped outside. 'Hello, darling. Haven't I done well today?'

She drew back. 'Well?'

'Yes. Getting the day off. I hadn't hoped for it but when I told them your Dad had had a setback they insisted I came. How is he today?'

She prayed his mood would last. 'He's not too bad. He said he might get up later. He enjoys your visits.'

'Good. I'll pop up and see him in a minute.' Then his tone changed. 'Hang on. Is something wrong?'

Her heart missed a beat. 'No. Why?'

He turned her to face him. 'You're looking

247

rather pale and tired. It's nothing to do with your father, is it?'

'No. I've just told you. The doctor's quite pleased with him.'

'Then what is it? Is something else worrying you?'

Ignoring the question she led him into the house. 'You're imagining things. Go up and see father while I make you a cup of tea. I know he's longing for a man to talk to.'

He glanced at her again and then kissed her. 'All right. Give me fifteen minutes and then call me. I like the old man but time with you is precious. Don't forget.'

She helped him off with his raincoat. 'I won't. Off you go.'

Cuffing her cheek he hurried towards the stairs. As he ran up them she heard him whistling. Not daring to think what would happen later that day she made her way into the kitchen.

She took the plunge after lunch. At first she had wondered if she should wait until after he had made love to her when she had given evidence that her feelings for him had not changed but then feared their physical intimacy might weaken her resolve. Better to face it earlier, she thought, when there would still be time left to prove her constancy.

Her father was another factor she had to

consider. Although he still did not look well he informed them both that he did not intend wasting Douglas's visit by spending the day in bed and so would be downstairs soon after lunch. Knowing he might be having second thoughts about his advice to consult Douglas, she decided she must face the issue beforehand in case Charles' presence compounded or complicated it in some way.

She chose the moment when Douglas was sitting in the lounge with the tea tray beside him. The sun, shining through the window opposite, was full on him and she thought how contented and handsome he was looking. The sight did nothing to aid her resolve. She accepted the cigarette he offered her, then took a deep, deep breath. 'Darling, I have something to ask you. Do you remember that pilot we once spoke about? The one I found trespassing on the estate?'

For a second he looked puzzled. Then he gave a start. 'That bolshie fellow? Yes, I do. He hasn't been back, has he?'

'No. He was shot down.'

His expression changed. 'Shot down? How do you know this?'

She swallowed to lubricate her throat. She had always known this was going to be the most difficult part of her confession. 'One of your colleagues told me. An officer who used to know him.'

'What officer?'

'One who used to be at your old station at Lemington.' Worried in case she would be dragging Phillips into some military embarrassment, she was forced into her first lie. 'I'm not sure but I think his name was Latimer.'

'Latimer? I don't remember anyone of that name at Lemington.'

'Perhaps I'm wrong but it doesn't matter. It was he who told me Sean Hammond had been shot down.'

He gave a start. 'Sean Hammond. I remember him. A good pilot but an odd character always at odds with the other men. Was that the bolshie's name?'

'Yes. It was Latimer who gave it to me. He said Hammond was shot down when escorting B17s over Germany.'

For the moment Douglas Martin's face was showing bewilderment. 'How the hell did you meet this chap Latimer? And why did he talk to you about Hammond?'

She had the panic stricken feeling she was sinking deeper and deeper into quicksands. 'Does it matter? I do get invited to parties occasionally when you're away and I met him at one of them. I must have mentioned about the pilot who'd trespassed here and he guessed it was Hammond. That's why he told me he'd been shot down.'

Curiosity was taking the place of bewilderment in Douglas's expression. 'I don't get this. Why would you talk about Hammond? What was he to you?'

The question dismayed her. 'I suppose I remembered him because of his odd views on religion and patriotism. Things like that stick in your mind.'

His voice turned dry. 'They seem to have stuck in yours. I remember at the time I wanted his name and you wouldn't give it to me.'

She was forced into her second lie. 'That's because I didn't know it then. It was only after I mentioned Hammond's odd views to Latimer that we knew it was the same man.'

He was staring at her as if she had suddenly become a stranger. 'Why haven't you told me all this before?'

'Because there was nothing to tell. I can't help meeting people when you're away, darling, but they're not worth talking about when you come home. Time's too precious then.'

She could not tell whether her words had placated him or added to his curiosity. 'But you're telling me now,' he said. 'Why?'

She knew it was her chance before he asked her more about her fictitious friends. At the same time she had to brace herself. 'It's because Latimer phoned me recently to tell the strangest story about Hammond. It seems news had come from the Swiss Red

Cross that he wasn't killed but only captured.' She went on to tell of Sean's escape and re-capture. 'I know it all sounds like fantasy but Latimer swears it is true. So now Hammond is going to the Gestapo unless efforts are made over here to save him.'

His expression had revealed a complex of emotions while she had been speaking. His first words shocked her. 'Do you believe all this bullshit?'

'Of course I do. It came from the Red Cross.'

'It sounds to me it's come from some fifth rate newspaper reporter. To begin with why would a German priest help him to escape? And how could the Red Cross have heard about it? It's all bloody nonsense, Linda.'

Her dismay grew. 'No, it's all true. Hammond is going to die unless an effort is made to save him.'

His sharp mind made an instant deduction. 'You're telling me this in the hope I can do something. Am I right?'

Although his reaction was alarming her, she had no option but to concur. 'Yes. I suppose I am. Can you?'

He ignored her question, instead asking the one she had feared. 'Tell me something. Why are you so interested in this chap Hammond?'

She tried to remember the answer she had rehearsed. 'He's a human being, Douglas, and one of your own kind. A fellow pilot who won the DFC and yet now might be tortured and killed by the Gestapo. Doesn't that make him someone we should all be concerned about?'

His eyes did not leave her face. 'I didn't ask why he should interest the rest of us. I asked why he should interest you. Particularly when you know he's an atheist with no love of his country.'

She knew she had to try to answer his question, perhaps as much for her own sake as for his. At the same time she knew she must not mention Sean's accident in France or her reasons would seem totally bizarre. 'I've asked myself that a dozen times and find I don't know. I found his ideas far fetched and his anti-religious ones shocking and yet some part of me says he is important and must be saved. I know it sounds crazy and it probably is. But I can't help it.' Her tears were close to the surface now. 'Don't blame me for it, darling. It's something I don't understand myself.'

He gazed at her and then his voice took on the tone she had feared. 'Perhaps you're searching too hard for an answer. Perhaps it's a simple one, that you've fallen in love with him. Have you considered that?'

It had happened, she thought. The thing she had dreaded. Somehow she kept her voice steady. 'Yes, I've given it thought.

What woman wouldn't? But my love for you hasn't changed in the slightest. I count the days to your coming home and long to feel your arms around me. So I must believe it is something else. Something I just don't understand.'

She realised as she finished speaking that she had been expressing her own mystification rather than giving him reassurance. Seeing his expression that betrayed the extent of his shock she wanted to run over and throw her arms around him. Instead his military discipline betrayed them both. With some remark she could not catch he stubbed out his cigarette and rose to his feet. 'Fair enough. At least you've been honest with me. So you want me to do what I can for this man? That's right, isn't it?'

Her eyes were wet with tears now. 'Yes. But at the same time you must believe I still love you. You mustn't think anything else. Do you hear me?'

He ignored her last words. 'To be honest I doubt if anything can be done but I'll have a word with old Ashcroft. He'll know the score better than anyone and he's in the top league. But he'll want to know all the details, like the real name of this chap Latimer and the contact who gives him this information. Can you get those for me?'

Realising he had seen through her lies, she nodded dully. 'I'll do my best. I'll try to

254

phone them today.' Her voice rose as he made for the door. 'Where are you going?'

He glanced back. 'If Hammond's in the hands of the Gestapo there's no time to waste, is there?'

She ran after him into the hall where he was already picking up his coat. 'Can't you wait just an hour or two? It'll give me time to get those details you need.'

He reached for his cap and then turned to her. His face was expressionless as he spoke. 'Ring them through to me when you have them. And say goodbye to your father for me.'

She caught his arm as he opened the front door. He did not pull away but the hand that removed her own relayed its own message. Then he was gone and the tears she had fought back for so long burst out in a flood.

She tried to phone Phillips twice that afternoon but each time a curt voice told her the squadron lines were cut until further notice. It was nearly six o'clock before Phillips rang her. 'Sorry, Linda, but we've had an operation today. The Duty Officer says you've rung twice. What can I do for you?'

She wondered how much she dared say over the phone. 'My husband paid us a visit today and I made him that request you and I discussed two days ago. He agreed to do all he can but among other things he needs to know your name. May I give it to him?'

Phillips' delay in answering and his wry tone told her all she needed to know. 'It could cause me a problem or two, but if it's absolutely necessary, yes, you can give it to him.'

'That isn't all,' she confessed. 'He also needs to know the name of your contact.'

The delay was considerably longer this time. 'That's rather different. Leave it with me and I'll come back to you later.'

It was nine o' clock when Phillips phoned again. 'I've had a word with my contact and he has so much to tell me that I think it better we meet again rather than talk over the phone. Can we do that if I run over to Longbridge? Around 3 pm tomorrow?'

'Yes, all right. But what about your contact's name and status. I need that to give to Douglas.'

'I'm afraid I can't give you that, Linda. It would compromise him too much.'

'But did you ask him?'

'Yes but he wouldn't agree. I can't blame him. He's taking too many risks as it is.'

She bit her lip. 'But Douglas probably can't do anything without these details. And every wasted minute could mean Sean's life.'

Phillips' voice lowered as if in fear of being overheard. 'I shouldn't worry about that too much, Mrs Martin. At the moment he's safe from the Gestapo.'

'Why? How do you know that?'

When Phillips' gave her the answer she nearly dropped the receiver in her surprise. 'But it seems impossible that could happen again. Are you sure it's true?'

'That's what my contact says. See me around 3 pm tomorrow and I'll give you all the details.'

She returned the receiver but stood motionless beside it, unable to separate the two emotions Phillips' news had given her. Sean's second escape, improbable though it seemed, had lifted the immediate nightmare of Gestapo sadism but it had also come too late to prevent her admission to Douglas, with all the negative complications that might involve. When she finally pulled herself together and made her way upstairs to check on Charles, some fanciful cell in her mind was reflecting that her personal star had not only lost its way but was plunging her into another galaxy where the universal laws of logic and probability were no longer valid.

TWENTY-FOUR

McNeil released the branch and turned to Sean. 'They've stopped a farmer's truck and are checking it. There must be fifty or more of the bastards.'

Wincing at the pain in his shoulder, Sean pushed himself up to look himself. At the foot of the road that ran down the shallow hillside he could see two uniformed soldiers examining a hay truck while its driver gesticulated his irritation. To the left and right of the vehicle armed soldiers could be seen spread out in a huge semicircle, combing every bush and ditch that led up to the small wood where he and McNeil were hiding. He cast a glance at the trees behind him. 'What's at the other side of this wood?'

'Just goddam fields,' McNeil told him.

'So if we break cover they're going to spot us as soon as they get up here?'

The American nodded. 'That's how I see it.' His question carried a hint of strain. 'You got any ideas, buddy?'

Sean drew aside the bush again to take another look at the advancing soldiers. They were perhaps half a mile away, he decided. Time for the two of them to clear the wood and start across the fields beyond but too little time for them to find safe cover. As his gaze turned up to the tree tops McNeil gave a sarcastic grin. 'You thinking of climbing up one and hiding?'

Sean nodded wryly at his injured shoulder. 'I wouldn't get far up with this, would I? But why don't you give it a try? If I tell them you've run off they might fall for it and push on after you.'

McNeil glanced up at the tall trees that surrounded them. 'Are you kidding? Those goddamned firs wouldn't even hide my ass. Even the birds keep away from 'em.' His eyes returned to Sean. 'Naw, we keep together, buddy. For better or worse.'

I couldn't have been luckier than to have met this man, Sean thought. A farmer's son from Idaho, there seemed nothing he did not know about wildlife and wood lore. No matter what field or wood they had encountered during their escape he had always found something they could eat or chew to ease their hunger. Nor was he less skilled at well judged theft. It had been he who had kept watch on isolated farms and washing lines and purloined piece after piece of clothing until the two of them could now pass muster as farm labourers. But even these gifts took a small place beside the man's loyalty. In spite of his physical toughness, Sean's earlier privations had taken their toll, and in the emergencies they had encountered the American's strength and willingness to help had proved a godsend.

By this combined effort, determination, and luck, they had managed to reach France and although both knew the odds were still stacked against them, the knowledge they were now in an occupied country had a heartening effect. Moreover both felt Sean's ability to speak French must be an asset. But things had gone wrong the night before when McNeil had snatched a bread roll from a boulangerie while Sean was talking to the baker. When McNeil had yelled at Sean in English to run, the news must have spread from the police to the German garrison because in no time kubelwagons had screamed into the small town and poured out troops into its narrow streets. Sean and McNeil had managed to break out before a cordon was thrown in place but weakened by inadequate food and sleep they had been only able to reach the adjacent wood before the troop commandant had realised his quarry had flown. Efficient and anxious to gain the kudos from capturing the two enemy airmen who so far had made fools of his colleagues, the German had strung his men out across the fields with orders the escapees must be captured at all costs. From Sean's viewpoint, with the helmeted figures advancing purposefully towards the wood and prodding every bush on their way with bayonets, that capture was only a matter of minutes away.

Down on the road the search had ended and the truck driver was climbing back into his cab. Noticing that no soldiers were climbing in after him, Sean watched the truck start up and begin climbing the shallow hill. Following the road with his eyes Sean saw it ran through the wood half kilometre to his right. Making his decision he turned and nudged McNeil. 'Let's get to that truck. It's our only chance.'

McNeil stared at him. 'But won't the driver give us away?'

'He might try. If he does we'll steal the bloody thing and made a run for it. Come on. We've nothing to lose.'

Realising he was right McNeil followed him through the wood. Although the firs were sparse in themselves the undergrowth was thick and, in their weakened condition, both men were struggling for breath when they reached the road and sank down out of sight. Round a bend in the road they could hear the sound of the truck's engine as it approached them. McNeil turned his sweating face to Sean and voiced his thoughts. 'If we have to take the goddamned thing we won't get very far. They'll catch us in a couple of miles.'

Sean nodded. 'Never mind. Let's play it as

it comes.'

The truck appeared round the road bend half a minute later. Sean saw it was an old Renault. Neglected mechanically because of the war, it looked to be running on will power alone. As it came within thirty yards of them Sean glanced at McNeil. 'OK?'

McNeil nodded and both men stepped out in front of the truck. It halted with a squeal of brakes. Both men ran to the cab. Sean called up in French to the driver, an elderly French countryman with unkempt beard and weather-beaten cheeks. 'Can we have a lift, monsieur?'

The driver leaned from the cab window. 'Qu'est ce que c'est?'

'We're trying to get to Toulouse,' Sean lied. 'We missed the bus this morning.'

The driver grinned, showing two rows of graveyard teeth. He jerked a tobacco stained thumb at the road behind him, following the gesture with another laugh, and then a jabber of French that made McNeil glance at Sean. 'What's he saying?'

'He knows we're not French because of my accent. He knows we're the airmen the Boche are searching for.'

McNeil waited to hear no more. 'Then let's throw him out and grab his truck. Before those Heinies reach us.'

Sean held up his hand. The driver, climbing down from his cab, began talking rapidly

262

to Sean and at the same time started pulling off bales of hay. McNeil turned to Sean. 'What the hell's he doing?'

Sean was showing excitement now. 'He says we can't get past the Jerries on our own because they've sent some men round the other side of the hill. So our only chance of escape is to go with him.'

McNeil stared at the truck's load of hay. 'How the hell can we do that? They're sure to search the hay again.'

The Frenchman was now showing anger at their procrastination. Chattering to Sean, he motioned at the bales of hay still to be removed. 'Qu'est ce que vous faites? Aidez moi! Vite, vite!'

'What the hell's he want?' McNeil muttered.

Sean grabbed his arm and pulled him towards the impatient Frenchman. 'He has a secret compartment under the hay that he uses to fool the Germans when they search him. If we hide in it he can get us away and into safe hands. But we must hurry.'

McNeil found himself pulling down a bale of hay. 'But can we trust him?'

'As I see it we've no choice,' Sean told him. 'So let's give it a try.'

The false floor came in sight half a minute later, a hinged replica that when unlocked and lifted revealed a compartment that ran the full length of the truck's floor but was no more than eighteen inches deep. McNeil's question was full of misgivings. 'How the hell are we going to fit in there?'

Neither man had time left to argue. The driver's French and urgent gestures told their own story. Lying in the shallow compartment the two men discovered the false floor could just settle on its seating if they lay flat on their backs with their arms at their sides. As they heard the Frenchman outside panting for breath as he replaced the bales, McNeil gave an apprehensive grunt. 'It feels like a goddamned coffin to me. What about breathing? You think the old guy's thought about that?'

Without knowing why, Sean found the comment amusing. 'I saw a few holes in the floor below us. Let's hope they're enough.'

A minute later they heard a cough as the engine started. Below them springs groaned as the truck began moving forward. A few seconds later McNeil stirred. 'You smell oil?'

'Yes. But isn't that a good sign? It must mean air's getting in from somewhere.'

'Yeah, that's true. Maybe the old guy knows what he's doing after all.'

The truck was moving faster now, suggesting they were now running down the opposite side of the hill. McNeil's voice came again. 'You think the Heinies will search the truck again?'

'Knowing we're around here somewhere they'll be stupid if they don't.'

'Yeah, that's what I figure. You got your fingers crossed?'

'All of them,' Sean told him. 'Toes as well.'

The sound they were dreading came five minutes later. The truck's brakes squealed again and the sense of movement ceased. As the engine cut off, an authoritarian voice shouted an order. Unsure of the Frenchman's allegiance, both of the listening men held their breath in fear of betrayal. Instead, to their relief, they heard the Frenchman grumbling at his second stoppage and the truck sway when, on a further order, he dismounted from his cab.

Their tension returned a few seconds later when sounds above gave evidence the hay was being searched again. Although they were unable to see the extent of the search or understand the orders given out, the sounds on the false floor and jerking of the truck suggested that instead of the bales being removed this time, bayonets were being thrust into and between them to flush out any quarry. The ruthlessness of the search, perhaps influenced by the truck's earlier examination, was a warning to the men of the treatment they could expect if they were found and captured.

But the very ruthlessness of the search proved to their benefit. Without the false floor exposed there was no way it could be detected and after a few minutes an order rang out and the thumping and prodding ceased.

When at last the grumbling Frenchman returned to the cab and the truck began rolling forward again, McNeil's whisper expressed both men's feelings. 'How come I didn't know it was Christmas? Can you believe this French guy? He's risked his life for us.'

'I think he's done this before,' Sean told him. 'This compartment isn't just to hide bits and pieces. My guess is he's in the Resistance.'

'Resistance? Does that mean he's taking us to someone who'll hide us?'

'I think so. He'll probably stop when he thinks it's safe and tell us his plans.'

'And of all the guys in France we run into him. What do you make of it, buddy? Why are we getting all the breaks like this?'

Sean did not answer. He was thinking of Libermann and the strange bargain they had made. So far the priest had kept his promises, inexplicable and improbable though they were. If he were spared he could do no less although for what purpose he could not even guess.

TWENTY-FIVE

Phillips was already in the White Hart when Linda arrived. A group of aircrew were clustered around the bar and she felt their eyes following her as she crossed the lounge. Seeing Etherington was not among them she wondered if he was a recent casualty. Relieved at the same time he was not there to complicate her arrival, she approached Phillips' table. He rose as she approached him. 'I hope you don't mind leaving your father, Linda. I'd no sooner asked you than I remembered he wasn't well.'

'No. It's all right,' she told him. 'I've asked our housekeeper to stay in the house until I get back.'

'Let me get you a drink,' he said.

She motioned him back into his chair. 'No. I want to hear this news about Sean. I couldn't believe it when you said he'd escaped again.'

He nodded. 'I wanted to tell you sooner but couldn't until the station came on line again.' His voice lowered. 'Am I right in thinking you've already mentioned his case to your husband?'

She lit a cigarette before answering him.

'Yes. He got a few hours off yesterday and because of Sean's danger I couldn't wait any longer. But I didn't give him your name.' Reading his thoughts, she went on quickly to save them both embarrassment: 'He made the ridiculous assumptions that I believed he'd make, but that couldn't be helped. Who would have thought Sean would escape again.'

To her relief he was sensitive enough not to ask her further questions about her confrontation with Douglas. Instead he took up the conversation from her last words. 'I agree. I was just as amazed. The air attack on the train seemed almost providential.'

'Is that how he escaped?'

'Yes. But that's not the whole story. The rest comes from the German officer who was on the train escorting Sean.'

She stared at him. 'A German officer?'

'I know. This is the part that's hard to believe. It was this officer who told the story to the Swiss.'

Her astonishment grew. 'The one Sean escaped from? Why on earth would he do that?'

'I know how incredible it sounds. But it seems he knew something about the priest who allowed Sean to escape, and after the attack on the train and his discovery that Sean had escaped, he contacted the arrested priest to find why he had arranged his first escape. It was because of what the priest told him that this officer notified the Swiss.'

Although the airmen at the bar were becoming louder as the beer flowed, she had the sensation the entire world was holding its breath to hear the reason. Her voice sounded hoarse as she asked her question. 'What did the priest tell him? Do you know?'

'Yes. He said God had ordered him to release Sean and so it had been his duty to obey.'

Her eyes opened wide. '*God* had ordered him?'

Phillips nodded. 'I know how it sounds. Yet the priest said Sean was one of the few men who understands the true meaning of religion and the needs of the world, and so it was essential he was freed to express and dispense them.'

She was bewildered. 'I can't believe all this. How could a priest come to such conclusions? Are you sure this officer isn't making fools of us all?'

She could not understand the look he was giving her. It was a mixture of puzzlement and embarrassment. 'Why are you looking like that, Peter? Are you doubtful about this German officer too?'

He seemed to take comfort from her question. 'No. Oddly enough I believe the things he told the Swiss. It fits in with what we knew already.'

'Then what else is there? Because there is something else, isn't there?'

He glanced away as if seeking help. 'It's probably nothing. With the story going through so many people it's probably had many changes.' Then, as if bracing himself, he glanced back at her. 'Yet it would give a powerful reason why the priest let Sean go.'

'Are you talking about that accident he had? When he was said to be clinically dead?'

'It could be an important factor. But the priest told the German he had another reason too.'

Her curiosity grew. 'What was that?'

As Phillips gazed at her she felt he was bracing himself. 'It was you, Linda. The priest believed it was vitally important that the two of you met again soon. That was why Sean had to make a promise to see you, before he was released.'

She stared at him 'Promise to see me? Why?'

'I don't know. But that's what the priest told the German officer.'

'But why? Did the priest believe we're lovers? But in any case why would a priest care about that? It doesn't make any sense, Peter.'

Phillips took a deep breath as if to steady himself. 'I know that. But the priest believed it was God's will that the two of you meet again. And he must believe that with his heart and soul to give his life for it.'

For Linda the lounge had gone deathly quiet. Her eyes were huge as she stared at Phillips. 'God's will? Do you believe all this, Peter? Or are they all making fools of us?'

Phillips looked afraid of the question. 'I don't know what to believe, Linda. But there is one thing I can't dismiss. The priest believed providence would ensure that Sean would get through to you. And he has escaped twice already.'

Without knowing why, she suddenly found herself trembling. 'But surely that's just due to luck or chance?'

Phillips' expression gave the lie to his words. 'Probably. But it's not what the priest would say.'

For the sake of her sanity she felt she must find a plausible answer. 'Perhaps this German officer who told this to the Swiss is playing some sort of game. Have you considered that?'

'Yes, I have. But what game could it be? He's an officer in the Abwahr. That's Germany's intelligent services? He could be court martialled and even shot for giving out information of this kind.'

'Not if it's part of a clever plan.'

'Yes, but what possible advantage could be gained from this type of information? My contact and I wondered if you could help us

271

here. We wondered about your relationship with Sean. Whether the two of you had made any kind of deal or promise to one another during your meetings.'

She was too dazed at the news to take offence. 'I only met Sean four times. And I've never seen or heard of this priest. Nor as far as I know has he ever seen or heard of me. So why'd he insist on Sean seeing me again?' Reason, reaction, and not a little suspicion changed her voice. 'None of this makes any sense at all. Are you sure your contact doesn't get carried away with things he hears? If you've mentioned me to him, couldn't he have made this up or dramatised it?'

For a moment Philips looked hurt at the inference behind her question. 'I don't use your name to anyone, Linda. Until my contact gave me this message from the German officer he had never heard your name mentioned. That's why it's so astonishing.'

Without being certain why, she found she believed him. 'I'm sorry. Only what other explanation is there?'

A few seconds passed before Phillips shook his head. 'I can't find one and am wondering if the German officer has the same problem. Could that be why he contacted the Red Cross?'

Her brow furrowed. 'You mean in the hope of finding an answer?'

'Yes. Perhaps he's interested in metaphysical problems and the priest's behaviour has fascinated him. It's the only reason I can think of.'

She shook her head in bewilderment. 'How can I tell all this to Douglas? On top of everything else he'll think I've gone insane.'

Phillips nodded. 'I wouldn't say any more to him just now. For the moment there isn't the need. I'd wait to see if we get any more news.'

'But Douglas is expecting me to give him the name of your contact!'

'I can't give you that, Linda. In any case, if I broke my word we'd never get any more news about Sean.'

With her thoughts in a hopeless tangle she needed a simple practical act of sanity to bring the world back on its axis again. 'If I may, I'll have that drink now. I've never needed one more.'

She left Phillips fifteen minutes later with her thoughts in a greater confusion than ever. She had met Phillips in the hope she would learn more about Sean's second escape but never in her wildest imaginings had she believed his freedom was related in some way to herself. How could that be? Why would a priest, of all people, see something so important in their brief relationship that he was giving his life for its resumption? And what was the significance, if any, of Sean's bizarre accident in France? Until now Linda Martin had been curious about her encounter with Hammond and tried without success to understand its importance to her. Today she was feeling a different emotion. It was something akin to fear.

TWENTY-SIX

Douglas phoned Linda at 10.30 the following morning. 'Linda. Have you got the name of that character who gives away all this gen from the Red Cross?'

It took her a moment to answer him. 'No. He won't allow his name to be released.'

'I don't wonder. He'll get the high drop if old Ashcroft finds out who he is.'

'Does that mean you've spoken to Ashcroft?'

'Yes, and to a point he's sympathetic. But he needs to be certain it's authentic and for that he needs names and rank. If you can't or won't get them there's nothing he can do.'

'I can't get them, darling. I tried yesterday. But now it mightn't he necessary.'

'Why not? Have you had another meeting with this fellow Latimer?'

274

She bit her lip. 'Yes. And he told me Hammond has escaped again. So the immediate danger is over.'

His exclamation told its own story. 'Again! Are you serious?'

'Yes. I believe it's true.'

'But how did the news come through?'

She knew if she told him the truth he would think she was having some kind of mental breakdown. 'I don't know the details. But I'm certain he has escaped again.'

It was too much for the sceptical Douglas. 'First he's released by some mad German priest. Then he is captured again but kills a German officer and is sent to the Gestapo. Now he escapes again. What's his next move? Killing Hitler and occupying his Eagle's Nest? Who's spinning you these yarns, for God's sake? Can't you see they're just making a fool of you?'

She was very close to tears. 'I know how it all sounds. But I believe it's true.'

'You believe it's true but you won't give me the names of the people behind it. Even although we might then be able to verify their story.'

'I can't, darling. I've given my word. But I'm certain I'm getting the truth. Why won't you trust me?'

There was no answer and she realised he had put the phone down.

She confessed it all to Charles that afternoon. She felt it was cowardly of her but with no other confidant than Phillips the temptation was too great. After letting Mrs Griffiths go home, she had gone upstairs to collect Charles's lunch tray and instead of taking it downstairs had set it on a nearby table and then seated herself along Charles's bed. 'Dad, I've got to talk to you. I shouldn't trouble you with it at this time but I've no one else to turn to.'

Charles, propped up with a pillow at his back, showed no surprise. 'I wondered why Douglas didn't say goodbye to me before he left. And you weren't in a mood last night to tell me. You'd told him about this Hammond chap, hadn't you?'

She nodded. 'Yes. And as we both expected he took it badly. In fact he went straight back to Group.'

Charles winced. 'He's a proud man, darling. He hates your sharing your thoughts and feelings with another man.'

'I know all that. But what else could I do when a man's life was in danger?'

Knowing his daughter well, Charles ignored the question. 'That isn't what you've come up to talk about, is it? Has it something to do with that Longbridge trip you made?'

At that moment Jason pushed open the bedroom door and padded to her side. Grateful for the diversion she patted the dog for a moment before turning back to Charles. 'Yes. I heard something that doesn't make any sense. No sense at all. And yet I've every reason to believe it.'

'Whom did you see?' Charles interrupted.

'That intelligence officer. Squadron Leader Phillips. He told me something so bizarre that I think I'll go crazy if I keep it to myself any longer.'

Charles frowned. 'Then go ahead. I won't interrupt.'

She told him everything, from Phillips' impressions of Sean to the news she had heard the previous day. She did not hold eye contact with him, she was too afraid what his expression would tell her. Instead she kept her eyes on Jason as the words came out. At the end of her story she raised her head with a shaky laugh of embarrassment. 'So it seems Sean, a confirmed atheist, has been released on condition he comes straight to me, and this by some priest who doesn't know me from Adam. Since then, by pure luck, Sean keeps escaping capture. Can you wonder I'm bewildered.'

It was a full fifteen seconds before Charles spoke. 'This man Phillips? Can you trust him?'

'Yes, I'm sure I can. He was a close friend of Sean.'

'He wouldn't tell you all this as a favour to Sean, would he?'

She frowned. 'I don't follow you.'

'He wouldn't keep you interested in Sean because he thinks you might be good for him if he survives the war?'

It was an aspect she had not considered. 'No. He's not the kind of person who'd do a thing like that. Anyway, when he knows Sean's an atheist, why would he invent this story about a priest believing God wants us to meet again.'

'Knowing you are religious he might think it will have a more powerful effect on you. It's possible, darling. After all it's already caused a tiff between you and Douglas. When you've lived as long as I have you know people are capable of any deceit.'

At that moment she wanted to believe him. 'I know that, Dad, but I don't believe Phillips is capable of contriving a story like that. In any case there's this thing I have myself. It's something I can't explain no matter how I try.'

One of Charles's bushy eyebrows lifted. 'What thing?'

'This wanting to see Sean myself, Dad.' At his look she went on quickly: 'No, it's not that. It's something much deeper and much stronger. Something I can't understand or fight.'

The silence in the room was broken only by Jason licking himself. Then Charles stirred. 'Have you thought about talking to

Father Clifford?'

'Yes, I have. But what could he tell me? That I'm having the same problem that's affecting millions of women today? That I'm lonely and having fantasies about other men?'

'Yet according to your sources it was another priest that released Sean,' Charles reminded her. 'So wouldn't Father Clifford be the one most likely to understand why?'

'I don't see how. Would Father Clifford release a German atheist to see some unknown woman in Germany? I wonder if he'd even believe me. There's something mysterious about this, Dad. Something that's frightening me more and more with every day that passes.'

In spite of her protest, Charles felt he must ask the question again. 'Are you sure that Douglas isn't right, darling? Are you sure you aren't in love with Sean and it's your religion and background that's keeping you from accepting it?'

Her self control broke down at the question. Sobbing she threw herself forward and buried her face in the bed quilt. 'I'm not sure about anything. I don't feel I belong to myself these days. I know I still love Douglas and yet something is telling me I must see Sean no matter what happens to my marriage. What is it, Dad? Am I losing my mind?'

Finding no answer to her questions Charles leaned over her, drew her head closer and kissed her hair. On the carpet below Jason gazed up at them with cocked head and made a small puzzled sound in his throat.

The wind was an icy razor that cut the two men's faces with merciless intent. They were taking a narrow contour path along a mountain face with a drop of a thousand feet below them and with the wind struggling to throw them down into the abyss.

Nor was the wind the only threat they faced. Far below, on a snow covered ridge that linked the mountain to its neighbour, tiny moving figures could be seen. German mountain troops, patrolling the Pyrenees, had long been notified of their escape and at last had the quarry in their vision.

Although as yet out of rifle range, the pursuing troops were confident their mountain training would ensure the capture or death of the two men before they reached the Spanish frontier. The post was a good three miles away and the two men's progress along the treacherous path was slow and painful. One of the pursuing group, better trained or fitter than the rest, had already reached the slope that ran up to the contour path and two of his colleagues were only a couple of hundred metres behind him. If the leader could reach the contour path before the two escapees rounded the distant mountain shoulder they would come within rifle range.

No one was more aware of this than Sean. Massively handicapped by his damaged shoulder he was finding it difficult to keep his balance on the narrow path and to help him McNeil was following close behind. Time and time again, risking his own life, he would grab hold of Sean to restore his balance. An equal number of times Sean cursed him.

'Go on ahead, you bloody fool. Get round that corner and you can make that frontier post.'

The reply was always the same. 'We'll both make it, buddy. Keep going and we'll be OK.'

Sean heard a distant order from the pursuers below. As it echoed back and forth he wondered if the cold and the dizzy drop were turning him delirious. He wanted to look back to see if the leading German had reached the path yet but McNeil's strong hands checked him. 'Keep going, buddy. Keep your eyes on that bend ahead.'

What fate had brought this man into his life, Sean wondered. He felt certain that without McNeil's rural knowledge and physical support he would never have survived the harsh and punitive escape across Germany. And even after their near miraculous introduction into the French Resistance the American's simple faith and optimism had invigorated not only Sean but the Frenchmen who had given them shelter until they could be passed down the rescue line to the Pyrenees. Although the last man on earth to believe in supernatural intervention, Sean was beginning to wonder if it were not more rational to believe in Father Libermann's faith than to believe that the roulette wheel of chance could continue doubling and redoubling the stakes in this way.

Another shouted order from below jerked him back to the perilous present. Perhaps, he thought, the mystery of it had come down to this. The final showdown. Escape or death. One or the other would surely provide the answer. He addressed the American behind him. 'Is that Jerry in sight yet? Because if he is you're going to get the first bullet. Do you realise that?'

In reply he received a push. 'Let's get to that goddamed corner. Then we've got a chance.'

Panting, legs aching, wet with sweat in spite of the cold, they at last reached and rounded the mountain shoulder. Ahead of them they saw the path continue round the mountain with a second steeper path leading down to a clump of snow-covered trees. On the mountain slope beyond the trees, diminished because of distance, was a cluster of huts. McNeil's yell set off echoes that must have reached their hunters. 'That's it. The post. Come on, buddy. We can make it now.'

Sean remembered little of their descent down the mountainside. The path was icy and because of their need to reach the trees before their hunter came within rifle range they had to force their aching legs into a stumbling run. Twice Sean slipped and fell, both times on his injured shoulder, and the pain was so intense he barely realised McNeil was half carrying him during the last fifty metres to the trees. It was only when he heard a rifle shot and a curse from the American that he realised the leading German had rounded the mountain shoulder and was now within rifle range.

Another shot sounded and then for the moment they were safe, with the trees showering snow on them. With bodies screaming for rest, they dropped down and fought for air. It was a full half minute before McNeil managed to speak. 'That bastard's coming after us. We must get him before the others come round that shoulder.'

Rolling over, Sean saw he was right. Knowing the two escapees were unarmed, the German, with rifle at the ready, had already started on the second path. If the two men picked themselves up and tried to make a dash for the frontier post they would present an easy target once the German reached the lower edge of the wood. Yet to remain inside it would mean certain capture if not by the first man then by the others close on his heels.

Sean jerked a thumb behind him. 'You go. He'll have to stay with me and that'll give you the time you need. Run like hell and you should make the post before the rest get here. Get going, for God's sake.'

McNeil dragged him to his feet. 'You've given me an idea.' He pushed Sean towards a clump of snow covered bushes. 'Lie here,' he panted. As Sean stared at him he ran deeper into the wood, leaving tracks in the snow swept in between the trees by the wind. Thinking for a moment he had taken his advice and made a dash for the frontier post, Sean turned his attention to the approaching German and saw he was now halfway down the path. As he watched the soldier's cautious approach he heard a hiss behind him and saw McNeil had reappeared and was crouching near the clump of bushes. Panting, he grinned at Sean. 'Get the idea? You lie here, point to those tracks I made, and suggest I've gone on to the post. I'll do the rest.' With that he dropped out of sight behind the bushes.

Sean had no time to argue. The armed German was no more than fifty yards away now, his alert eyes scanning the trees where he knew the two men were hiding, his rifle swinging in an arc from side to side. Beside him Sean heard a whisper. 'Where's the bastard now?'

'Getting close,' Sean whispered back. 'I'm going to break a twig to bring him over here.'

'OK. I'm ready.'

Fumbling beside him, Sean found a small branch and snapped it between both hands. Instantly alerted, the German halted and turned, his rifle pointing in the direction of the sound. Breath held, Sean watched him move forward again, foot by foot this time. Sean was not unaware of his danger. After the fools he and McNeil had made of the enemy since their escape from Germany it was quite possible the orders had gone out that they were to be shot on sight and this lone soldier might well feel that one dead escapee would be the insurance for his own safety.

Whatever the outcome Sean knew there was no turning back now. Raising his head he gave a cough. Seeing him, the German went into a crouch, his rifle pointing at Sean. Cautiously Sean lifted his arm, a gesture of surrender. 'It's OK,' he said. 'The other man's gone.'

Although he doubted the German understood him, his tone seemed to bring reassurance. Although still cautious he approached Sean until he was standing over him. Twisting round, Sean pointed at the footprints behind him. 'He's gone! Kaput!'

From the German's eyes Sean could see that he understood. As he turned back to Sean and lowered his rifle, it seemed for a moment his intention was to dispatch one escapee so that he could pursue the other. But whatever his plan it was never tested. As Sean braced himself, McNeil came from behind the bushes like a battering ram, swung a broken-off tree branch, and knocked the German to the ground. As Sean grabbed the rifle, McNeil jerked a knife from the half-stunned soldier's belt and dragged back his head. Seeing he was about to slit his throat. Sean grabbed his arm. 'No! Don't kill him!'

Still holding the German in a headlock, McNeil stared at Sean. 'You gone crazy? He'll tell the others about us.'

Sean shook his head. 'No. He was only following orders. If we take his rifle he can't harm us. And in any case the others know where we are.'

McNeil stared at him a moment longer, then hurled the German to the ground. 'You are crazy,' he fumed. Snatching up the rifle, he pushed Sean deeper into the wood. 'Come on then. We gotta clear that open ground to the post before the rest of the Heinies get in range. So run like hell.'

Stumbling, slipping, they cleared the small wood and started down the mountain slope to the distant group of huts. The descent was steep and treacherous and both men had difficulty keeping their feet. Reaching a pile of rocks both were forced to pause to catch their breath. 'You OK?' McNeil panted.

Slumped against a rock, Sean found it an effort even to nod his head. The pain from his shoulder, already compounded by the falls he had made, was an agony that exploded with every gasping breath he took. McNeil's question was anxious. 'You going to make it, buddy?'

The answer that came into Sean's mind bore no relation to his pain or distress. Nor in its urgency did it brook disagreement. Almost in spite of himself Sean nodded again and pushed himself from the rock. At the same moment there was the crack of a rifle and a bullet whined eerily from one of the rocks. It brought a curse from McNeil. 'The bastards have reached the wood. We gotta go, buddy, or they'll pick us off before we reach that post.'

He could see what Sean could not, a dozen figures who had run out of the frontier post and were now frantically waving them on. As another rifle cracked, McNeil grabbed Sean's arm and the two men, now resembling disjointed puppets rather than human beings, stumbled towards the huts that meant safety while behind them soldiers emerged from the wood and under frantic orders from an NCO dropped to their knees and took careful aim.

TWENTY-SEVEN

Linda had never known longer or more interminable days. Although Phillips had promised to contact her if any more news came through, her patience broke on the third day and she phoned him at Lemington. His voice told her immediately that somehing was wrong although at first she attributed it to news about Sean. 'Have you heard anything more of him?' she asked. 'It seems so long since you heard he had escaped again.'

'I'm sorry, Linda. I don't expect we will hear until he is captured again. Then in time we might get news from the Red Cross.'

'You sound as if you expect him to be captured. Do you?'

'Sorry. I didn't mean it that way. It's just that while he's on the run we won't get any news. You can see that, can't you?'

Was he reproving her, she wondered. 'Is something wrong, Peter? I know I shouldn't bother you this way but I've no one else to discuss it with. And I can hardly talk about it to my husband.'

His reply puzzled her. 'I thought you had. At least that was the impression I had yesterday when he called me to Group to see him.'

Her heart missed a beat. 'Douglas sent for you? Why?'

'Why? Once you'd given him my name he was bound to question me. Didn't you expect that?'

She was shocked. 'I never gave him your name. Did he tell you so?'

'No. But how else could he get it?'

'I don't know. But it wasn't from me.'

Phillips's voice changed. 'Then he must have been making inquiries or he remembered Sean and I had been friends when we were together at Lemington. Anyway, it doesn't matter. He gave orders he wanted to see me.'

'Has it got you into trouble?' she asked.

Phillips sounded rueful. 'He's not pleased with me for giving you news of Sean and he's even less pleased that I won't give the name of my contact. But I expect I'll live with it.'

She was chastising herself for underestimating Douglas's intelligence.

'What did he ask you about Sean?'

'Just about everything one could think of.'

'But he must have remembered him from Lemington,' she interrupted.

'Yes. But only as a fine pilot. Now he

wanted to know about his religion, his relationships with his colleagues, and his views in general.'

She was almost too afraid to ask the question. 'Did he ask about his relationship with me?'

'Yes. I said I knew nothing about that. He didn't believe a word of it, of course, but I gave nothing away.'

She mentally thanked him. 'So now he knows all about Sean?'

'Only the best and positive things. Although whether he thinks they're as admirable as I do I can't say.'

'Has all this got you in trouble?' she asked.

Phillips' reply was a mixture of ruefulness and humour. 'I can't honestly say. I shouldn't think I'll be getting any recommendations for promotion in the near future, but I can live with that. I've always got the bank when all this is over.'

She wished at that moment she was with him in the flesh to express her appreciation. 'You've been a genuine friend. I couldn't have done without you. But I mustn't get you into any further trouble.'

'Don't worry, Linda. I'll survive. If I can get any more news I'll ring you right away.'

So Douglas was building up a picture of Sean, she thought as she replaced the receiver. What was his purpose? And where was Sean at this moment? A captive again or still on the run? Why did the thought of their planned rendezvous obsess her so much when at the same time she feared his return might herald the break-up of her marriage? As each question burned her mind without giving the hint of an answer she felt she would have a breakdown if the puzzle did not unravel itself soon.

It was another six endless days before she heard from Douglas again. She had just returned from taking Jason for a walk when Mrs Griffiths met her at the front door. 'Your husband phoned about fifteen minutes ago, Mrs Martin. He left a number for you. It's by the phone. He says you must phone him before eleven.'

Needing time to think and to brace herself she cleaned Jason's muddy paws before going to the telephone. Even then she lit a cigarette before dialling the number. As a woman's voice enquired her name she steadied herself. 'I would like to speak to Group Captain Martin, please. This is his wife speaking.'

A silence followed in which she heard brusque background voices and the occasional ringing of telephones. Then she heard the receiver being picked up and Douglas's clipped voice. 'Hello. Is that you, Linda?'

She could feel the nervous beating of her heart as she answered him. 'Hello, darling.

You left a message for me to call.'

'That's right.' The lowering of his voice made her guess the Waaf secretary was nearby. 'I've got news about Sean Hammond.'

She felt her entire body stiffen. She took a moment to find her voice. 'What's happened?'

'You're not going to believe this. He's in England.'

She nearly dropped the receiver. 'In England? Who's told you this?'

'The usual sources. He and an American are in hospital getting medical treatment. The news came through early this morning.'

'But how is it possible?'

'Apparently they got French help to the Pyrenees and then managed to escape into Spain. The American was wounded and Sean Hammond had an injured shoulder. Our Air Attaché in Spain got news of them and after first aid treatment they were flown to England three days ago. They're now in military hospitals in Portsmouth.'

She felt she was in some bizarre dream not knowing what words to use and what questions to ask. 'What will happen to Sean now?' was the best she could manage.

'He'll receive the usual interrogation given to all escapees. Then I want a talk with him myself.'

Trying to think what a confrontation between them would entail was too much for her imagination. Aware of his difficulty in speaking freely with Waafs and fellow officers close by, she tried to make her question innocuous. 'Darling, can't I see you beforehand? There's so much to say and I haven't had the chance since your last visit.'

It was a few seconds before he answered her. 'I'd like that myself but I doubt if I'll get the chance. We're up to our eyebrows at the present and I can't log a visit to Smalloaks as official business.'

She was desperately trying to analyse his voice as well as his reply. Although negative in words she felt it had a conciliatory tone somewhere. Knowing their voices might be overheard if not recorded, she struggled to find the right reply. 'Please keep me in touch, darling. And try to remember the things I told you.'

His voice became clipped again. 'I haven't forgotten. Take care of yourself and give my regards to your father.'

It was happening, she told herself as she stubbed out her cigarette in the tray beside the phone. Like a dozen coloured pieces, all the dramatic but seemingly irrelevant incidents of the past weeks and months were now slipping into their allotted places in the giant jigsaw. What the outcome would be when the final picture was completed she could not guess but instinct warned her it would change their lives forever.

TWENTY-EIGHT

The young pilot officer opened the office door and addressed its single inmate. 'He'll be here in a moment, sir. He's just having a word with the ward sister.'

Sean, wearing pyjamas and a dressing gown, with his left arm in a sling, nodded back. 'Thanks. Is anyone with him?'

'No, sir. There's only a Waaf driver and she's gone to the canteen.'

'OK. I'm ready to see the big man when he's ready.'

Looking unsure how to take the remark, the young officer nodded and withdrew. Left alone Sean reached for a cigarette and then changed his mind. As a patient he might get away with some informality but this was hardly likely to be a welcome home visit from a staff officer to one of his underlings. To be involved with a superior officer's wife was never a convivial situation but at least it had its structure and its boundaries. In a situation like this one, without any structure that made any sense, the possibilities defeated his imagination.

A tap on the door broke into his thoughts. The young pilot officer appeared again, very formal this time. 'Group Captain Martin, sir.'

Sean rose to his feet and came to attention. Douglas Martin, handsome, erect, immaculate, a briefcase under one arm, gave him a nod. 'Hello, Hammond. At ease.' As Sean relaxed, Douglas nodded at the pilot officer. 'Thanks. You can go now.'

A snappy salute, a glance at Sean, and then the young officer withdrew and closed the door. Douglas glanced back at Sean. 'You can sit down, Hammond. How are you feeling?'

Sean, who had been trying to decide whether it was curiosity, hostility or just plain puzzlement in the staff officer's eyes, sank back in his chair. 'I'm fine, thank you.'

'I'm told you were in bad shape when you reached that Spanish post. They've operated on that shoulder, haven't they?'

'Yes, sir. It's coming on well.'

'I'm glad to hear it. Anyway, congratulations on your escape. It was quite a feat.'

Sean was wondering when the prelims were going to end. 'Thank you, sir. Although I did have a great deal of help.'

Douglas seated himself on a second chair, balancing his briefcase on his tailored trousers. 'So it seems. Or are you referring to the American who crossed the Pyrenees with you?'

'He was a part of it, yes. He saved me time

and time.'

Douglas nodded. 'The staff sister tells me you've been asking about him every day. You know, of course, that he's in an American hospital?' When Sean nodded he went on: 'He's doing well and sends his regards.'

Sean tried to hide his surprise. 'You've seen him yourself?'

'Yes. We had a long talk yesterday. He thinks well of you, Hammond. In his words he says you're a hell of a guy. Also the luckiest man he's ever met.'

Sean managed a smile. 'We did have some luck. We'd never have escaped without it.'

'So I believe. If all we hear is true your luck was phenomenal.' As he was talking Douglas opened his briefcase. 'Am I right in thinking a German priest contrived your first escape?'

It was coming now, Sean thought. 'Yes, sir. He did.'

'Why, Hammond? What was his reason?'

'I don't know how to answer that, sir. Perhaps it was because he saw me spare a German pilot before I was shot down.'

Douglas drew out a sheaf of papers from his briefcase. 'That isn't the reason I've been given. The priest himself says he released you because God needed you for his own purposes.' Douglas's expression was a complex mixture of scepticism, scorn, and curiosity. 'Didn't he tell you that before letting you go?'

Sean's confession was not without embarrassment. 'Yes, he did talk in those terms. I couldn't make any sense of it but at the same time I wasn't going to throw away my chance of escape.'

'But he did believe it was his Christian duty to release you?'

'So he said,' Sean admitted.

Douglas leaned forward. 'Why, Hammond? Why among all our crews shot down did you deserve this special treatment? Particularly when I'm told you're an atheist.'

Realising the trap he was in Sean could only fall back on a lie. 'I honestly don't know. Perhaps he wasn't well or perhaps he didn't like Hitler and his gang. How can I know?'

Douglas took a look at the closed door behind him. As he turned back on Sean, the pilot saw his expression had turned hostile. 'I want the truth, Hammond. Not a pack of lies. You were released on the promise you would see my wife if you escaped to England. Isn't that right?'

Sean's surprise gave him away. 'How did you hear this?'

'Because the priest told it to a certain German officer who had been on the train with you. This officer claimed the priest's reasons fascinated him and he interviewed the priest before the man was handed to the Gestapo.'

Sean's bewilderment grew. 'How can you know this?'

'We know it because the German officer informed the Swiss Red Cross.' Seeing Sean's expression of disbelief. Douglas went on: 'He gave his reason as curiosity, his need to know the answer to the puzzle. Does that surprise you?'

Sean shook his head in disbelief. 'I don't think anything surprises me any more. Who told you all this?'

Ignoring the question, Douglas's voice turned dry. 'You're not alone in being surprised, Hammond. Others are having the same problem after hearing the things that have happened to you. Your very escapes seem to have something providential about them.'

Douglas's use of providential confused Sean for a moment until he caught the officer's true meaning. Then he gave a jerk of shock. 'Good God, you don't think I'm a spy, do you?'

Douglas's tailored shoulders lifted. 'It's not what I believe. It's what others of higher rank are asking. That's why there's a guard on the hospital and why you may face a Board of Enquiry when your doctors give permission.'

Sean could not believe what he was hearing. 'For Christ's sake, I flew in your squadron. I shot down enemy aircraft. Remember?'

'True, but on your own admission you spared the life of an enemy pilot over Germany. You also refused to let your American colleague kill a German soldier. In addition you have weird and wonderful ideas about our armed forces.' He patted the pile of papers on his lap. 'It's all in here. Your views on religion, patriotism, nationhood, and the rest. You're hardly an outstanding example of British military manhood, are you?'

All the disciplines of rank had gone now, Sean thought. The tips were off the rapiers and the thrusts were now meant to wound or kill. In the way he had always lived, Sean welcomed the end of the foreplay. 'This is all because I saw your wife a few times, isn't it? And for some reason better known to himself the priest made me promise to see her again. One way or the other you're going to fix me, aren't you?'

To his surprise Douglas did not respond aggressively. Instead he leaned forward again with a look in his eyes Sean could not immediately analyse. 'Why did this priest want you to see my wife again? What reason did he give?'

For a moment Sean had the sensation the question had momentarily turned the two of them into allies. 'I can't give you the reason. It didn't make any sense to me either.'

Douglas made an angry, impatient gesture. 'Let me decide that. What was it?' As Sean shook his head, his voice turned hoarse. 'You must tell me, Hammond. I have to know.'

To his astonishment Sean was now feeling sympathy for him. 'He had some crazy idea that it was God's purpose. I know. It sounds pure nonsense. But he wouldn't let me go until I promised I would see her.'

Douglas made an exclamation. To his surprise Sean saw the papers in his hand were shaking. His hoarse voice attacked Sean. 'Why did you make that promise?'

'Isn't it obvious? It allowed me to escape?'

'But what happens now you're back in England?'

Sean braced himself. 'I have to keep that promise. What else can I do?'

'You can't see her. I can't allow it.'

Sean made an effort to restore the conversation from the abstract to the concrete. 'Sir, whatever that priest's reason it seems to have cost him his life. How can I break a promise to a man like that?'

Douglas shook his head. 'I'm sorry but I can't allow it. Not now or ever.'

Sean's voice turned bitter. 'Why? Because I don't fit into your matrix of an ideal citizen with my views on patriotism, nationhood and the armed forces?'

To his surprise Douglas showed no resentment. 'No. It's because I'm afraid of what might happen to Linda.'

'Linda? What can happen to her? She told

me a dozen times she's in love with you.'

'Perhaps she does believe it. But it doesn't explain her obsession to see you again.'

Sean stared at him. 'Obsession?'

'Yes. I don't think she understands it herself. But according to her she's had it ever since you were shot down.'

Sean discovered he was sweating. 'That seems to fit with what the priest said. But how could he know and what could it mean?'

Once more they were allies searching for the inexplicable. Douglas was the first to speak. 'Did the two of you have an affair? That's the only thing that makes any sense.'

Sean's reply was emphatic. 'Never. In fact most of the time we argued. And she always made it clear how much she loved you.'

Douglas' bitterness returned. 'She has an odd way of showing it, telling me she must see you no matter how much I resent it.'

Sean's reply was more to himself than to Douglas. 'I can't agree with that. Whatever rubbish the romantics say, we're all capable of loving more than one man or woman at the same time.'

It was a mistake. Douglas's voice was instantly hostile. 'Then she is in love with you?'

'No. At least I don't think so. She was helpful to me when I needed help. I admit that. But we never had an affair or discussed having one. In other words she was never unfaithful to you. I give you my word on that.'

A long silence followed and then Douglas began stuffing the papers back in his brief-case. When the task was finished he glanced back at Sean. 'Regarding this talk of your being a spy, I want you to know I don't believe it. Do you know why?' When Sean shook his head he went on: 'It's because of Linda. Knowing her as I do, I don't believe she could feel this way towards a liar and a cheat.'

It took a moment for Sean to register his words. 'You're saying it isn't you who is behind this farce?'

'No. It's come from the things I've found out about you but I never intended it to go this way. It's how others are seeing it.'

Have I misjudged this man, Sean was thinking? Am I prejudiced because he is in love with Linda? 'I still want to see Linda again,' he said.

'I know. And that's what I can't let happen. I want you to promise to stay away from her and I'll do everything I can to free you of suspicion.'

Once again Sean found he was sweating. 'But that priest has given his life for our meeting. Don't ask me why. It's never made sense to me but how can I let him down?'

'You must.'

Sean shook his head. 'I can't. I don't blame you for your feelings but it's something that has to happen. Every day during my escape I've felt it drawing me.'

'Because you wanted it,' Douglas said bitterly.

'No. That wasn't the reason. I've even fought against it but it still stayed with me.'

He received a look of scorn. 'You're saying that's because God wants it. How hypocritical can you get?'

'I know. It sounds like madness. But it got me back to England, didn't it? No one can deny that.'

Douglas gazed at him, then rose and went to the door. There he turned. 'Is this your last word?'

Sean rose to his feet. 'Yes. In a way I wish it wasn't because I believe you're a decent human being. But I'm not a free man in this. And it doesn't sound as if Linda is either.'

Douglas seemed about to say a last word. Instead he took another long look at Sean and then walked away, leaving Sean reaching for the cigarette he had denied himself earlier. He was still drawing in smoke and gazing from the office window when the young pilot office arrived to take him back to his ward.

TWENTY-NINE

To Linda's relief the doctor allowed Charles out of bed that week. 'I think he's fully recovered now, Linda. I feel it was only his age that set him back. Make sure he takes it easy for the next few days and I believe he'll be good for a few more years yet.'

No one was more relieved than Charles to return to his old routine. 'There never was anything wrong with me, darling. These damned doctors fuss too much. In any case I intended being up for your birthday. It's on Friday, isn't it?' When she nodded. 'I wonder if Douglas'll be able to get here. He did say that he'd try.'

'I think it's unlikely,' she told him. 'From all he says they're working at full pressure these days.'

'Then why don't you ring up a few friends and either invite them round or spend the evening with them? You don't want to spend a birthday with just an old fogie like me.'

'I like old fogies like you,' she told him. 'Sometimes I think you're the only people who talk any sense.'

He chuckled at that. 'I've been telling you that for years. What's come over you? Are you growing up at last?'

That was the moment the telephone rang. She answered it and recognised Phillips voice. 'Linda. I've got some news for you. I think you'll find it rather startling.'

Although her heart began to race she managed to keep her voice steady. 'Go on,' she said. 'I'm used to startling news by this time.'

'This isn't just startling. It's absurd. Sean's under house arrest for being a spy.'

Her eyes widened. 'A spy. Have they all gone mad?'

'That was my first thought when I heard it. It seems they've decided his escapes have all been too good to be true and so he has to face a Board of Enquiry.'

'Has my husband anything to do with this?' It was her first suspicion.

'No, I don't think so. It's officers above him. But believe it or not the news doesn't stop there.'

She took a grip on herself. 'Don't tell me they're putting him in the Tower of London.'

'No, it's more dramatic than that. I've just been told of it and felt you must know immediately.' As his voice ran on she gave a gasp of disbelief. 'This can't be true. It's not possible.'

'I know. It does sound like fantasy doesn't it? But it's true all right. You can imagine the stir it's causing at Staff Headquarters.'

She put the phone down thirty seconds later and had to steady herself against the table. What could it mean? Unless the affair had turned into pure madness or farce, it meant only one thing. She gave it thought for another minute and then went into the lounge where Charles was having his morning coffee. 'Dad, I've just had a phone call that's made me change my mind. If you'll be all right for a couple of days I think I will go up to Scotland to see Susan. She's always asking me to go and it'll be a bit of a change for both of us.'

Charles returned his cup to its saucer and nodded his approval. 'Good idea. It'll do you the world of good to get away from this place and its problems. But what about the Ration Office?'

'I'm not going to let them know until the weekend that you're better. I know it's fibbing but a few more days won't make any difference to them.'

'When will you leave?'

'I thought I might go tomorrow. Is that all right?'

'Of course it is, darling. You go and enjoy yourself.'

She sighted Douglas's staff car that afternoon just as she was about to take Jason for his walk. Drawing the dog back into the house, she waited at the door while he parked in the courtyard. As he left the car she saw he was carrying a small suitcase. Uncertain of him she tried to read his expression as he climbed the steps towards her. Then, to her immense relief, he gave a smile. 'Hello, darling. How are you?'

She managed a smile. 'I'm all right.' She nodded at the suitcase. 'What's that for? Have you got some leave?'

'Yes. Haven't I done well?' Taking hold of her arm he drew her closer and kissed her. 'Five whole days. Can you believe it?'

His kiss made her want to fling her arms around him but somehow she held herself back. 'How did you work it?'

Out of habit he glanced round before answering her. 'As you can guess we're all going to be under full pressure soon. So everyone's been given a few days leave before it starts. I got mine because of your birthday. Isn't it wonderful?'

'Yes, it is,' she managed. 'I never expected it either.'

For a moment he looked uncertain. 'You are pleased, aren't you?'

'Yes. Yes, of course I am. Why wouldn't I be?'

He examined her expression for a moment, then drew her close and hugged her. 'I'm sorry about what happened the other week. It's all over now, isn't it?'

She brushed back tears. 'Of course it is. Now come and say hello to Dad.'

She waited until after lunch to tell Douglas about her proposed trip to Scotland. 'Susan seemed quite excited at the idea. She said she was going to have a party and invite friends.'

Douglas showed sympathy. 'Then you'd better get her on the phone right away. You don't want her to make plans and then be disappointed.'

It had to be now, she thought. The test that was necessary but had to be made. 'Yes. I'm afraid she will be disappointed.' She watched his handsome face for the slightest change of expression as she went on: 'Darling, would you mind terribly if I still went? I'd come straight back the following day.'

His face seemed to cloud. 'You mean to be there on your birthday?'

'Yes. Just the one day. I'd never have arranged it if I'd known you were coming but she's having a party and has invited all her friends. She'll be terribly disappointed if I let her down.'

He dropped a hand on his knee in disgust. 'For God's sake, must it be this week? Couldn't she wait a few more days?'

He was good, she thought, but the tiniest flicker of his eyes had given her the answer she wanted. 'I'm not happy about it myself. It would be such a change to go out together again. If only I'd known before that you were coming.'

'I didn't know myself until last night,' he said. 'You know what it's like these days. You have to take what you can get.'

She nodded. 'I know, darling. Then do you want me to phone her and tell her to cancel everything?'

He gazed at her and then shook his head. 'No, you can't do that. Not at such short notice. But how long would you stay there?'

'As I said, I'd come back the next day. We could celebrate then. But are you sure? It's such a shame this has happened.'

His face cleared and his gesture was one of generous surrender.

'No, you go ahead. Keep your promise and we'll go to dinner on Saturday. Let's make that a firm date.'

She took him upstairs to her bedroom that afternoon and made love to him with all the passion she could engender. When it was over and they were lying side by side on the bed his voice broke the silence. 'That was wonderful, darling.'

Her hand stroked his warm cheek. 'Are you happier now?'

He nodded. 'I've been so damned miserable since we had that quarrel. I couldn't bear the thought of your seeing Hammond again.'

'Then you were silly, weren't you? It had nothing to do with my love for you.'

'So you said but I couldn't accept it. I still can't. I can't share my love with another man. It's not the way we humans are made.'

The things had to be said, she thought. It would be like walking in a minefield but she could not delay them any longer. 'Are men and women really that way? Or is it the way we've been brought up?'

He stirred. 'What do you mean by that?'

She eased his head back on the pillow. 'I mean love doesn't work that way, darling. It's not a finite thing. It doesn't diminish by giving someone else sympathy and under-standing. It grows instead.'

He frowned. 'That's the kind of thing Hammond would say. He seems to disagree with everything normal people accept or feel.'

His mention of Sean gave her the opening she needed, although at the same time she trod with great care. 'He does see things differently, darling. But is that such a bad thing?'

He gave a half laugh. 'It's not to be recom-mended if you're a member of the Armed Forces. He's a fighter pilot and yet they say he despises patriotism. Is there any wonder he's under suspicion for treachery?'

She feigned ignorance of Sean's plight. 'Treachery? Sean? That's ridiculous. He was one of your best pilots, wasn't he?'

He nodded. 'I don't believe it either. But those escapes of his have put him under suspicion. And this talk about the wrongs of patriotism haven't exactly strengthened his case.'

'That's because they don't understand him. He dislikes patriotism because it's divisive. It pits nation against nation. Whereas he believes the only hope for the world is for us all to settle our disputes under one governing body.'

'Did he tell you this?'

'He might have done. I can't remember. But I know he's contemptuous of the way nations strut around boasting and acting as if they're the best and not seeing how it leads to jealousy and dislike.'

He gave a half smile. 'In other words he doesn't think much of the human race?'

She was both heartened and grateful for the tolerance he had shown so far. 'No, I don't think he does. But that doesn't make him a spy. I've never heard anything more ridiculous.'

There was a long silence before his question came. 'It sounds as if he's converted you. Has he?'

Knowing she was right inside the mine-field now she took great care with her answer. 'I don't think conversion is the right word. I often disagreed with him but later I began seeing there was some truth in every criticism he made. But does that matter? It doesn't change anything between us.'

'Except it could be making you into a different person,' he said. 'Have you thought of that?'

Unprepared for the question, she hesitated before her reply. 'Have I changed towards you? Has it shown today?' Before he could answer she bent down and kissed him. 'You know I haven't. So does it matter if I grow up a little in other ways?'

'It depends in which ways, doesn't it? I like you as you are.'

She kissed him again. 'Yes, but these days I'm realising how blind I've been about some things. I've gone along with the others and seen life the same way but now I'm having doubts and asking questions.'

'What kind of questions?'

'Blind patriotism is one. Religion's another.'

He frowned. 'But religion's always been a comfort to you.'

'It still is, darling. Only in a different way.'

'But Hammond's an atheist. I'm no tub thumper myself but I believe the world would be a poorer world without religion.'

She shook her head. 'Sean's not an atheist. He only thinks he's one. In fact he believes in the things told us two thousand years ago. I believe that's one reason the German priest released him.'

'What do you mean, he only thinks he is?'

'You have to look at his reasons, not his words. He despises modern religion for its acceptance of wealth and power. Also don't forget what it did to his sister and his best friend.'

He made a gesture of impatience. 'A sane man doesn't become an atheist because of one racist priest.'

She shook her head. 'Life isn't that simple, darling. One thing leads to another. You start to think, to ask yourself questions, and then things begin to unravel. It's like pulling a thread from a carpet. In no time at all there's no carpet but just wool all around you.'

He stirred again. 'Is that what's happened to you?'

'Yes,' she admitted. 'It began first with religion. I began studying it again and began to realise how much it had changed. It doesn't unite people today. It divides them. And its basic beliefs have changed. In some cases disastrously. Like usury. Once it was a mortal sin to lend money for profit. Now our entire economic system is based on it.'

'Is this another of Hammond's ideas?'

'I don't know. But I wouldn't have thought of it if he hadn't encouraged me to give that first tug of the wool.'

'Yet he doesn't seem to have had this effect on his colleagues. From all I hear they thought him a misfit although they admired his courage and flying skills.' Before she could reply he went on: 'Did you know I've seen him?'

She gave a start. 'No. What happened? How is he?'

'Thin and battle scarred. But as stubborn as ever when I told him he wasn't to see you again.'

She swallowed to moisten her dry throat. 'What did he say to that?'

'He said he had to see you. That was the condition of his release by the priest.' Douglas raised his head to gaze at her. 'What the hell could he have said to the priest about you to have that effect?'

Afraid his tolerance might be coming to an end, she shook her head. 'I don't know. I honestly don't. All I ever did was argue against his outbursts and on his last visit sympathise with him.'

'What about?'

'He'd shot down a German pilot and seen him burn in his cockpit. He was very distressed about that.'

She half expected sarcasm at her use of the word sympathy but after gazing at her a moment Douglas sank back on his pillow. 'You're impressed by him, aren't you?'

Although astonished at his forbearance, she still took a deep breath before giving her answer. 'Yes, I am. Perhaps it's because he has ideas a thousand years ahead of our time. Or perhaps it's the effect his criticisms have had on me. It's as if he is some kind of a catalyst, awakening thoughts and ideas I've never had before.'

'What sort of thoughts?'

'It's difficult to explain. It's like sparks flying off from a Catherine wheel. Thoughts bringing in turn other thoughts. Like thoughts about our education. How we should be taught from the day we're born to question every assumption in our culture. How we should be taught ethics in schools. How we should be taught never to blame another race for the sins of its forebears. How we have made money our God today. A whole host of thoughts like that.'

His eyes searched her face. 'You suddenly want to change the world, don't you?'

'I hadn't once,' she said. 'But I'd like to now.'

'And this is because of Sean?'

She bent down and kissed him. 'Yes.'

In the silence that fell she could hear the chiming on the grandfather clock in the hall below. It brought with it a sudden need to tell Douglas about Sean's accident in France. She knew it was a betrayal of confidence and yet some impulse stronger than herself told her the admission had to be made. She braced herself. 'You don't know anything about the accident Sean had in France before the war, do you?'

'Accident? No. What kind of accident?'

Not without embarrassment she told him. His expression when she finished was not the one she expected. For the moment it told her he was as shocked and chilled as she had been herself at the revelation. Then he gave a grimace. 'Then isn't that the answer? It scrambled his wits and gave him all these crazy ideas.'

She gazed down at him. 'Isn't that rather unkind?'

To his credit he nodded. 'Yes, I suppose it is. But what's your point in telling me?' Then he gave a start. 'You're not suggesting that's why the priest released him, are you?'

She shook her head. 'I don't know anything about the priest. I just feel you should know he is different from the rest of us.'

'How do you mean, different?' As he spoke she could sense again his shock at the news. 'He got knocked out for a few minutes and that was all. It probably happens everyday to one poor bastard or another.' Then his tone changed. 'Is this why you're so impressed by him? Have you some religious idea that he was given a message before coming back to life?'

'No. I was impressed by his opinions long

before I knew about his accident. Since then I've grown to believe they're valid.'

He frowned. 'You don't believe they'll change the world, do you?'

'Not in our lifetime. Perhaps never.'

'Then is it worth all this soul searching? Isn't it better to live with what we have and make the best of it?'

A fair question, she thought, and yet it illustrated the difference between one man and the millions of others of his kind. 'Easier, yes. And far less painful. But not better. That's why I admire him.'

He cleared his throat. 'Is this why you want to see him again?'

Here it was, she thought. The question to which she had no answer. 'It's not a matter of wanting, Douglas. I have to. Don't ask me why because I don't know myself. I'm even scared of it. But, yes, I must see him again.'

'And all this has come from only four meetings?'

'Yes. It doesn't make any sense, does it.' Before he could reply, she went on: 'What will happen to him now?'

'If he gets off the Enquiry he still can't fly over Germany again. Escapees aren't allowed to. If you hadn't told me about that head injury he might have been sent to the Far East. Now he'll probably get a desk job.'

She thought about that for a moment, then gazed down at Douglas again. 'We were stupid to quarrel about him the other week, darling, because I love you very much. You won't ever forget that, will you?'

He frowned. 'You talk as if you intended staying in Scotland.'

Her eyes were stinging with tears he could not see. 'Don't you sometimes say silly things when you're making love? Of course I'm not staying in Scotland.' She stretched out her long beautiful body and pressed herself against him. 'Let's live for today, darling. Let's pretend it's already my birthday, that the war's over, and the lights have come on again all over the world.'

THIRTY

Charles looked up from the book he was reading. The sound of claws scratching at the front door came again. 'Jason,' he called. 'What's the matter with you tonight? Stop it and come here.'

A whining sound and more scratching was his answer. He called again. 'Jason. Come here.'

It took a few seconds for the dog to obey him. Giving a sigh it flopped down beside his armchair. Charles reached down and patted its head. 'What the matter, old lad?

Are you missing Linda?'

As the dog whimpered again, Charles lowered the book to his knee. The dog wasn't the only one missing her, he thought. If it hadn't been for this Hammond affair he wouldn't have wanted her in Scotland on her birthday either. But although the possibility of her keeping her rendezvous with Hammond now seemed unlikely if not impossible, it had seemed prudent to let Linda have her own way. No doubt, he thought, Douglas was thinking along the same lines. Otherwise his behaviour in not contesting her trip made no sense.

The whimpering of Jason once more interrupted Charles's thoughts. As he reached down to comfort the dog again, it suddenly leapt to its feet and dashed back into the hall. At the same moment, Charles heard the sound of a key in the door lock. Believing it was Douglas returning, he heard the sound of a woman's voice instead. Puzzled he rose to his feet only to start as Linda entered the room. 'Linda! What on earth's happened?'

She put a finger to her lips. 'Douglas isn't here, is he? I see his car's missing.'

'No. He's gone to see friends. He said he might stay the night so he took his case with him. But what are you doing here?'

'I came from the station by taxi. Can't you guess why?'

Charles frowned. 'I hope it's not what I think.'

She hugged his arm. 'I had to be here, Dad. Don't be cross with me. It's something I can't help.'

'But he can't come, love. He's under surveillance. Douglas told me yesterday.'

She nodded. 'I know. But there's something else Douglas didn't tell you, Dad. Sean's got away.'

Charles gave another start. 'You mean he's absconded?'

'Yes. Phillips told me yesterday. That's why I pretended to go to see Susan. Originally I thought it would prevent your being worried and involved if Sean came. But when Douglas arrived and said he had got leave, I realised I'd set up the chance I needed. That's why I didn't cancel it.'

'Does Douglas know he's absconded?'

'Of course he does. Phillips told me. But Douglas hasn't said a word about it.'

Charles sighed. 'You can't blame him, darling. He's scared to death you'll leave him for Hammond.'

'I'm not blaming him, Dad. In any case I've lied to him myself about going to see Susan. But once I heard Sean had escaped I knew I had to be here.'

Charles's distress came to the surface. 'You mustn't go through with this, darling. Douglas isn't the man to forgive deceit.'

'I know that, Dad. That's why he mustn't find out.'

'But, darling, you're taking the risk for nothing. Hammond isn't likely to come. Not if he's on the run. He'll be far too busy avoiding the provos and the MPs.'

She shook her head. 'If he's alive he'll come tonight. I can't explain why but I know it.' She kissed him and then drew back. 'Don't worry. I'll stay in a hotel after I've seen Sean and arrive back tomorrow as if nothing had happened.'

'But it's cold tonight. You'll freeze out there.'

She indicated the thick coat she was wearing. 'I'll be all right. You settle down with your book. I'll come back and say goodnight if Douglas doesn't return.'

Charles had never felt more helpless. 'What do I say to him if he does come back or phones me?'

She kissed him again. 'You don't say anything. I'll arrive tomorrow as planned, as if nothing had happened.' Before he could reply she bent down to the joyous Jason. 'Yes, you can come, darling. He'll want to see you too.' Then, with a last smile she and Jason had gone, leaving Charles dropping back into his armchair with a groan.

There was frost in the glade. It sparkled on the lilies on the lake, on the bushes, and on the roof of the gazebo. It crackled beneath Linda's feet as she walked round the pond and it lay like a silver cloth on the table between the two benches. It enriched the sky with a million ice particles and gave a brilliance to the new moon resting on the upper branches of the ageing oak.

She reached the table and paused beside it. There was no sound, she realised. Not even the far off sound of a train or car. The night seemed to beholding its breath as if expecting an event beyond time and space.

It was all in her mind, she told herself. It had been that way since her first meeting with Sean. Some inexplicable thing had been said or done that had steered her off the path of normality and given her thoughts and ideas that were in conflict with those near and dear to her. It had given her nothing but confusion and concern and her common sense should have led her back to her old and conformist life style. Instead she had listened to the siren voice until it had led her to this act that if discovered might end the marriage she valued so much. Every protective instinct told her to leave the glade while there was still time and yet that compelling voice that had guided her, often against her will, was now demanding and insisting on her presence. Finding no strength to resist, she drew up her coat collar and waited.

The crescent moon began climbing from its resting place on the ageing oak. A distant jay gave a cry and then settled down to sleep again. The faintest of breezes sent a whisper though the surrounding trees. Jason grumbled at her inactivity but settled down at her feet. She glanced at her watch and told herself it had all been a grand deception. The Gods had been amused at her life style and decided to make a fool of her. And yet, although the night air was penetrating her coat and chilling her entire body, the voice that brooked no argument gave its orders. She would leave only at midnight when she would know one way or the other the truth of her obsession.

It was then that Jason stirred and cocked his head. The dog's movement brought every chilled nerve in her body back to life. A moment later Jason gave a startled bark. Dropping her hand on his head to quieten him, she stood listening. For a moment her eyes closed, whether in fear or thanksgiving she did not know. She listened but the silence seemed like a finger pressing against her lips as if warning her from any speech or movement that could break the spell. A minute passed and then she heard a distant sound as if from a breaking twig. Beneath her hand she could feel Jason trembling. As she tried to restrain him he suddenly broke free and ran towards the boundary bushes.

As a man's figure appeared through them and leaned down to pat the joyous dog, she let out a cry of astonishment and relief and ran herself towards the smiling newcomer.

THIRTY-ONE

Parking his car on the forecourt Douglas was about to pull out his suitcase when he saw light blaze out from the house as the front door opened. Puzzled he hurried up the steps and saw Charles standing in the doorway. 'You all right, Dad?'

Charles's voice was hoarse with concern. 'Yes. I heard your car and wondered who it was. I thought you were staying out the night.'

'I intended to but then I realised they weren't expecting to put me up. So I let them believe I intended coming back.' When Charles didn't withdraw into the house his concern grew. 'You're sure you're all right? You shouldn't keep that door open like that, you know. There's always the chance some air raid warden might spot it.'

Charles was not listening. 'I wanted to know who had come to see me. I also intended to bring Jason back into the house.'

'Is he out?' When Charles nodded, Douglas

324

went on: 'Don't worry about the dog. I'll go myself and bring him in.'

'No.' The urgency of Charles's cry made Douglas stare at him. 'Leave the dog. He's only been out a few minutes. I'll go for him myself later on. You get your case in and then have a drink with me.'

Douglas moved up the steps. 'You have to close that door, Dad, or someone's going to complain. Go inside and leave the dog to me.'

To his surprise Charles hurried down the steps towards him. 'No. He's been locked up all day. Leave him out for a while.'

As he stumbled and almost fell Douglas caught hold of him. 'What is it, Dad? I've never known you fuss about the dog like this.' Then his voice changed. 'You're trembling. What's the matter? Why are you acting like this?'

Charles could think of nothing but a lie. 'I don't know. I'm not feeling well. Help me back into the house, will you? I need a drink.'

Douglas stared at him, then led him into the house and to his armchair. He then poured him a whisky. 'Feel better now?' he asked as Charles sipped at the glass.

Charles nodded. 'I think so. Sit down and pour yourself one.'

'No. I'm going to fetch Jason in.' As Charles protested again and rose from his chair,

Douglas shook his head and moved towards the hall. 'It's no use, Dad. I have to go and see what's happening out there.'

Charles made a last effort. 'Leave things alone, Douglas. It's better for everyone that way. Believe me, it is.'

Douglas nodded. 'You might well be right. But I must know the truth.'

With that he was gone, with Charles dropping back into his armchair and staring blindly at the blacked out window opposite.

Douglas wondered why he was making for Linda's haven as he crossed the lawn. Why was he so sure Jason had gone there? What were the suspicions that Charles's uncharacteristic behaviour had aroused in him?

By the time he reached the wood he believed the first question was resolved. He had seen Linda to her train: he had even waited until it had pulled out of the station. It was true that could have been a deception but that only made sense if she believed Hammond could keep his rendezvous. He had been careful not to mention his escape to Linda and even if she had known about it she would almost certainly have brought it up during their earlier conversation, if only to plead for his absolvement.

Then what could be the reason for Charles's concern? It had been genuine enough: he had no doubts about that. Could it have anything to do with Hammond? Was it possible that, in his need to see Linda, the pilot had come up to the house and spoken to Charles. That Charles had sent him away but Hammond had returned to the glade in the hope Linda might still keep her appointment? It was a far fetched possibility but the only one that could explain Charles' undoubted concern.

Douglas wondered what he would do if Hammond was waiting in the glade. Would he arrest him? Professionally that was his duty but what effect would that have on Linda? Would she ever forgive him if he made impossible the reunion that both of them seemed to want and need so much? Or would he tell Sean that his courage and persistence had all been in vain but nevertheless let him escape to face whatever life had in store for him? The distant sound of engines brought him relief from his thoughts. As it grew louder he paused and glanced up at the frosty sky. As the throbbing grew louder his professionalism made assessments. Possibly Lancasters making another attack on the Ruhr. It would be cold and lonely up in that sky tonight. At the same time he envied the crews.

Their decision lacked the complexity of not knowing what was right and what was wrong. They had a job to do and their training and sense of duty would see them through to death or victory. He found comfort in the thought. Whatever shocks might befall him he had at least a career that made no such demands on his integrity.

The massive thunder of engines died away. He reached the wood and found the path that led though the trees to the lake. As he started down it he felt his heart beating faster. What would he do if Hammond was there? What was right for Linda? What was right for their marriage? What was right for his military status and his duty?

He was close to the glade now and he believed he heard Jason give an enquiring bark. Although he knew it might be the dog's reaction at his own approach he also sensed it might have another cause and he felt his stomach tightening, an experience so unusual for him that at first he did not recognise it as fear. Then, bracing himself, he was about to start along the path again when he heard the rustle of bushes behind him. Turning sharply he saw the stumbling figure of Charles trying to reach him. Before he could admonish him, the old man made a frantic gesture for silence. At the same moment, Jason let out a series of barks, followed by the incredulous but equally joyous voices of a man and a woman. Shocked by the implications, Douglas spun round to enter the glade when a desperate hand caught his arm. As Charles stumbled making the effort, Douglas was forced to grab hold of him. Before he could speak the old man made a frantic gesture for silence and urged Douglas to withdraw along the path. Supporting him as he was, the younger man had little option but to obey. As they stumbled back along the path, any sound they made was drowned by the barking of Jason and the excited voices from the far side of the lake.

They were back on the car forecourt and in the moonlit shadow of the house before Charles spoke in anything other than hushed whispers. 'Thank you, lad. I know how hard it was for you.'

Douglas' reply was a mixture of anger and disbelief. 'That was Linda's voice. How the hell has she worked it?'

'She never went to Scotland. She came back here tonight. She couldn't help it, lad.'

'What do you mean, she couldn't help it? Why is she lying and cheating like this?'

'I can't explain. And neither can she. Something strange is happening, Douglas. It makes you wonder if that German priest is right about divine intervention.'

Douglas stared at the old man who was now leaning against his car for support. 'Divine intervention? Have you all gone crazy?'

'I know it must seem like that but how else can you explain what has happened? Hammond's many escapes and Linda's behaviour. None of it makes any sense otherwise.'

Douglas' reply was harsh and bitter. 'It does to me. They've got a hell of a crush on one another. God has nothing to do with it.' He turned towards the moonlit wood. 'I'm going to settle this thing for once and all. Sorry, Dad, but I must.'

Charles grabbed his arm, only to stumble and fall. His protest was frantic. 'No, you mustn't. Please, Douglas. Don't. Don't go.'

Cursing, the younger man helped him back on his feet. 'I have to go. It's my wife over there. Sit in the car until I bring her back.'

Charles's plea was distraught and panic stricken. 'No, you mustn't. It could harm you all.' Then his tone changed. 'Are you still a Catholic, Douglas?'

Douglas stared at him. 'What has that to do with it?'

'If that German priest is right it could have everything to do with it. Aren't we taught to believe God is all powerful and can change the world if He so wishes?'

The younger man's laugh was bitter again. 'We're taught it but often wonder why He doesn't. So where's the relevance?'

'Two people, lad. Linda and Hammond. Totally different in almost every way. And yet both getting the same message and one going through almost unbelievable experiences to fulfil them. Doesn't that say anything to you?'

This time there was a slight pause before the younger man's reply came. 'Yes. It says they are having a red-hot affair. Don't tell me God approves of illicit sex.'

Charles's hoarse voice suggested he was close to collapse from his efforts. 'You're wrong, Douglas. Linda's not having a sexual affair. She loves you too much.'

'Then she has a hell of a way of showing it. Lying and cheating in the hope of seeing that bastard again.'

'She knows this, Douglas. She hates the lies she's had to make. But what choice did she have when she knew how jealous you are? Leave it alone, lad. She won't leave you. But she's been given some task and so has Hammond. Let them both serve it and one day you'll be proud of her.'

Douglas's eyes were intent on Charles's expression. His voice betrayed a moment of uncertainty. 'You really believe this, don't you? You really believe it has some kind of divine purpose.'

'I didn't until I heard what that German priest said and did. He believed it with his life, Douglas. And everything he prophesied has come true. That has to mean something.'

In the distance the joyous barking of Jason could be heard again. The sound seemed to snap Douglas' brief uncertainty and with an exclamation he started back towards the wood. Then, as Charles let out a despairing cry, he took a deep breath, and halted. When he turned back to the pleading Charles, his voice was a mixture of perplexity and self-disgust. 'I know I'm going as crazy as everyone else but it doesn't seem a situation I can win. So I'm going to leave them to it and not let Linda know I've been here. Presumably she'll arrive back officially tomorrow and you can phone me at Group to tell me the score. If she wants me back, I'll have to give it thought. But until then let's play it as it comes.'

The old man's eyes were moist with tears as he held out his hand 'She'll want you back, lad. I can vouch for that. Bless you for your understanding. I know God will reward you for it.'

Douglas' reply was dry. 'Let's hope she does. Otherwise my faith will go where my waste paper and rubbish go.' He motioned at the house above the forecourt. 'Will you be able to get back on your own?'

'Yes. I'll be all right now. Thank you once more, lad. You won't regret it.'

Douglas took a final glance at the wood. 'I can only hope you're right.'

As he climbed into the car Charles reached out and gripped his arm. 'Bless you, Douglas. You're a good man.'

Douglas shook his head. 'You're wrong, Dad. I'm a fool. Take care of yourself.'

With that he started up the engine and with a last wave at Charles drove away. As the sound of the engine faded and then died away, the night seemed to have an import of its own to the old man standing there. The hushed silence seemed to be paying homage to a far-off priest who had given his life for this moment.

Stirring himself, Charles made his unsteady way to the house. As he climbed the steps and reached the door, he heard Jason barking again. Turning and glancing back at the distant wood he gave a start. A faint luminous glow had appeared inside it and, as he watched, it began to grow as if it were a tree outgrowing the others around it. Shaking his head at the mystery of it all, Charles stood watching while the luminous glow rose like a benediction over the wood and the magical glade from whence it came.